Provence
— To Die For

Provence
— To Die For

A *Murder, She Wrote* Mystery

A Novel by Jessica Fletcher
and Donald Bain
based on the
Universal television series
created by Peter S. Fischer,
Richard Levinson & William Link

Wheeler Publishing • Chivers Press
Waterville, Maine USA   Bath, England

This Large Print edition is published by Wheeler Publishing, USA
and by Chivers Press, England.

Published in 2002 in the U.S. by arrangement with
NAL Signet, a member of Penguin Putnam Inc.

Published in 2002 in the U.K. by arrangement with
Universal Studios International B.V., Consumer Products Division.

U.S.	Softcover	1-58724-284-2 (Wheeler Softcover Series)
U.K.	Hardcover	0-7540-7458-7 (Chivers Large Print)
U.K.	Softcover	0-7540-7459-5 (Camden Large Print)

The text of this Large Print edition is unabridged.
Other aspects of the book may vary from the original edition.

Set in 16 pt. Plantin by Al Chase.

Printed in the United States on permanent paper.

British Library Cataloguing-in-Publication Data available

ISBN 1-58724-284-2 (lg. print : sc : alk. paper)

For Marisa and Ron
and
Billy and Jessica

Chapter One

"*Bonsoir,* madame. So nice to see you again," said the pretty young woman in lightly accented English.

"Good evening," I replied as I shrugged out of my warm woolen coat, handed it to her with my large case, and pocketed the coat-check ticket. "I'm happy to be back."

Guillaume, the maitre d', smiled. "Madame Fletcher, *c'est un plaisir de vous revoir.*"

"It's a pleasure to see you again, too."

"Monsieur awaits." He led me across the brown-and-white-tile floor and up two steps to a table in the corner, where my agent, Matt Miller, had already risen from his seat.

"Jessica! Glad you could make it." He gave me a brief hug, then stepped to the side so Guillaume could pull out the table. I settled into the leather banquette and tucked my handbag on the seat beside me.

Guillaume handed us menus and wished us *bon appétit.*

"Let's decide what to eat, and then we can chat," Matt suggested. "A French meal can go on for hours, and I don't want to make you late."

"That's fine with me," I said, opening my menu.

Matt looked down at the list of specials. "How's your French?"

"Pretty good, if I'm with someone who doesn't speak too quickly. I've been taking lessons."

I scanned the menu and decided on an appetizer and a salad. I wasn't very hungry, and my stomach was still a bit shaky after a particularly turbulent flight. But this was the beginning of my vacation. I was going to spend eight weeks in France, focusing on my own much-needed three R's: reading, resting, and relaxing. Just the contemplation of it slowed my pulse, loosened the tension in my shoulder muscles and, I was sure, lowered my blood pressure. Matt and I had selected the restaurant L'Absinthe on the Upper East Side of New York City. It had the perfect atmosphere to launch my holiday even though it was an ocean away from France.

I was coming off a particularly hectic summer in which friends, some invited and some not, had decided Cabot Cove was a great place to visit in July and August. That's peak tourist season for every village along the Maine coastline, and even though my hometown is short on public attractions, the lure of the Atlantic Ocean, lobster dinners, and "quaint" New England architecture is enough to fill up our motels, inns, and bed-and-breakfast homes. One couple, cheerfully escaping the sweltering heat in Florida, had shown up at my door, suitcases in hand, without prior notice. I'd met them only once before. As it happened, I already had houseguests, and spent a frantic hour on the telephone trying to find these new arrivals a bed for the night. I can't say whether or not I would have accommodated them even had my guest room been unoccupied. Presuming that people will welcome you without the courtesy of a call to see if they're otherwise engaged is high on my list of inconsiderate behavior. But fortunately for them — and for me — I didn't have to resort to my backup plan: spreading a sleeping bag on the living room floor. Seth Hazlitt, our local doctor and a dear friend of many years, responding to a note of panic in my voice, convinced a recently widowed patient of his, Mrs. Bloomquist, that her pool house would make delightful guest quarters. She could earn a bit of extra money, my unexpected visitors would have a roof over their heads, and Cabot Cove's restaurants would benefit from two more mouths to feed. It all worked out in the end, and I heard recently that Mrs. Bloomquist has registered with a group that promotes New England's bed-and-breakfast trade.

I didn't know where September and October had gone. My hopes to fit in a few days of fishing before the season's end went begging as various projects, some work-related and some community-based, seemed to vacuum up all the hours in the days, until I began to feel I would never have time to sit down.

But that was all behind me now, and the French countryside beckoned. While Matt studied his menu, I took in my surroundings.

The decor in the elegant brasserie was just as you might imagine a Parisian restaurant to look. Warm wood paneling rose to meet cream-colored walls on which were displayed elaborately framed mirrors and advertisements for a variety of French events and products, including L'Absinthe, the notorious aperitif reputed to have driven Van Gogh to slice off his ear, and for which the restaurant was named. Crisp white napery covered the tables. Huge flower arrangements lent drama, but not fragrance, to the corners and center of the dining room. The only scents were the wonderful aromas that wafted behind the trays of food carried by the waiters coming from the kitchen.

I ordered escargots in puff pastry, a specialty of the house, and a green salad to follow. I'd learned to eat snails on a previous trip to France. Once I'd overcome my aversion to the idea, I'd discovered that I really enjoyed the mollusks, especially when they were prepared in the Provençal manner with lots of garlic. Matt opted for trout with braised endives and a side of *frites,* the Gallic name for what is perhaps France's best-known contribution to the American diet and waistline — French fries.

"White all right with you?" he asked as he pored over the wine list. The sommelier, who'd been hovering nearby, came to Matt's elbow.

"Are you sure you want to order a whole bottle?" I asked in reply. "One glass will be sufficient for me."

"You'll have to do better than that in Provence," he said. He pointed to a bottle on the list and nodded at the wine steward.

"Très bien, monsieur."

Matt turned to me. "When Susan and I were in Provence a few years ago, our host opened two bottles, a red and a white, every day at lunch, and at least four each night for dinner."

"Yes, but your host owned a vineyard," I pointed out. "Martine is an artist, and her farmhouse is next to an olive grove."

"So that's where you're staying. Who is this lady?"

"Her name is Martine Devries. Her sister lives in Cabot Cove. Have I ever mentioned Elise Edman?"

Matt shook his head, tearing off a hunk of crusty roll and popping it in his mouth.

"She's married to Rudy Edman; he teaches earth science in the high school. She's been helping me brush up on my French, and vows that I'll sound like a native by the time I get back."

"You have hidden talents, Jessica. I didn't know you could speak French that well."

"I'm sure she was exaggerating, but I'll find out soon. Anyway, Elise and her sister, Martine, were 'army brats' — that's what they call themselves. Their father was a major who met his wife in Paris. The family moved around a lot. When he was stationed in France, the girls got to travel all over the country with their mother. Martine said Provence was her favorite region. She always wanted to live there."

"She's American, then?"

"Yes, and half French. She speaks both languages fluently."

"That's great for you," he said, grinning ruefully. "I took Spanish in high school, so I was no help at all when we visited Provence. Sue remembered enough French to figure out how to ask directions, but not enough to understand the answers. We got lost a lot. Fortunately for us, our hosts had a better grasp of English than we had of French."

The wine steward returned with a bottle of chardonnay, and presented the label to Matt, who nodded his assent. We watched as he uncorked the wine and poured a small amount in Matt's glass, carefully wiping off the lip of the bottle with an immaculate white linen towel. Matt, who was well versed in the customs of wine tasting, swirled the wine around in the glass, held it up to the light, took a sip, swished the liquid over his tongue, and finally swallowed. *"Bon!"* he pronounced. "Good!"

The wine steward filled my glass halfway, added more to Matt's glass, and shoved the bottle into a bucket of ice on a stand next to our table. Matt and I raised our glasses and clinked. "To a wonderful stay in Provence," he said. "I know you'll love it."

"Thank you. I'm sure I will."

The waiter arrived with our dishes, and conversation temporarily ceased as we concentrated on the wonderful flavors. The snails were as good as I'd remembered them, and the lemony dressing on my salad was the perfect counterpoint to the butter and garlic of the classic dish.

"When do you head south?" Matt asked, pulling the wine from the ice without waiting for the steward.

"The day after tomorrow." I covered my glass with my hand to keep him from filling it again. "I'm taking the noon train to Avignon. It's only a little over three hours."

"And how long will you be staying there?"

"About two months. I gave Martine's address and phone number to Paulette last week," I said, referring to Matt's assistant. "So if you need to reach me, you can."

"I'll try not to do that. What good's a vacation if you keep getting calls from the office?"

"I appreciate the thought," I said, smiling. "Although I may get a yen to hear my native language after immersing myself in French for a while."

"What about Martine? She speaks English."

"Yes, but she won't be there for the first month."

"She won't? Why not?"

"We're swapping houses," I said. "She'll be settling into mine in Cabot Cove at the same time I move into hers in Provence."

The waiter removed our plates, and returned shortly with a dome-topped cart containing a selection of cheeses.

"I've had enough for now," I told Matt. "But you go ahead."

He picked out a small, round white goat cheese, a creamy Brie, and a French cheese I didn't know, a Cantal. The waiter cut wedges of the cheese, arranged them on a plate, garnished with some slices of pear, and set it in front of Matt with a flourish. He looked across at me, in case I'd changed my mind.

"Non, merci," I said.

The waiter smiled wistfully and pushed the cart away.

Matt picked up a piece of Brie with his fork. "How come Martine's not staying with her sister and brother-in-law?" he asked, balancing a sliver of pear on top of the cheese.

"She told me that a month is too long to impose on them," I replied. "But I think she also likes the idea of being able to get away and give them — and herself — some privacy. With Martine staying at my house, she can have a nice long visit without worrying about wearing out her welcome. And I get to live in a French farmhouse."

"Yes, but it's November," Matt pointed out, frowning. "It's not exactly tourist season. A lot of places will be closed. What are you going to do all by yourself? You don't even drive."

"Oh, I think I can manage," I said, already envisioning morning excursions to the market for fresh vegetables, brisk afternoon walks, and curling up by the fire with a pile of books I'd been meaning to read. "It's been a long time since I've had the opportunity to go away and relax. When I travel for business, well, that's business. At home — you know how it is — there are always chores to be done, correspondence to write, errands to run, and people to see — and that doesn't even count work. But in Provence there's no pressure, no computer or fax machine; everything is quiet and uncomplicated. I'm looking forward to the solitude, living a simpler life, reading and resting, cooking for myself, and enjoying the occasional day shopping in Avignon or visiting a museum. It's quite a cosmopolitan city, I understand."

"You'll go stir-crazy in a week," Matt predicted as he speared the Cantal. "You're a social person, Jessica. You'll be bored with no one to talk to."

"I'm perfectly capable of entertaining myself," I said. "But in any case, I won't be entirely alone."

"Aha! What haven't you told me?"

"Nothing shocking, I assure you," I said. "I'm planning to take cooking classes in Avignon."

"Cooking? I thought you were already a pretty good cook." He gathered the remaining crumbs of goat cheese with the back of his fork. "Your homemade baked beans and clam chowder never last long around my house. And that blueberry crumb cake you sent last Christmas was the best." His eyes became dreamy as he remembered the crumb cake, the cheese forgotten as the waiter removed his plate.

"Thanks for the vote of confidence," I said. "Like most cooks, I guess, the dishes I know how to make, I make very well. But I don't know much about French cooking. Provence is renowned for its cuisine. Lucky for me, cooking classes are available year-round. I've already signed up for one course."

"Are you going into competition with me?" said a male voice other than Matt's.

It was Jean-Michel Bergougnoux, the chef and owner of L'Absinthe, who'd been stopping at each table to greet his customers. He wore his kitchen uniform of white jacket and dark pants, but was without his toque, the tall white hat that's the symbol of his trade.

Matt and I laughed. "You're in no danger, Jean-Michel," I said. "What a wonderful meal, as always, of course."

"*Merci, madame.*" He bowed and winked at me. "I heard you say you go to Avignon."

"That's right."

"You cannot miss the restaurant of my good friend, Christian Étienne. He's a *maître cuisinier de France,* a master chef, like me."

"I'd be delighted to visit him, and bring your regards."

"*Merveilleux!* And you must eat at his restaurant, too. He will make you something very special. If you like, I can call him and make a reservation for you. Just tell me which day you would like to go."

"What a great idea, Jessica," Matt put in. "Can't get a better recommendation than that, can you? From one great chef to another."

"You're right," I said. I pulled my datebook from my handbag and we consulted on which day would be good to visit his friend's restaurant. "My cooking class in Avignon starts on a Wednesday. I'll already be in town, so that would work well."

"If you are cooking in the morning, it will include lunch," he said. "I will make your reservation for eight o'clock. It's a bit early, but . . ."

"Eight o'clock it is," I said, making a note and circling it.

"We French eat later than you Americans do. But by eight there should be a few people at the restaurant. Is a good time for you, *n'est-ce pas?*"

"Perfect."

"I will call Christian tomorrow." Jean-Michel looked down at our empty table and frowned. "I have interrupted your meal," he said sorrowfully. "You must let me buy you dessert." Our protestations that he'd already been helpful and that we were finished eating were ignored. He gestured to our waiter. "Alain! *Les desserts, s'il vous plaît.*"

Alain hurried to a sideboard and returned with a tray laden with a selection of pastries, tarts, creams, and cakes that promised to have me loosening my belt at least a notch. Jean-Michel looked over the tray and adjusted the angle of a walnut torte so we could see where a slice had been removed, revealing the layers of cake and cream. He patted Alain on the shoulder, excused himself, and turned to greet a party taking a table across from ours.

Matt eyed the tray and groaned, but succumbed to a macadamia-nut crème brûlée. I declined dessert, but knew I'd still get a taste of something sweet; Jean-Michel always had a few chocolate truffles brought to the table at the end of dinner.

Alain put Matt's dish in front of him. *"Café? Madame? Monsieur?"*

"Oui! Deux," Matt replied, holding up two fingers. "You want coffee, don't you, Jessica?"

"Decaf, if you have it," I said, looking up.

"Certainement, madame," the waiter said.

"Well, I feel better now that I know you'll have at least one evening out on the town, Jessica. That was very considerate of Jean-Michel."

"It was. The trip is shaping up nicely. I'll have my cooking classes, and now I have a special occasion to look forward to."

"So you have a month on your own before Martine returns. What happens after that?"

"My leisurely vacation will end at that point. She's already planned a full schedule of sightseeing for us. By that time, I should be truly rested. It'll be fun to see all the places listed in my guidebook, especially with someone who knows them so well."

Over our coffees, Matt brought me up to date on business. He was off to Frankfurt, Germany, the next day to negotiate German rights on some books, including two of mine. Sales were going well. The publisher was already asking where the next mystery would take place. Not to worry, Matt assured me. When I returned home from France, there would be plenty of time to start thinking about that project.

Out on the street in front of L'Absinthe, Matt hailed a Yellow Cab for me. "Kennedy Airport," he told the driver, who hefted my bag into the trunk. Matt held the door as I climbed into the taxi. "Have a great trip, Jessica. Get out and meet the people. Go dancing. Read a lot of books."

"I have at least one of those items on my agenda," I replied. "Thanks, Matt. This was a great bon voyage dinner. L'Absinthe was the perfect place to put me in the mood for France."

Chapter Two

The train to Avignon left Paris at a little after noon from the Gare de Leon, a huge open depot bustling with people. Porters pushed carts laden with luggage. Young people sprawled on the floor, lounging against backpacks while waiting for their trains. Mothers, with bags hanging from both shoulders, cautioned their children to stay close. Businesspeople, encumbered only by the weight of a briefcase, strode purposefully past the myriad cafés and food stalls where pigeons and sparrows fluttered down from the rafters to seek crumbs. I inhaled deeply and let go, my breath a soft cloud in the chilly station. Daylight flooded in from the glass roof but did little to warm the air, which felt several degrees colder than outside.

I rolled my case to the head of the platform and paused to punch my ticket in a machine, following the example of my fellow passengers. As a frequent flyer on promotional tours for my books, I'd gotten used to traveling light; I could manage well for a week, perhaps a few days more, with one small suitcase and a carry-on bag. But two months in Provence, not to mention stops in Paris at either end of the trip, required a bit more packing. Even the suitcase-on-wheels I now steered alongside the train would never hold all I'd want for two months. I'd sent ahead a duffel bag of belongings to Martine's

20

farmhouse; hopefully it would arrive before I did. My books, except for the one in my handbag, were in that duffel, along with boots and heavier clothes in the event the mistrals, the legendary fierce winds that whip down through the mountains and across the valleys of Provence, were blowing.

I showed the conductor my ticket. He waited while I climbed aboard, then lifted my heavy suitcase as if it weighed nothing and deposited it next to me. A small space for luggage was provided at one end of the car, and I maneuvered my awkward case into a gap between two bulging garment bags. Relieved of my burden, I heaved a grateful sigh and walked down the carpeted aisle.

The train was arranged with pairs of seats down one side of the car, and a row of singles down the other. Here and there, between facing seats, were small tables. Two long hinges allowed the sides of the top to be folded over, narrowing the table to make it easier to sit down. My seat was at one of these tables. I removed my coat, folded it carefully, slipped it into the lower of the two overhead racks, and took my place by the window. Across from me was a young woman, her overstuffed backpack propped on the seat beside her. I guessed her age to be seventeen or eighteen. She had unfolded the panel on her side of the table and was earnestly writing in a small notebook that I assumed was her journal. Her elbows were splayed across the table's surface, her head resting on one arm. She had fine light brown hair pulled back into a ragged braid, and wore wire-rimmed glasses. When she looked up, I saw that her eyes were hazel and rimmed in red with faint shadows beneath them.

"*Bonjour,*" she said softly.

"*Bonjour,*" I replied with a smile, and asked her how she was: "*Comment allez-vous?*"

A spark of interest flickered in her tired eyes. "You're American, too, aren't you?" she said in English, sitting up straight.

I laughed. "Is it that obvious?"

She grinned. "Well, you speak French with an American accent. You don't hold your mouth like the French people do, kind of pushed forward a little — at least that's what I have to do to sound French — and they make '*bonjour*' sound like 'boojoo,' real quick." She pursed her lips to demonstrate. "And when you asked me how I was, you spoke very formally to me. Most adults don't."

"You're very perceptive," I said. "It sounds as if you've made quite a study of the language."

She shrugged. "I'm almost fluent, but I still can't read a newspaper very well."

"How long have you been traveling in France?" I asked, folding down my side of the table and resting my book on it.

"How do you know I'm traveling?" she asked coyly. "Maybe I live here and I'm on my way to school."

"Maybe you are," I conceded. "But your

backpack is a new American brand, and while that might not be unusual, it's too large to be simply a school bag or a substitute for a handbag. It's lumpy, but there aren't any hard edges protruding, so it's doubtful you've got schoolbooks in there. My guess is you're carrying clothing, perhaps even a sleeping bag. Plus, you still have the airline tag tied to the handle."

"You're pretty perceptive yourself," she said. "I've been here since August." She closed her journal and zipped it into a small compartment in her backpack. "I took a course at the Sorbonne, which was okay, but I was really here to see Paris, and the city was dead in August. I hung around to see what happened when everyone came back from vacation. I've been here ever since."

"Have you been in Paris all this time?"

"A group of us from school went to Versailles once with our professor. That was cool, although I don't know why anyone would want to live in such a fussy place." She pulled her braid around her shoulder and started playing with the wispy end. "And I took the train to Lyon with my boyfriend for a weekend. And once we went up to Rouen. But I really haven't been anywhere else. There's a big ex-pat community in Paris — you know, expatriates — and most of them speak English and they're a lot of fun. So I hung out with them."

I wondered why she wasn't in school and how

she supported herself all these months, but couldn't raise such a personal question. Instead I asked, "Where are you going now?"

"Down to Marseilles for bouillabaisse. I figured it's time I saw a little more of France before I have to go home."

"Where are you from in the States?"

"Portland."

"Maine or Oregon?"

She chuckled. "I forgot Maine has a Portland. I'm from Oregon."

"Well, as it happens, I'm from Maine," I said. "I'm not likely to forget about our Portland. I'm Jessica Fletcher, by the way." I extended my hand across the table.

"Mallory Cartright," she said, shaking my hand quickly, then busying herself with the rubber band on the end of her braid. "Where are you going?"

I told her about my house-swapping with Martine, and my plans to take cooking classes at the Hotel Melissande in Avignon a week from Wednesday. We chatted for a while longer, but her eyes became heavy and she yawned widely, patting a hand over her mouth. "Oh, excuse me. I don't mean to be rude. I was awake a lot last night. I think the train is rocking me to sleep."

"You look tired," I said. "Why don't you take a nap?"

"I wanted to see the French countryside," she protested. But she had removed her glasses and was settling herself against her backpack in preparation for sleep. "Would you mind waking me in an hour?"

"Are you sure that's long enough? It's three hours to Avignon. I could wake you when I get off."

"I'll never sleep that long," she said, snuggling into the canvas. "I put my ticket in the slot up there." Her eyes indicated a piece of molding under the rack above, into which other passengers had tucked their tickets. When I looked back, her eyes were closed.

The countryside as we left Paris unraveled southward with mile after mile of flat plain, broken only by rows of trees marking off farmers' fields. Hovering over the landscape, which had been scraped bare by harvesting machinery, were low gray clouds canceling any shadows that might have given the land definition. A few blackbirds, scavenging for scraps of grain on the barren ground, jumped into the air at the blast of sound and current generated by the train, only to settle back to their repast when the threat went unrealized. I studied the view as the train sped past trees and fields and clumps of buildings that might have been villages. How different from the stands of tall evergreen forest that led down to the rocky shore of eastern Maine, and our coastal villages with Victorian houses crowded around the bays.

I flicked on the overhead light and opened my book. The train was remarkably quiet — it had none of the usual sounds I associate with rail

25

travel — and the ride was smooth, altogether an impressive technological achievement by the French. But despite the perfect atmosphere for reading, the words on the page made no impression as my mind wandered to the past two days.

I'd gone straight to the airport following my dinner with Matt. The Air France overnight flight to Paris had been full, and I counted myself lucky that a month earlier I'd secured a seat in business class, after trading in a hefty chunk of my frequent-flyer miles for the upgrade. The staff was friendly and attentive, and the food surprisingly good, what little I'd tasted of it. I've never slept easily on a plane, but I managed to fit in a few catnaps, and felt almost refreshed by the flight's early-morning arrival at Charles de Gaulle airport.

My travel agent had arranged for a car to pick me up, and I was grateful to see the hand-lettered board with MME. FLETCHER held up by a middle-aged man with a beard. He was neatly dressed in a blue blazer and gray slacks, and his car was equally tidy, if smaller than most American models. On the ride into town, he switched on the windshield wipers, and bemoaned the timing of my trip in accented but clear English.

"You are here on business, yes?"

"Not at all," I said cheerfully. "I'm on vacation. I'm going to Provence tomorrow."

He scowled. "The weather there is no better than here, madame. You may as well stay in

Paris, where at least there is entertainment."

"Paris is a lovely city," I said noncommittally. I wasn't going to allow his grumpiness to affect me.

"You Americans come to Paris in all seasons. For the spring and the summer, I can understand. The fall, maybe, too. But now? It's almost winter. It is strange," he said, clicking his tongue. "I don't complain. It's good for business. I am driving many, many of your countrymen to hotels each day. But look." He swept his arm in front of the windshield as the wipers methodically cleared the spatters of rain from two small wedges of glass. "When I go on holiday, I go where it's warm and there's sun." He thumped the steering wheel, punctuating what he obviously considered his more sensible attitude on places to vacation.

"I don't mind the weather," I said. "There are plenty of inviting indoor activities. I'll probably go to a museum."

He shook his head as if unable to fathom the peculiarities of these visitors. He was correct about the numbers of Americans in Paris, however. My hotel, the Pont Royal, was full, and the accents around me in the lobby and at breakfast the next morning were mostly American. The cordial English-speaking staff may have had a lot to do with the hotel's popularity, as, I'm sure, did the wonderful views over the rooftops of Paris from the long windows on the top floors. I'd thrown open the French doors in my room and stepped up onto the small balcony that over-looked the intersection of Rue de Montalembert and Rue du Bac. The sun had punched holes in the clouds and lit up patches of blue sky over the Eiffel Tower, away to my left, and Montmartre, at some distance on my right. I decided a museum visit would have to be put off. Better to take advantage of the partial sunshine, and spend my one day strolling the city.

I stopped at the front desk for a map, and ad-mired the oval lobby and the slice of warm, wood-paneled bar I could glimpse through its curtained portal. The Pont Royal had once been a leg-endary Left Bank gathering place for well-known authors. Crowding into its bar and signing its guest list were such famous names as the French writers Jean-Paul Sartre, Albert Camus, and Simone de Beauvoir. Aldous Huxley, Arthur Miller, and Truman Capote visited, as did T. S. Eliot, James Baldwin, Oscar Wilde, and Gabriel García Márquez. In the lobby, the faces of some of those regulars could be seen peering down from their portraits at the current guests, perhaps less celebrated but equally enthusiastic recipients of the hotel's hospitality.

The hotel was located in the heart of Saint-Germain-des-Prés, a section of the city named after a famous church, and home to the narrow, winding streets and outdoor cafés that evoke the image of Paris around the world. I'd left my suit-case packed, removing only those items I'd need for the night, slipped a small umbrella into my raincoat pocket, and stepped out into the crisp, fresh air. The rain had washed the empty streets clean, and many other people had responded to the break in the weather as I had, spilling outside and tilting their faces to the sun. I walked, map in hand, all over the neighborhood, window-shopping in the elegant boutiques of world-famous designers, sampling the heady scents on offer in the *parfumeries,* and admiring the antique stores filled with furniture and objets d'art centuries older than what was usually available at home. Finally, jet lag caught up to me. I found a vacant chair at a sidewalk café on a street closed to traffic, sipped a strong café au lait, and watched the parade of tourists and natives examining the wares of an outdoor market.

The train entered the station at Lyon, and I looked up from my musings. Mallory was sleeping soundly; her face in repose was soft and very young. I revised my guess at her age downward. Seventeen at most, I thought, perhaps fifteen or sixteen. I leaned across the table and tapped her shoulder.

"Mallory, you wanted to be awakened in an hour," I said. "I'm afraid it's a bit after that. We're already at Lyon."

She mumbled something and snuggled into her backpack.

"Mallory, shall I wake you at Avignon?"

She smiled slightly and nodded, and was asleep once more.

I opened my book, and was surprised when, in a short time, the conductor announced Avignon as the next stop. This time my efforts to rouse the teenager were more successful. She sat up, eyes still bleary, and smiled.

"I'm sorry to interrupt your sleep," I said, "but you did say you wanted me to wake you."

She rubbed her eyes and stretched her arms over her head, cocking her head first to one side and then the other. "I'm up now," she said, blinking rapidly. "Thank you. I hope I didn't give you a hard time. I'm a sound sleeper."

"No trouble at all," I replied. "I don't wish to pry, but do you have a place to stay in Marseilles?"

"There are youth hostels all over, so I'll probably stay in one of those," she said, pulling off the rubber band and releasing her braid. She hesitated and looked at me. "Do you mind?" she asked.

"Mind what?"

"If I redo my hair."

"No, go ahead."

"My folks would have a fit if they saw me braiding my hair at a table, even though there's no food here." She combed her fingers through her silky locks and divided her hair into three sections to begin replaiting, concentrating on catching the loose strands in her new braid.

"Does your family know how to reach you?" I asked.

She shrugged and avoided meeting my eyes.

"I've got my cell phone. I can give them a call once I'm there."

I knew she was reluctant to discuss the situation with me, but I was uncomfortable seeing her so young and adrift.

"Well, on your way north again," I offered, "you're welcome to spend a night or two with me in St. Marc." I tore a blank page from the back of my datebook, and wrote down Martine's address and telephone number.

"That's very generous of you, Mrs. Fletcher, but I don't know my plans right now."

"Just keep that in your back pocket, in case you need it," I said. I doubted she'd call, but wanted her to know she had a responsive adult nearby if she ran into any problems. I folded over my side of the tabletop and put my book away. The train slowed, and I pulled my coat from the overhead rack.

"It was nice to meet you, Mrs. Fletcher," Mallory said, tossing her newly remade braid across her shoulder. She rose from her seat and put out her hand. Someone had taught this child manners.

"It was my pleasure to meet you too, Mallory," I said, taking her warm fingers in mine. "Be careful in Marseilles. And don't hesitate to use that number I gave you."

She gave me a wide smile and dropped back onto her seat. "Thanks."

I walked slowly to the end of the car, holding on to the seat backs to keep from losing my balance as the train entered the station and shuddered to a halt. I was afraid I was going to have to manhandle my suitcase all by myself, and was pleasantly surprised to see the conductor standing in the luggage area and handing down bags to their owners. I pointed out mine, followed it down to the platform, and moved out of the way so the conductor could assist other disembarking passengers.

The sky was threatening, and I felt the first drops of rain on my head. I pulled out my umbrella and walked up the platform, trailing after the other passengers, who seemed to know where they were going. I hoped they'd lead me to a taxi stand. Knowing that I would arrive late in the afternoon, I'd made arrangements to stay overnight in the hotel where my cooking classes would be conducted the following week. I didn't want to have to familiarize myself with new surroundings while it was getting dark. My plan was to leave for Martine's house in St. Marc in the morning.

The Hotel Melissande on Rue de Melissande in Avignon was off a one-way street so small I wasn't certain the taxi would be able to make the turn without putting a sizable scratch in the white paint of the door. If other towns were similarly laid out with such narrow and twisting streets, it would explain the French preference for tiny cars. Somehow the driver avoided the sharp corners of the buildings that intruded on the intersection and pulled up to the glass front door of an ancient edifice that ran the length of the block.

Weary and grateful to be near the end of my travels, I barely noticed the lovely stone floor and walls of the entrance hall. On the second floor, a porter wheeled my bag down several halls overlooking a first-floor atrium, where I'd been told breakfast would be served, and showed me to my quarters. It was a beautiful room with floral wallpaper over polished wainscoting. An Oriental rug stretched beneath a king-size bed that had already been turned down, a disk of chocolate perched on the pillow. I was tempted to leave my suitcase standing near the door and simply collapse onto the smooth white linens, but long habit had me hanging up my coat, unpacking what I needed for the next day, and setting out my toilet articles in the elegant marble bathroom.

I had a quiet dinner in the hotel dining room; only two other tables were occupied, both by Americans. My waiter explained that the restaurant was fully booked later in the evening, but that Americans seemed to dine earlier than the French. And in fact, when I'd finished my meal and had risen to leave, many of the tables were newly occupied, and the sounds of clinking glasses and animated conversation followed me out. By that time, however, more than two days of travel and the six-hour time difference between Avignon, France, and Cabot Cove, Maine, were having their full effect. I sank gratefully between the sheets of my king-size bed and fell asleep instantly.

"You know he's only amused that you're a beautiful young woman who admires him. The old bull! He's not good enough for you."

"Shhh! He'll hear you."

"I don't care."

"Maybe so, but if he gets angry, he'll make trouble for you."

"If you realize that, why do you stay with him?"

"He needs me. He's sensitive and sad."

"Apparently there are several women he needs."

"That's not so."

The conversation was in French, and I heard a rush of air escape the man's lips in the characteristically Gallic expression of disgust. I couldn't see his face — he was in the office behind the hotel's front desk — but the young woman he was chiding had her back to me, standing in the doorway just past the battery of numbered wooden slots that held messages and room keys for the hotel's guests. I cleared my throat and she started when she saw me, immediately flushing a bright red.

"*Oh, madame, je suis désolé.*" She immediately switched to English. "I'm so sorry. I didn't know you were waiting."

"Not a problem," I replied.

"I am so embarrassed," she said, crossing to

the front desk. She fussed with the hotel computer, staring at the keyboard. "Did you sleep well? Was your room all right? Was everything to your liking?" she asked, gray eyes under dark lashes looking everywhere but at me.

"I slept like a log, thank you. My room is beautiful, and breakfast was fine. The coffee is delicious, the best I've ever had," I said, prattling on, hoping to stave off any more questions, and giving her another moment to collect herself. "Your English is excellent, by the way. Where did you learn to speak so well?"

She smiled up at me, cheeks still pink. "I was an AFS student," she said, referring to the American Field Service, which arranges student exchanges, placing American students with families abroad and foreign students in American homes. "I stayed with a family in Ohio and went to the high school there."

"You learned well," I said.

"You are very kind," she said, the blush beginning to fade. "Is there something I can assist you with this morning?"

"Yes," I replied. "I'm checking out today. In fact the bellman can bring down my bag whenever it's convenient."

"I will let him know," she said.

"And another thing." I opened my handbag and pulled out a piece of paper on which my travel agent, Susan Shevlin, had printed my itinerary. I put on my reading glasses and scanned the page. "A car is supposed to come for me at ten. Is there any way you can see if that arrangement has been made?"

"Yes, of course," she said. "I will look it up for you right now. Your room number, madame?"

I gave her the number, and she tapped the keys skillfully, secure in the task. While she researched my ride, I studied her. Her name was Claire, according to the pin she wore on her right shoulder. She was tall and lissome, with a cap of dark, curly hair. She had a short nose and a full mouth, and was not especially beautiful, but there was something interesting about her angular face that was very attractive. Right now she was looking distressed again.

"Marcel will be a little late, I'm afraid," she said. "Will that be terrible if he comes at twenty past the hour?"

"No. That will be fine."

"Is there anything else?"

"Yes, there is," I said. "I'm taking one of your three-day cooking courses next week, starting on Wednesday. Can you check to see if there's a record of my registration?"

"Certainement." She pulled a heavy appointment book from a shelf under her desk, laid it on the marble counter between us, flipped through the pages till she found the proper date, and ran her index finger down the list of names for the Wednesday class. *"Oui, madame,* here it is. J. B. Fletcher, this is you, yes?"

"Yes. I'm J. B. Fletcher, Jessica Fletcher."

"The class is being taught by Chef Bertrand,

owner of the restaurant L'Homme Qui Court. It has a Michelin star," she said proudly. She coughed delicately, and excused herself. "He is an excellent chef."

"And an excellent teacher, you must tell her," a hearty voice said from a few feet away. The man was dressed in white, and was wearing a toque. Probably in his fifties, he was ruggedly handsome; lines like curved spokes reached across his high cheekbones from startling sky blue eyes topped by black brows, and deep grooves bracketed his thin-lipped mouth. He appeared very fit, built like a boxer, broad across the chest and solid, with heavily muscled forearms extending from his rolled-up sleeves. A pair of reading glasses hung from a gold chain around his neck. The sides of his head were shaved, the stubble more gray than black.

"Madame Fletcher," said Claire, "this is Chef Bertrand." Her face was getting pink again, and I wondered if this was the man under discussion earlier, the one who'd been accused of being unfaithful. He was old enough to be her father.

"*Enchanté, madame,*" he said, smiling broadly, taking my hand in both of his and bowing slightly. "I shall be delighted to have such a lovely student in my classes — and such a famous one. You are the American mystery writer?"

"Yes. I write mysteries." I was astonished that he knew my name.

"Ah, I see from your eyes that I surprise you.

But even here in southern France, we have heard of J. B. Fletcher. But I must confess, I thought J. B. Fletcher was a man. I did not know *he* would be such a beautiful woman."

His eyes peered deeply into mine as if I were the only person present. Claire stood quietly watching. I thought to myself that she wouldn't be the only woman to blush today. Chef Bertrand certainly was a flatterer.

"Alas, if you look for adventure in Provence, you must go to Marseilles. *C'est une ville notoire* — how do you say? — a notorious city. Here in Avignon, we are peaceful and calm."

"I'm not looking for adventure," I said crisply, "just a nice relaxing vacation."

"That you can find here," he said, giving my hand a final pat, then releasing it. "Is this your first trip to France?"

"I've been to Paris several times, and years ago, when my husband was alive, we came to the south of France, but not in this part of Provence."

He made a *tsk*ing noise with his tongue. "It is very beautiful here," he said, "but perhaps not so much at this time of the year. We must have you come back when the sun shines and the lavender is in bloom. Isn't that so, Claire?" He smiled sweetly at her.

"*Oui,* Emil," she said, returning his smile.

"I would like that," I said, "but I'm sure I'll enjoy this visit as well."

"*Absolument! Provence, c'est merveilleuse tout le*

temps." He looked perplexed. "How does one say this in English?"

"Provence is marvelous all the time," Claire translated.

"*Oui! Vraiment.* Truly. And we shall make sure this visit is wonderful for you. Have you taken cooking courses before?"

"Not for a very long time," I replied, laughing, and thinking that my high school home economics classes probably wouldn't qualify.

"In that case, I am honored you have chosen to attend my class," he said, closing his eyes and putting his hand over his heart.

I had a feeling that he would have been "honored" whatever my answer had been. He was very charming, in the manner French men have historically been credited with, confident, flirtatious, attentive, and sure of his attractiveness. This couldn't be the same man Claire had described as sensitive and sad.

"Guy, come out here. *Vite!*" he called into the open office door.

A bespectacled man in his mid-thirties, also wearing kitchen whites, emerged frowning from the back room. He was tall and very thin, and his movements were awkward, like those of a teenager who hasn't become accustomed to his changing body. Catching sight of me, he put on a pleasant expression. "*Bonjour, madame.*"

"*Bonjour.*"

"This is Guy Lavande, sous chef in my restaurant and for my cooking courses," Chef

39

Bertrand said. "He also speaks very good English. *N'est-ce pas, Guy?* Isn't that so?"

"*Oui, c'est ca,*" Guy said, blinking. Behind his thick glasses, he had one eye that turned in, giving his face an off-balance appearance, but his friendly expression was ingratiating. "It's true," he continued in English. "I attended university in your country for one year. This makes me an expert. If you have any questions, I will be happy to assist you." Guy was taller and thinner than the master chef, with straight brown hair streaked with gray and a bushy mustache, his easy manner in contrast to the palpable magnetism of the chef. I was sure his was the voice I'd heard talking with Claire, warning her "the old bull" wasn't good enough for her.

"*Bon!*" boomed out Bertrand. "Claire, *ma petite,* tell me, do we have other Americans in Madame Fletcher's class?"

Claire reviewed the list of students again, and I detected the slightest tremor in her fingers as she moved them down the page. "I don't think so, but you have a British couple, the Thomases," she told Bertrand. "And Monsieur Bonassé will be back, as will Madame Poutine. You also have a student from the Institut de Cuisine but I don't have the name yet, and Madame Fletcher. There will be six, no more, as you prefer."

"*Parfait!* You have done well," he said in a soft growl, tipping his head and gazing at her until her face was suffused with high color again. He turned to me. "You must excuse me, madame. I have to inspect this morning's purchases from the market to see what we will cook today." He looked quizzically at his assistant, who was frowning at Claire. "Guy!" The younger man jumped. "Why don't you give Madame Fletcher a tour of the classroom? That is, if you have the time, madame. We have a very beautiful kitchen to teach in. It is located in an old part of the building that dates back many centuries. I'm sure you will enjoy to see it."

I glanced at my watch. It was a quarter to ten. "I would like to see it very much," I said, "as long as I'm back here in time to check out and meet my driver."

Guy came around the desk and poked out his elbow for me to take. The sleeves of his jacket were too short for his long arms, stopping well short of his bony wrists and hands that were red and chapped. "I can give you the short tour or the long tour." He was smiling again. "I will keep my good eye on the time, and you will tell me when I have bored you enough."

Laughing, I took his arm. I thanked Claire and Chef Bertrand, and Guy and I crossed the stone entry to a small vestibule to the right of a beautifully curved staircase that led to the upper floors. We took the elevator down, and when the door opened I stepped out into a low-ceilinged corridor with stone walls. The air was cool and damp and musty-smelling. Down the hall to the left was an open doorway. From it, fluorescent light flooded across the dark passage and painted a bright rectangle on the facing wall. Sounds of running water and the clunk of metal hitting metal emanated from the room.

"That's the hotel kitchen," Guy informed me. "You can see this another time. But first you must see ours."

Ahead of us was a wide stone arch. Guy guided me through it, down a step, and into a cold and dark room. Two wall sconces were insufficient to illuminate all the corners. Beneath our feet were huge blocks of dusty stone, scarred and uneven from the many feet that had trodden over them through the years. I shivered from the chill.

"This part of the building is very old," Guy said in a low voice. "Can you perhaps feel the spirits of the past?"

"Do you have ghosts here?" I replied playfully, trying to shake off an odd feeling that the room aroused in me.

Guy shrugged. "When you have old buildings, there are always unexplained things. This building dates from the time the city became official home to the popes. Did you know Avignon was the capital of Christendom in the fourteenth century?"

"Yes. I read about it. The Palace of the Popes isn't far from here, is it?"

"It is very close by. You should pay a visit before you leave us. As every schoolchild in Avignon can tell you, Pope Clement the Fifth abandoned Rome and settled here in 1309.

Later his successor, Clement the Sixth, brought his whole court here. For seventy years this city was the home of the papacy, and an important economic center as well."

"I can imagine. Was this building built at that time?" I rubbed my hands up and down my arms to warm up a bit.

Guy strode to the wall on the right and slapped it, releasing a cloud of dust. "Yes. This was at one time a courthouse and later a private residence." He wiped his hands on the side of his trousers. "The stonework is beautiful, is it not?"

"Yes," I said slowly, casting my eyes over the rough limestone walls. What was different here?

"Ah, something is not right." He was pleased. "Can you tell what it is?"

"This is a strange room," I said. "What function did it have?"

"See if you can guess."

We walked to the center of the area where a long wooden table with a battered top stood in solitary splendor on the stone floor. Piles of plates, bowls, flatware, and napkins had been arranged neatly on its rough surface. On one end, laid out on a white linen towel, was an array of large kitchen knives in size order. A short earthenware pitcher held a bouquet of what I presumed were small knives; I could see only their black, brown, and white handles. The table, a bench along one side, and several high-backed chairs drawn up to the other were the only pieces of furniture in the room. The light in the sconces flickered and dimmed.

"Oh, dear," I said, resting my hand on the corner of the table.

"Don't be concerned. It's a temporary malfunction. They do this from time to time. Someone must have switched on the dishwasher."

I turned to scan the room. There were three arches in the masonry walls. Those on the right and left had been fitted with heavy wooden doors; the open one behind us led back to the hallway. High on the walls were sets of shutters covering what might be storage cupboards. *Peculiar places for storage*, I thought. They'd be inaccessible without a ladder. On the other side of the table, up a step, was a multipaned glass window looking into another room.

Guy picked up one of the large knives and idly tested its point with the pad of his thumb. "There is a mystery here, eh?"

"Why are those storage cabinets so high?" I asked. "Can you reach them from another room?"

"You have a keen eye," he said, replacing the knife and aligning its blade so it matched the others. He was enjoying the game. "I give you a hint." He tapped the floor with his foot. "This stone was laid in the thirteenth century."

"But you said the building was built in the fourteenth century," I said, pointing to the wall.

"*Exactement.* The floor is older because it isn't a floor at all. We are right now in the middle of a medieval street. Do you see the outside of the houses?" He waved a long arm at the walls.

I looked up and realized that we stood in what appeared to be a courtyard with buildings all around. Those possible storage cupboards were at one time windows overlooking this small square. The table was standing in the street. Perhaps the glass window on the other side had been the window of a shop. It was only the beamed wooden ceiling, high above our heads, that had transformed the spaces into an interior room.

"Those arches," I said. "Were they passageways leading to other streets?"

"*Oui!* And, like our streets, they are narrow because there were no cars in those days, only mules."

"Yes, I can see the square," I said slowly. "It's obvious now that you point it out."

The knowledge of the room's origins, however, did not lessen my uneasiness. I made a mental note to bring a warm sweater to the cooking class. Perhaps it was just the cold that was bothering me. Stone walls and floors, especially in a subterranean room, will hold a frosty temperature for a long time.

"The room above this is the same," Guy continued, oblivious to my discomfort. "It is the atrium, where we serve breakfast and tea."

"And what do you use this room for?" I asked.

"This is where we consume the fruits of our labor. It's the dining room for our kitchen over there." He pointed at the room beyond the multipaned window. "When we have spent all morning cooking our meal, we sit down together here, and drink wine and eat up all we have made. Chef Bertrand always makes a complete meal, including dessert."

"I look forward to it," I said, moving around the table and climbing the step to peer through the window into the darkened kitchen.

Guy patted his jacket pockets and frowned. "I don't have the keys to open the kitchen," he said. "Emil must have them."

"Do you mean Chef Bertrand?" I said, cupping my hands on the glass to see inside.

"*Oui*. He is always forgetting his keys and taking mine."

I looked back at him. "Have you worked for him for a long time?"

"Unfortunately, yes," he replied with a wry smile.

"He's a demanding boss, I gather."

Guy's eyes flew up to the ceiling. "The worst."

"But there must be some benefits or you wouldn't stay, would you?"

"He is a tyrant in the kitchen, but also a genius," he said. "Not everyone gets a chance to work for a chef who has a Michelin star. I am very lucky, so he tells me. And he promises to make me a partner someday. I am hoping to take over his restaurant in Avignon when he opens one in Paris. But you cannot tell anyone that. It's still a secret."

"I won't say a word."

"Till then, I work for him at the restaurant and also here as his sous chef when he teaches in the cooking school."

"Is Monsieur Bertrand the only chef to teach at the cooking school?"

"Oh, no," Guy said, shaking his head. "He is one of many. Daniel Aubertin, the head chef here at the hotel, invites all the *maîtres de cuisiniers,* master chefs, in Provence to teach, even the ones he doesn't like. It is a matter of honor to make sure the school has only the top chefs in the region."

"Even the ones he doesn't like?" I said, teasing. "That's certainly dedication."

"It is indeed," Guy said, his smile back in place.

The light in the sconces wavered and then went out, plunging us into total darkness. Disoriented, I turned so my back was to the window and stood absolutely still, trying to remember the layout of the room. "A temporary malfunction, I believe you said."

"Ah, madame. It's just a momentary gap. Wait. I'm sure they will come back on."

We stood in the inky darkness waiting for the sconces to flicker to life again, but it soon became apparent that there was a problem with the electricity.

"This never happens, I promise you," Guy said. "I will see if I can find a flashlight in the kitchen."

I heard him shuffle his shoes across the stone

toward the archway through which we'd entered. Then I heard a thump and a muffled curse as he stumbled on the step. His footsteps faded as he made his way down the hall toward the hotel kitchen, until I could hear nothing at all.

Without the lights, the room seemed even colder. I waited, running my hands up and down my arms from shoulder to elbow, trying to counter the icy air. There was no sound of footsteps returning. The colder I grew, the less patient I became. I inched one foot forward, conscious of the narrow step I'd climbed to look through the window. My toe found the drop and I eased my foot down to the floor, twisting my shoe back and forth on the uneven footing till I felt secure. I patted the air with my hands, groping for the end of the table. I swung my other foot down and started to move forward, but my heel was wedged in the gap between two stones and I went flying sideways. One hand caught the end of the table, and in my efforts to gain purchase my fingers closed around the white towel and I fell, twisting around, landing on my bottom, and pulling along the kitchen knives that had rested on the linen. They jangled loudly as they hit the floor around me just as the dim light of the sconces came back on.

I heard someone sprinting down the hall. Guy rounded the corner and ran to assist me as I climbed to my feet and surveyed the damage. He took my elbow and bent down to examine my face. The thick lenses of his glasses magnified his eyes.

"Madame, how terrible. Are you hurt? It is very difficult, this floor, so rough. I have tripped myself sometimes." He pulled out a chair and pressed me to sit down.

"I seem to be fine," I said, more embarrassed than injured. I brushed the dust off the legs of my pantsuit, and looked around for the shoe I'd lost in my tumble. The knives were scattered across the floor, but fortunately not one had landed on me, and except for some bruises I would be sure to feel later, I was unscathed.

Guy knelt to retrieve my shoe, rotating it to free the heel from the grip of the boulders, and brought it to where I sat.

"Guy. Oh, Guy," a soft voice called from the hallway.

I looked up to see Claire hurrying into the room.

"Madame, I am so sorry about the lights," she said, slightly out of breath. "The new dish-washer cut off the electricity. The whole hotel went out. You are all right, I hope. We are calling the electrician to have it repaired right away."

"Madame Fletcher tripped in the dark and fell down," Guy said, as I pushed my foot into the shoe he held for me. He straightened up and stepped back, his foot knocking against one of the knives.

Claire gasped. "Oh, madame. Are you hurt?"

She rushed to my side and leaned over me. "Would you like me to call the doctor? These old floors are just awful. May I bring you some coffee or tea?"

"I'm really okay," I said. "I was just clumsy, and, as you see, I've made a mess."

"Not at all, madame," Guy said. "Don't upset yourself. Let Claire take care of you. I will only be a moment. Stay where you are." He bent his long body in half and moved around the room, bobbing up and down, picking up the knives and the linen towel. He reminded me of the birds I see at home on the shore, pecking at the sand.

Claire hovered over me. "You're certain I cannot get you anything? A glass of brandy? Perhaps you would like to lie down."

"No, no," I said, chuckling. "Really, I'm fine." I stood up, mentally inventoried my body — no real harm done — and slid the chair back into place at the table.

"But, madame, you must rest and —"

"Now then," I said, interrupting her, "you were looking for Guy when you came downstairs, weren't you?"

"Actually, I was looking for you," she said. Her hands flew to her cheeks. "Oh, my goodness. I almost forgot. Your car, it is here."

I looked at my watch. It was ten o'clock, exactly when the car was originally scheduled to come. An unexpected wave of relief came over me.

Guy dumped the knives on the table and took

50

my arm as we walked back to the hall and rang for the elevator.

"Marcel, he arrives on time after all," Claire said apologetically, "but I have your bill prepared, and the man has brought your luggage to the front. Marcel puts it in the car, even now."

"I am so sorry for your fall, madame," Guy said.

"Not your fault," I said, patting his arm. "It was an accident. I'll wear my sneakers next time."

He shook his head. "I have been a poor host," he said. "You haven't even seen our wonderful kitchen."

"You'll show it to me when I come for the class."

"Yes, Guy," Claire added. "Madame Fletcher will be back."

He smiled at Claire, reached out, and touched her cheek with one finger. To me he said, "Our Claire will take good care of you. I look forward to seeing you again. *Au revoir.*"

He turned and loped back through the arch toward the table. The knives would need washing again.

"Too bad you have not had the opportunity to see the school kitchen. It is very old and charming."

"Yes, too bad," I echoed.

The elevator came and we stepped inside. I turned around and watched the door close on the ancient courtyard. I wasn't at all sorry my car had come early. I was ready to leave.

Chapter Three

Marcel was a very confident driver, but I was not his equal as a passenger. As his little car hurtled down the country road, I held tight to the side of the seat near the door, and tried not to close my eyes. The combination of crooked streets and traffic had kept his driving to a crawl in Avignon, but once outside the city's crenellated walls — a legacy from the later years of the papal occupation — he was liberated. He stomped the accelerator to the floor with his right foot, and I doubt he ever lifted it the entire trip to Martine's.

An unlit, unfiltered cigarette hung from the corner of his mouth, and as he talked, it bounced up and down. He was a carpenter by trade, but it was winter. The summer tenants had gone back to their homes in Paris, London, and New York, and things were slow. He filled in by providing transportation to those who lacked it.

He pulled a card from his shirt pocket, letting go of the steering wheel and inspiring what I was certain was a stream of colorful language from the driver of a truck he nearly sideswiped. "This is the number of Madame Roulandet," he said. "She runs the village bakery." He handed me the card and pulled the car back into the lane ahead of the truck to an accompaniment of blaring horns. "When you need a ride, you call her the day before, and she will find me.

Est-ce compris? Understand?"

I took the card but vowed I would find another way to get to Avignon for my cooking class. I didn't think I'd live through a repeat of this harrowing ride. Even if I arrived alive — which was up for debate — my nerves couldn't take it again.

"You look worried," he charged, his bushy black brows rising over his tinted glasses. "I am a very safe driver. I never have accidents. Martine, she didn't tell you?"

"I think she forgot to mention it."

"Everyone drives like this in France. It's normal."

The car flew past a cluster of yellow stone buildings up a hill that Marcel indicated was the village of St. Marc, careened around a corner, and jounced off the pavement onto a dirt road. Fortunately, no human or animal was nearby. The plume of dust in our wake would surely have choked any living thing engulfed by it. As we aimed for a building on a rise just ahead — I prayed it was Martine's farmhouse — I saw olive trees whizzing by my window.

Marcel skidded to a halt before a graceful two-story building nestled among bare-branched shrubs and trees. Its facade appeared to have been stucco at one time, but over the years chunks had fallen off, and patches of brown showed through the dingy white paint. Martine had ignored the aging walls, but had painted the wooden shutters a bright turquoise and the front door a deep red. The effect was eccentric, like an elegant dowager wearing vivid makeup.

Marcel climbed out of the car and went around to the trunk to haul out my suitcase, while I groped around the floor of the car to retrieve my handbag, which had fallen off my lap during the wild ride. I paid him, nodded as he repeated his instructions to call the baker if I needed him again, and watched as he steered the car around a large tree and drove back toward the village in a cloud of his own making. In a few moments the growl of his engine faded away, and silence descended.

I stood still, listening to the whoosh of the wind and the skitter of dried leaves across the dusty driveway. I'd been waiting a long time for this trip, relishing the anticipated peace in the hectic months that preceded it, and eager to put the planes and trains and cars behind me so I could begin my "vacation." You'd think that someone who traveled quite a bit for business would just as soon stay put when the opportunity arose. But my natural curiosity about other cultures, and the opportunity to live in a foreign country — even for so short a time as two months — was an exciting prospect. Combined with ample time to walk and read and cook and sharpen my French skills, away from the hustle-bustle of small-town Maine life and the technological intrusions I'd allowed to take up residence in my home, this was going to be a wonderful new experience. Chef Bertrand had said Provence was marvelous all the time, and I believed him. I would not be deterred by a little rain or cold. After all, Cabot Cove was probably wetter and colder, and I fared very well there.

I walked across the concrete patio that led to an entrance flanked by a pair of empty urns. Faint stem prints from long-removed vines had left a delicate tracery on the wall around the door. Martine had sent me a key. I inserted it into the keyhole and followed her written instructions on how to jiggle it in the lock. The lock cooperated and the door swung inward with a soft groan. I pulled my suitcase into the house behind me and turned on a light. Yesterday's rain in Avignon had skipped St. Marc — if the state of the dusty drive was any indication — but the solid bank of dark clouds in the sky above Martine's house promised wet weather to come, and permitted only a pale light to pass through the windows. I parked my suitcase next to the door, threw my coat and handbag over the back of a chair, and took in my new accommodations.

The downstairs of the farmhouse consisted of a single long space. The kitchen stood to the right of the front door and the living room to its left, separated only by a deep beam that seemed to indicate where one room stopped and the other began. The low ceiling was made up of alternating stripes of wooden beams with some kind of mud or stucco filling the gaps between them. The walls were painted a light mustard, the perfect backdrop for Martine's large, colorful canvases, which filled most of the wall space that wasn't occupied by the fireplace or windows. The floor was an expanse of dark square tiles, although in the living room they had been covered with a profusion of colorful rugs, Oriental, shag, and broadloom. Facing sofas on either side of a massive stone hearth were covered in the same small blue-and-yellow-print fabric and strewn with an assortment of pillows, no two alike. None of it matched but somehow it all worked together. The artist's eye, I thought. What other decorating surprises did Martine have in store for me?

A flight of wooden stairs off the kitchen gave access to the second floor, which was a mirror of the first except for the steeply sloping ceilings. The same dark tiles ran from one end of the room to the other. Martine had covered the walls with smaller paintings here; most appeared to be hers, but there was a smattering of work by other artists as well. The upstairs consisted of two small bedrooms, each with a double bed under a pile of quilts; a good-sized bathroom stood between them. The first room was obviously Martine's; I took the other down the hall. I turned on the bedside lamp and nearly tripped over the duffel bag I'd sent ahead. It had arrived — thank goodness — and someone had lugged it upstairs for me. I hoped it hadn't been Martine. I could barely lift the thing, and she was a small woman.

I hung up my suit jacket in the empty wardrobe and went downstairs to find the key to the duffel. At the base of the stairs, next to the back door, were a series of hooks about eye level that I hadn't noticed on my way up. Hanging from one was what we used to call a "barn jacket" in my youth. I had a similar boxy, flannel-lined jacket pegged up by my kitchen door at home, and had left it there for Martine. Apparently she'd done the same for me.

The next hour was spent settling in and ferrying clothes from my luggage up the stairs to the bedroom I now thought of as mine. The suitcase was too heavy and awkward to maneuver in the small stairwell, and I wasn't willing to risk a wrenched back just to make unpacking a little easier. Plus, I was a bit sore from my tumble at the hotel. Half the contents from the duffel had to come downstairs anyway. I lined up my winter boots on the floor under the hooks and put a pile of books on an end table in the living room, making efficient use of the round-trips.

As I'd done for her, Martine had left a letter for me in the kitchen detailing useful information, such as where things could be found in the house, and who the neighbors were.

M. Telloir will stop by with fresh eggs. He takes my olives to market in the picking season; we have a fair exchange. No need to pay him. Mme. Arlenne has a house directly across the paved road from our driveway. She will be happy to sell you root vegetables if you run out before the market day, which is Friday. I left you some food in the refrigerator, so you won't have to shop right away. Help yourself to anything in the pantry, and anywhere else, for that matter. The bakery in the village opens at seven. It's best to go in the morning when there's a good selection, and make sure to count your change! You're welcome to use my car. It's in the barn. The key is under the mat.

I wouldn't take her up on this last offer. Martine had forgotten I don't drive.

I found milk, butter, eggs, and a loaf of sliced bread in the refrigerator, and laughed at the irony as I made myself French toast for lunch. I wondered what the French called this dish. Following my first meal as a temporary resident of Provence, I wandered around the house, Martine's note in hand, locating the references on her list, starting in the kitchen. The "pantry" turned out to be a large bookcase covered by a yellow-and-white curtain that hung from a rod secured to the top. One shelf held rows of fruit preserves, another jars of olives, tomatoes, onions, cauliflower, and other vegetables; a third was filled with tins of fish and meats, boxes of pasta, and dry soup and other staples. Suspended from the side of the pantry was a narrow fabric bag with a flap at the top like an envelope. There wasn't anything in it, and I wondered what it was for.

The pantry stood to the left of the kitchen fireplace, which had a small, square, raised hearth.

A massive mantel supported by carved wood columns framed the blackened grate. Resting on top was a squat yellow flashlight. Martine had told me that she'd had a new heating system installed, but because of the expense, she usually used both the downstairs fireplaces to combat the cold. Since hot air rises, the heat they generated would warm the bedrooms, at least for an hour or two, plenty of time to get comfortable under the quilts. I checked the stack of wood to the right of the fireplace. There were enough logs for one night of burning but not more than that. I assumed there was a woodpile outside.

I slipped into my boots, pulled on Martine's barn jacket, and tied the scarf I found in her pocket over my hair. While I'd been unpacking, the threatened storm had come through. The full brunt of the weather had passed, but clouds still obscured the sun and a stinging mist hung in the air. I let myself out the front door, crossed the patio, and headed toward the barn, really more of a low stable, catty-corner to the house. The barn doors were on well-oiled hinges, and one easily yielded to my tug. Happily, it was the side of the barn without the car. Daylight spilled in through the open door, illuminating the accumulation of old tools, discarded furniture, paint cans, and tarpaulins. It was like finding a private junk shop. I pulled the scarf from my hair and wandered among the flotsam and jetsam that had washed up in Martine's garage.

The barn smelled like a combination of gasoline and hay, not at all an unpleasant aroma. Martine's navy-colored car sat on one side of the dirt floor, a veteran of the French road wars, with scars to prove it. It was old and battered, but as she'd once said to me, "It runs, and that's all you should ask of a vehicle." The other half of the barn was what interested me. I picked my way among wobbly chairs, unloved tables, empty picture frames, and rusted hulks of equipment, the purpose for which defied my imagination. Stopping to examine a blue-and-white pitcher with a small chip, I heard a soft mewing. I peered into the corner in the back where a rickety staircase led to the loft, and saw a sleek gray cat slip into the barn through a hole near the bottom step. We stared at each other, both of us sizing up whether this stranger was friend or foe. Finally I crooned, "Here, kitty, pretty kitty." The cat gracefully leaped over several toppled paint cans to get to me, and wound its damp body between my ankles, purring loudly.

"What a beauty you are," I said, stooping to scratch my new friend behind the ears. "Where do you live?" The cat wore no collar, and I hoped it had a home. Too often I'd heard about summer visitors who'd abandoned their pets at season's end, leaving them to fend for themselves. But this cat appeared healthy and well fed, with a soft coat and clear eyes.

I love animals, but I haven't owned a cat or dog since I was a child. When we were married, my husband Frank and I had no four-footed pets. His allergies limited our choice of animals to fish, beautiful and entertaining but not what you cuddle up with. After his death I'd concentrated on my writing career, and even though my business trips were infrequent at first, I'd never found the opportunity to bring an animal into my home. But having a cat or a dog, while impractical for me now, was still a sweet dream I hadn't let go. If this cat were to become a regular visitor, I mused, perhaps that dream would come true for two months in Provence. I looked forward to finding out.

Grateful for the quiet company, I continued to explore the barn with my feline companion. In the back, partially obscured by a stack of warped boards, we found a treasure. It was dirty and rusty and its tires needed air, but there it was — a bicycle. It even had a dusty wicker basket dangling by a wire from one handlebar. Martine had said to help myself to anything. Surely she wouldn't begrudge me riding her old bike.

I pulled the bicycle out of the barn to inspect it in better light. The tires were flat but the wheels weren't warped. Since it had no kickstand, I leaned it against a tree while I went back in the barn to search out an air pump, finding one on a shelf on the other side of Martine's blue car. The air valve was rusty, but with persistence I managed to unscrew the cap. Kneeling on the damp earth, I worked the hand pump up and down to push enough air into the tires to determine whether there was an unfixable leak. There wasn't. A short time later the tires were plump and firm, and I was dirty and exhilarated. I'd give the bike a good cleaning tomorrow before testing it out, I promised myself. I rolled the bike back into the barn, leaned it against one of the mystery tools, and wiped my hands on an already greasy cloth thrown over a toolbox. My cat friend had left the way she'd come in, through the hole in the back of the barn. I hoped she would give me the gift of her friendship again.

I closed the barn door. The sun was setting behind the clouds, painting streaks of orange and lavender across the sky. It would be dark soon. I looked around, regretful there wasn't more time to explore. But I'd already had a very satisfying day, and the expectation of another good one tomorrow.

That night, after a hot bath had soothed away the sore muscles brought on by my fall at the hotel, and following a supper of salad, bread, and a country pâté Martine had thoughtfully left for me, I made a fire in the living room fireplace and curled up to read. The book I'd chosen was a mystery by a popular author I'd never read before. His descriptions of eerie atmospheres and sinister characters were very well done, but the graphic descriptions of blood and gore had me skipping paragraphs. His hero was following a trail of blood on the floor, the crimson drops leading to . . . A chill raced up my spine and I shivered. Outside, the wind wailed and rattled the shutters. The old house creaked. I heard two thuds. Instantly I became acutely aware of the sounds around me. The crackle of the fire and the pop when the flames hit a pocket of sap. The mantel clock with its slightly offbeat ticking to the time of its swinging pendulum. The scratching of a branch brushing against an outside wall. I was in an unfamiliar house, out in the country, isolated, my nearest neighbor, whom I hadn't even met yet, down the road past the orchard.

"You're doing a good job of scaring yourself, Jessica," I told myself out loud. "It's time you went to bed."

I marked my place in the book and left it on the living room table. This was not a good bedtime story. Better to tackle it during the day, and save the night for a different kind of book, maybe the novel by Rosamunde Pilcher that took place in Scotland, or perhaps the book of French poetry I'd picked up in the airport.

I banked the fire in the hearth, checked the locks on the front door and the one in the kitchen, and went upstairs to my new bedroom. I changed into my nightclothes, washed up, and climbed under the covers. The sky had cleared. Moonlight spilled through the single window opposite my bed. The shadowed patterns on the cold white disk were sharply delineated. Off in the distance, an animal howled. A wolf?

"You'll never get to sleep with the moonlight in your eyes," I grumbled, flinging back the quilts and feeling around on the floor for my slippers. I crossed the room to the window and knelt on the window seat to keep from banging my head on the sloped ceiling. Tiebacks held the curtains open. I released them from the hooks, and started to pull the panels of fabric together when a movement caught my eye. A large tree in the front obscured my view of the barn, but I thought I saw the shadow of its door closing. Was someone sneaking around out there? I sank down on the window seat and stared through the branches, daring the prowler, if there was one, to show himself. The tree swayed with each gust of wind, and leaves rolled over the concrete patio outside the front door below, but no other shadows materialized.

"This is ridiculous," I told myself. "You can't spend half the night watching out the window." Without turning on a light, I pulled my coat from the wardrobe, put it on over my night-clothes, and padded downstairs. Now where had I seen that flashlight? *Right! The mantel.* I pocketed the light, crossed the kitchen, opened the front door as quietly as I could, and slid out. Moonlight filled the patio and illuminated the front of the garage.

I walked quietly to the big barn doors and opened the one on the right. The wind grabbed the door and threatened to slam it back against the garage. I held on tight and peered into the gloomy interior, endeavoring to see if someone was hiding behind the rusting tools. I flicked on the flashlight and played the beam over the metal hulks and discarded furniture. The garage was empty. I shone the light on the ground. Were those smudges on the damp ground footprints? They appeared to lead to the left.

Feeling a bit foolish but determined not to take any chances, I grabbed the nearby bicycle pump, latched the barn door, and tiptoed stealthily around the side of the garage. A trail led past the building, uphill between tall trees, and into the woods. The moonlight was fainter here — as was the wind — but by now my eyes had become accustomed to the dark.

I listened to the sounds of the night. Was that some wild creature making those snuffling noises? I moved forward slowly, stopping every few steps, straining to hear over the rustling leaves. The moisture from the wet ground and soggy leaves underfoot seeped into my slippers. "Next time you chase a prowler, Jessica," I told myself, "remember to put on your shoes." A sound up ahead put all my senses on alert. I crept up the wooded path, gripping the pump like a baseball bat for protection, squinting to detect any movement that might give away the intruder. I crested the rise and stopped. About thirty feet in front of me, someone was kneeling on the ground, digging under a tree. A small dog was circling the person and whining.

"You there!" I called out, forgetting to speak French. From the top of the hill, I directed the flashlight toward the kneeling figure. "What are you doing? This is private property." I held the bicycle pump aloft. "You have no business here."

The dog barked sharply but backed away from this advancing apparition wielding an unknown weapon. The animal's owner, dressed in a dark hooded jacket that concealed his face, cursed fluently and took off down the hill, a white canvas bag flapping on his back, the yapping dog running ahead of him. A moment later I heard the revving of a car engine and the whoosh of tires on the sand and gravel road below as the human and canine trespassers made their escape.

I lowered the bicycle pump and stood for a moment, waiting for my pulse to slow. Well, it was nice to know it wasn't just my heated imagination that had conjured an intruder, wasn't it? What could he have been burying under the tree? Loot from a robbery, perhaps? I shone the light on the ground beneath the tree, but there was nothing to see, except a shallow hole with an earth pile next to it. A distant bark sounded, followed by a howl, and then more barking. Coyotes? Did they have coyotes in France? Suddenly aware of my damp slippers and cold feet, I hurried to return to the house, not even stopping to replace the bicycle pump in the garage. Tomorrow, I pledged to myself, I would come back and see if there was anything more I could find.

Early the next morning, as I scrubbed down the bicycle in front of the house, M. Telloir arrived. I was dressed in my running outfit, gray sweatshirt and sweatpants, with an apron protecting the front of my clothes and a scarf around my neck for warmth. It was not exactly what I'd choose to wear to greet company, but since I hadn't known he was coming, I couldn't very well have prepared.

"Philippe Telloir at your service, madame," he said with a slight bow. He held a wire basket with a half dozen eggs nestled in hay. He had workman's hands, rough and red, with large knuckles and grease worked into the lines of his fingertips.

"I'm Jessica Fletcher," I said, drying my wet hands on a dishtowel I'd slung over one shoulder. "I'm pleased to meet you. Martine said you'd stop by."

He smiled at my greeting, his dark face lined from many years in the Provençal sun and wind, and wiped his right hand on his trousers before shaking mine. His eyes strayed to the half-washed bike. "It's not bad, eh? You are doing a good job of it."

"Thank you."

"But Martine, she 'as a car, you know," he said, winking at me.

"I know," I said, "but I don't drive. This will help me get around a bit faster than on foot. And if I can fix this basket, I'll have a place to put packages."

"Ah," he said, contemplating my predicament. "Marcel Oland can drive you. 'E 'as a good car. Very fast."

I cleared my throat to hold back a laugh. "Yes, it certainly is," I said. "Marcel drove me here from Avignon. Is he the only person who offers driving services?"

"In St. Marc? *Oui.*" He stuck his hand under his tweed cap and scratched his head, revealing sparse strands of gray-and-black hair combed over his mostly bald pate. "There is old Peristolle's son, but 'e is very reckless. You are safer with Marcel."

I sighed. Without an alternative, I would have to ask Marcel to drive me to Avignon next week.

M. Telloir put down his eggs, squatted in front of the bike, and tipped his head from side to side. His blue hooded jacket was unzipped, allowing his solid stomach to push out over his belt. He pinched his nose. "How are you going to attach that?" he asked, pointing to the wicker basket, which dangled from the handlebar by a thread of wire.

"I'm not sure," I said. "I should be able to find something in the garage, but I haven't looked yet."

"Let me see," he said, putting his hands on his knees and pushing up. He walked toward the barn before I could say not to bother, moving with the ease of someone accustomed to working outside, his bowed legs giving him a rocking gait that reminded me of a children's toy.

I picked up the wet rag I'd been using to wipe down the saddle seat, and continued my chore, keeping an ear toward the barn where I could hear M. Telloir rummaging through the toolbox. The front half of the bicycle was indeed *"pas mal,"* or "not bad," as he'd said, but the rust on the wheel spokes resisted my scrubbing. I'd finished removing the encrusted dirt and was wiping the bike with a clean, dry cloth when M. Telloir emerged from the barn. He clipped the wire holding one side of the basket to the bike, banged the basket against his leg, dislodging a sprinkle of dirt, and handed it to me. "It 'ave to be rinsed," he said. "Then I attach it for you."

"Thank you. I appreciate that," I said, straightening from my polishing. "May I offer you something to drink, Monsieur Telloir? Martine has some English breakfast tea, and I think there's a bit of cake as well."

"I wouldn't say no to some tea," he replied. He followed me into the kitchen, and while I filled the kettle, he removed a bowl from the cupboard, put his eggs in it, and deposited the bowl in the refrigerator. It was a familiar routine for him, I imagined, Martine entertaining him just as I was about to do. I put the kettle on the stove and took the bicycle basket to the sink. M. Telloir shambled over to the side door off the kitchen as I poured water over the grimy wicker.

"I will be right back," he said. The side door squealed as he opened it, and cold air circled around the kitchen, raising goose bumps on my arms. Two minutes later he reentered with an armload of wood and proceeded to fill the wood boxes next to the fireplaces.

"Would you like for me to lay a fire?" he asked.

"Are you cold?" I asked, placing two cups and saucers on the table.

"No. No, I'm fine," he protested. "But you . . ."

"I'm planning to go for a walk this morning," I said, "and I wouldn't want to leave a fire burning. But thank you for bringing in the wood. I'd wondered where the woodpile was."

"It is just outside your door," he said, pulling out a chair and dropping into it. "The wind was bad last night, eh? It knocked down a few of your logs."

Okay, I told myself. *Those were the thuds I heard. There's always a rational explanation for everything,* I thought. But why was someone digging in the woods behind the house? I eyed M. Telloir's hooded jacket. *No,* I thought, *I doubt he would be able to move as fast as my nocturnal prowler, but better not say anything yet.* I poured water over the tea, sliced a small cake Martine had left in the fridge, and put plates and silverware on the table along with a pitcher of cream and a bowl of sugar.

"I'm sorry," I said. "There's no lemon."

"Don't take it," he replied around a mouthful of cake.

We sipped and chewed in companionable silence, enjoying the early morning sunlight streaming in at an angle through the kitchen window.

"I thought I heard a wolf howling last night," I

said to open the conversation. "Are there wolves in Provence?"

His eyes flicked up from his cup. "Probably a dog," he said. "At what time?"

"Around ten or eleven, I think."

"Did it sound close or far?"

"Far, I think. But it was hard to tell with the wind so loud."

M. Telloir studied his cup, swirling the tea absently. "Thieves have been stealing dogs lately," he finally said, "and that's not all."

"They have! Why would someone want to steal a dog?"

"They can be very valuable," he mumbled into his cup, sipping the last of his tea.

"Are they a special breed?" I asked, standing to get him some more tea.

"No. Most of them are of many breeds, all mixed together."

"I'm afraid I don't understand," I said, refilling his cup. "What makes them so valuable?"

"Truffles," he said.

"Truffles," I echoed, referring to the exotic French fungus that grows underground on the roots of oak trees and is a delicacy prized by chefs the world over. Perhaps that's what my trespasser was after. "I thought they were hunted with pigs," I said.

"Pigs get stolen, too, but mostly it is the dogs now."

"The thieves are stealing dogs that are good at finding truffles?"

He grunted his assent. "Last week they beat up a farmer who was selling a dog. Took the dog and left the man all bloody."

"How terrible."

"It's the start of the season, you know."

"No, I didn't know," I said. "Are you a truffle hunter?"

There was a long pause; he seemed hesitant to trust me with this information. At last he said, "My dog was stolen, too."

"Are you all right? Did they hurt you, too?"

"Wasn't there. They make a hole in my fence and take my dog. 'E had a good nose. Trained him myself."

"What did you do? Are the police any help?"

He blew a stream of air through his lips and looked away from me. "*Bon à rien!* Useless," he said. "The thieves take our dogs over the mountains. And if a farmer in St. Marc buys a new truffle dog, 'e tells no one because 'e knows it could be stolen from somewhere else. Next week I go to the market in Carpentras. There's a man I know who might sell me his dog."

"What will you do in the meantime? Can you find truffles without a dog?"

"There are ways," he said. "If it's warm enough, I watch for *les mouches*."

"Flies?"

"*Oui!* They like very much the scent of truffles. One watches where they land under the tree, and dig there."

"And you've found truffles that way?"

"Oh, yes. My dog, 'e was faster, but the flies, they know, too."

I thought about the stolen dogs later that day while tramping in the woods behind Martine's house. M. Telloir had fastened the clean basket to my newly shined bike, and promised to bring more eggs later in the week. He'd also indicated that the baker had a special cake I should try. It had powdered sugar on top. I took the hint, and added the cake to the shopping list I'd compiled for my first venture into St. Marc.

After M. Telloir had left and I'd washed up our few dishes, I put on a heavy sweater and further explored my surroundings. I located the woodpile on the same side of the house as the kitchen door. The wood was split and stacked three logs deep, as high as my shoulder. There was more than enough to last two months, and probably a sufficient supply for the whole winter.

The view down the driveway confirmed the first impression I'd had from Marcel's car. Rows of olive trees stretched out on both sides, most of their silvery leaves still clinging to the branches but dry now, from the mistral, the constant wind that came from the north.

On the side of the garage, I found the trail I'd already explored in the dark. It led through a row of soaring trees and into a sparse forest of mixed growth. The tall cypresses may have been planted by a previous tenant, but the oaks and planes and pines beyond them had been put there by nature. I followed the well-traveled path that meandered uphill. When I stopped several times to look around or admire the view, I noticed little piles of dirt mounded around holes in the ground circling the trunks of oak trees. A truffle hunter had obviously been pursuing his quarry on Martine's property. I doubted she'd given him permission.

"I'd like two croissants, one for now with some coffee, and one to take home. And a baguette, please," I said in French, eyeing the tall, thin, crusty loaves of bread that stood on end in a crockery canister. "I think I'll get a little cake as well." A quiet day yesterday and a restful night's sleep at last had inspired this morning visit to St. Marc — that and the diminishing supply of food in the refrigerator. I had taken Martine's bicycle — she would never recognize its cleaned and polished frame — and walked the last half mile to the village, set atop a steep hill.

The baker, Mme Roulandet, was a birdlike woman, small and thin, with a pointy nose and narrow chin. Her dark hair was pulled back from her face and tied at the nape of her neck with a long scarf. She plucked two croissants from the pile, put one on a plate, and wrapped the other, twisting the ends of the white paper to seal it closed. She pulled a baguette from the canister and tied a piece of paper in the middle, leaving both ends of the bread uncovered.

"What else?" she demanded, as my eyes

scanned the array of tempting cakes and tarts. "I haven't got all day."

I looked up. The only other person in the shop was a young man wearing a white jacket and black-and-white-checked pants, who was reading a newspaper at a table in a small adjoining room.

"I'll take the one on the end," I said, pointing at a rectangular cake. "No, not that one. The one with the sugar on top."

Mme Roulandet shoved a flat knife under the little block I'd selected and wrapped it in another piece of white paper, this time deftly folding the ends and securing the little package with a piece of string. She put the three items in a plastic bag, and passed it over the counter; half the bread stuck up out of the opening. She looked at me impatiently.

Confused, I opened my bag to get out some francs, thinking she was waiting to be paid.

She clicked her tongue and barked, "What kind of coffee do you want?"

"Café au lait," I said, handing her some money. "Will that be enough?"

She grunted at the bills, pocketed them, handed me the paper plate with my croissant, and waved me away. "Take a seat anywhere. I'll bring you the coffee in a moment."

I turned toward the room next door just as the young man was leaving.

"*À demain*, Marie," he called out to the baker, telling her he'd see her tomorrow.

75

"*Attends,* Charles." She quickly gathered some of her baked goods, put them in a bag, came around the counter, and handed it to him. "Send your mother my regards. Tell her I hope her liver will improve." She kissed him on both cheeks and smiled as she watched him lope down the street. Her expression sobered immediately when she caught me observing her. Had I said something to offend her, or did she simply dislike Americans, or perhaps all foreigners?

The bakery was divided into two parts; on one side was the shop with its baskets of breads and large glass case displaying trays of breakfast pastries, cakes, tarts, and rolls. On the other side was a small room that served as a café. On the café side there was barely room for the four tables and twelve chairs. They shared the space with a tall glass-front refrigerator filled with juices, sodas, and teas, not so very different from the beverages offered in Cabot Cove's village deli.

I walked to a table by the plate-glass window facing the street, and put down my croissant. I hung my bag of bread and cake from the top of a chair, took off my jacket, and folded it over the seat. The ride into town had given me an appetite that hadn't been diminished by visiting several food stores. Without waiting for the coffee, I tore off a corner of the croissant and ate it. It was delicious, the dough crisp, light, and rich, crumbling in my mouth. I savored the unique flavor, thinking, *This can only be had in France,* and looked around for a napkin to wipe off the film of butter the croissant had left on my fingers. There was no napkin holder in sight. I went back to the bakery.

"May I have a napkin, please?"

"I'll bring it with your coffee. Go sit down."

"I'd like one now, please."

Irritation plain on her face, Mme Roulandet handed me a small piece of folded paper. I thanked her and went back to my seat, wiped the grease from my fingers, and patted my mouth. I'd heard rumors about the French being rude, but my recent experiences in Paris and Avignon had contradicted them. I'd been greeted warmly and made to feel at home. Certainly M. Telloir had been agreeable. Here was my first encounter with someone who was less than welcoming.

"So Martine is gone for a month," Mme Roulandet said crisply, setting down my coffee in a plastic foam cup. She pulled a bowl of wrapped sugar cubes from another table and placed it in front of me along with a knife and fork wrapped in a paper napkin. She frowned in disapproval at my cornerless croissant, and pursed her lips.

"Yes. She's visiting her sister."

"And you stay in her house?" she asked, as if this were a disturbing development.

"Yes," I replied. There was a long silence, and I had the feeling that *she* wouldn't trust me with Martine's house. "She's staying at *my* house in Maine," I added, immediately annoyed at myself that this woman had put me on the defensive.

"Where is this Maine?"

"Maine is one of the states in the United States," I explained, trying to be pleasant. "It's in the northeast, at the top of the map, just below Canada." I wasn't surprised that she hadn't heard of Maine — geography isn't as popular a school subject as it once was — but I was a bit taken aback by her hostile attitude toward me. Mme Roulandet owned the only bakery in St. Marc. I would be a customer of hers for two months. Yet there she stood, glaring at me as if I'd told her I'd come to steal her bread.

"Her sister should come here instead," she said, pulling my change and a wrinkled sales slip from her apron pocket and dropping them on the table.

I was grateful when she marched back behind the counter and left me in peace to contemplate the prospect of eight weeks of cold shoulders from the village baker. At least Martine would be back the second month. Hopefully Mme Roulandet's attitude would change then. I unrolled the napkin from the silverware and finished my croissant. A knife and fork. Did the French really use a knife and fork to eat their croissants?

The view from the bakery window was considerably more pleasing than its proprietor. On the other side of the square was Brasserie St. Marc, a restaurant and bar with chairs lined up outside for those hardy souls who liked their wine accompanied by a brisk breeze. It was open for lunch and dinner. Marcel had told me it was worth a visit. "Ask when the chef will make bouillabaisse. Then go," he'd said, "but go for lunch. It will be all gone by dinner." Beyond the brasserie was a *charcuterie,* a shop that sold cooked meats, like hams and sausages and pâtés, and beyond that an *épicerie,* a grocery, both of which I had visited earlier.

I would see the rest of the village another time, perhaps on Friday morning when the outdoor market was open. Idly I pulled my change over to the edge of the table and swept it into my hand. I looked at the wrinkled sales slip Mme Roulandet had left with the coins. I counted the coins and looked at the bill again. She had shortchanged me by a franc. I debated whether or not to tell her, and decided I would.

I finished my coffee, dropped the cup, plate, and napkin in a large wastebasket, and donned my jacket. I took my bag of bread and went to the bakery counter.

"Madame, you owe me another franc," I said, holding out the change in the palm of my hand so she could count it.

She looked at my hand and huffed. "You can afford it," she muttered.

"And so can you," I replied.

She pulled a franc from her pocket and slid it over the counter. I took the coin, walked back to the table, and left it as a tip along with some other coins. Buoyed that I hadn't been cheated, I left the shop. On the ride back to Martine's, I reviewed the scene in my mind and started to laugh. I had confronted the "enemy" over one franc, girded my loins to make a fuss over an amount less than twenty cents. But it was the principle of the thing, I told myself, shaking my head. She'd been so disagreeable. *Count the change*, Martine had said in her note. Now I knew why.

Chapter Four

"Did you go to the market in St. Marc?" Claire asked when I signed in for the first day of my cooking course at the Hotel Melissande.

"I did, last Friday. It was wonderful," I replied. "I've never seen so many different kinds of olives. And I finally learned the purpose of the long bag hanging on the side of my pantry."

"You didn't know?" Her eyes widened. "It's a *sac à pain;* it's to hold the baguettes, of course." She was trying not to smile at my foolishness.

"I'd been wondering what it was all week. I thought it might be a laundry bag for the dishtowels. Now don't you laugh at me," I said, starting to laugh myself. "I'd never seen one before."

"But where have you been putting the baguettes?"

"I cut them in half and put them in the refrigerator."

The giggle she'd been holding in burst forth, and she covered her mouth with both hands.

"I hope you will share the joke," said a stylish matron who'd come up to the desk, her gaze fixed on Claire.

The young woman struggled to contain her smile. "*Bonjour,* Madame Poutine."

"*Bonjour,* Claire." She turned to me. "And who is this?"

Mme Poutine had a beautiful but cold face, with classically chiseled features only slightly softened by age. Her chin-length platinum blond hair was tucked behind her ears; large gold earrings were clipped to her lobes. She was dressed in a black silk blouse, and an amethyst bouclé jacket and skirt with matching heels. A large diamond ring sparkled on her left hand. Her attire seemed more suited to an afternoon at the theater than a morning in a cooking class. I was considerably less turned out in my taupe pantsuit and heather pullover.

Claire stood up straight and adopted a formal tone. "Madame Fletcher, may I introduce Madame Poutine. She is attending Monsieur Bertrand's class today." She turned to the other woman. "Madame Poutine, this is Madame Fletcher. She will be in the class with you."

"It's nice to meet you," I said.

"You are American?" Mme Poutine said to me in English.

"Yes. I'm from Maine."

"I've never heard of it. Do you cook?"

"Yes, but I don't know a lot about French cooking."

"Then you don't cook," she said imperiously. "How do you find Provence?"

"I'm enjoying it very much," I said, starting to wonder if it was really true.

"An odd time of year to come, don't you think?"

"I think it's an excellent time of year," I replied.

"Well, I suppose there are fewer tourists, and that's certainly a benefit," she said, signing her name in Claire's book.

"I find there are just enough," I said.

"I suppose," she said, smiling vaguely at me. "I will see you downstairs."

As she crossed the hall, Guy came around the corner holding a tray with a coffee service on it. He gave her a wide smile and stopped to inquire about her health. She nodded in acknowledgment, and sailed past him to the elevator.

We're a lot nicer to visitors in Maine, I thought, *even if we don't know where you're from. What a frosty lady!* I much preferred the open antagonism of the baker in St. Marc to the veiled insults of Mme Poutine. What was it about French women? Were they all this way? No, of course not. Claire was delightful. Then again, she was barely out of her teens. Perhaps the peevish veneer came with age — and disillusionment.

"Madame Poutine attends all of Chef Bertrand's classes," Claire told me, apparently unaware of my churning resentment.

"She must be an excellent cook by now," I said.

"She used to demonstrate cosmetics on television. She has a beautiful complexion, doesn't she?"

"She certainly has no smile lines," I said.

"Madame, how are you today?" Guy said, coming to the desk and sliding the tray on top. "No lingering bruises, I hope."

"None whatsoever, thank you. How are you?"

"Good. Good," he said. "I've brought some coffee for my girlfriend over here." He winked at Claire.

"You are being silly, Guy," she said.

"I am a man in love, but she doesn't see me," he said. For a fleeting moment, the dark eyes behind his thick glasses looked sad. Then he shrugged and looked down at Claire over his shoulder, teasing her. "She has this beau with gray hair. Her heart is only for him."

"Guy!" Claire's cheeks were bright red.

"Ah, here are more of your classmates," he said. He looked back at a middle-aged couple descending the grand staircase. The man waved at Guy, and took his wife's elbow to keep her from going toward the elevator. "Good morning. Good morning, all," he said cheerily, rubbing his hands together. "Great day for cooking. Thank goodness the sun's not out. It's such a rare occurrence, I'd hate to waste time inside when the sun's shining. But this weather? Certainly makes me feel at home." They were dressed as informally as I, he in a striped shirt and slacks, his wife in a khaki shirtwaist dress and flats, the arms of a sweater tied around her neck.

Guy introduced me to Craig and Jill Thomas, visiting from Sheffield, England.

"Retired now," Craig said, "but used to work for the government."

"Yes, you were a boring sot," his wife Jill

teased him, poking his arm. "Much better now that you've got your head out of those books."

"She just likes the fact that I've got more time to escort her," he said, winking at me. "Someone to carry the bundles when she shops. Someone to stagger under the masses of linens, boxes of soaps, and tins of olives we're bringing back to a family desperate for a whiff of Provence in their deprived homes." He mimed a man staggering under a pile of packages, trying to juggle them before they fell.

Jill laughed at her husband's dramatic performance. "Oh, you," she said fondly. Still smiling, she asked me, "Where in the States are you from?"

"Tell them while we go downstairs," urged Guy, shepherding us toward the elevator. "The class is about to begin. The chef will be upset if we're late."

"But we haven't signed yet," Craig said, hurrying back to the desk, then returning a moment later. "Signed for you, too, my dear," he said to Jill. "Do you think it's legal?"

"I doubt they'll arrest us," she replied.

The elevator door opened downstairs, and I felt a shiver of trepidation as we walked through the arch into the damp and dim interior courtyard. The table was set for eight, with several unopened bottles of wine at one end.

"Creepy-looking place, isn't it?" Jill whispered to me.

"I feel the same way."

"It looks as if they should have torches burning here and instruments of torture rather than a dinner table."

In contrast to the medieval dining room, the kitchen classroom was brightly lit and inviting, but uncomfortably warm. I removed my jacket. Chef Bertrand was busy preparing his ingredients in the front of the room, a white apron covering him from chin to knees. Mme Poutine had already taken a seat on one side of the wooden table in the center of the kitchen. Next to her was a young man in a green sweater over a business shirt. The Thomases and I filled the three empty seats opposite him and Mme Poutine. The last student had not yet arrived.

I began to relax. No decorating magazine could have created a more appealing space for a cooking class. We sat on high stools around a large butcher-block table. Two of the walls were filled with pale green shelves, displaying an array of kitchen paraphernalia, from antique pottery to copper pans, to baskets of clean towels, to glassware, to dishes in myriad shapes and sizes. Everything was within reach and attractively arranged, like a culinary still-life. Across from me, white tile formed a wainscoting on the wall beneath the many-paned window that overlooked the strange square where we would later share our lunch. On the fourth wall was a massive black iron stove with a hood faced with blue and white tiles. A shelf jutting out from the skirt of the hood held a row of tall, two-handled, wide-necked, white porcelain olive jars with rounded caps, lined up handle to handle so the triangular decorative design that had been painted on each one was exactly centered.

"You know what is this design?" Guy asked me, seeing the direction of my gaze.

I shook my head. "It's not familiar."

"It is the hermine, the symbol of Brittany. Anne of Brittany was the queen of France. So this is a symbol of royalty."

"They're so perfectly lined up," I said.

"In a kitchen, it is important to be precise," Guy said.

"Do you have everything ready?" Bertrand demanded.

"*Oui.*" The sous chef jumped from his seat and nervously scanned the table, chewing on the edge of his mustache. He mentally tabulated the items that had been positioned around its surface, his head bobbing up and down as he accounted for each one. "*Oui,*" he repeated.

"Then it's time to start," Bertrand said.

Guy leaned over the empty stool, and with his long arm pressed the door closed. He continued talking to me. "We must have complete order in the kitchen, and know where everything is. That's essential in a restaurant. It ensures that the cooking goes smoothly and the dish comes out the same every time."

"Well, the jars are beautiful. In fact, the whole kitchen is charming."

Guy smoothed his mustache with a thumb and

forefinger. He looked at his watch, glanced at the empty place, and proceeded with the introductions. The young man next to Mme Poutine was René Bonassé, a businessman who had come south for the class. This was his second time observing Chef Bertrand.

"The banker," Bertrand said, pointing at the young man with a whisk covered in frothy egg whites that he had been whipping in a copper bowl.

Bonassé frowned. "Not really."

Despite his youth — mid-twenties was my guess — he was very reserved and immaculately groomed. Tall and athletically built, he had the faint scent of starch about him, and the collar and cuffs of the shirt beneath his sweater were blindingly white. His closely cut jet-black hair was a startling contrast to robin's-egg blue eyes. Serious about cooking, he was making notes on the pages in a folder in front of him. I noticed that the foreigners, myself and the Thomases, were lined up across from the natives, Mme Poutine and M. Bonassé. I wondered who would take the last seat on their side. Would it be another traveler? If so, Mme Poutine would find herself outnumbered by the dreaded tourists.

Obviously familiar with the routine, she'd removed her jacket and now wore a long white apron over her skirt and blouse. Reading the material in a folder at her place, she absently pulled the gold earrings from her lobes and set them on the table.

Bertrand, who was still whipping the egg whites by hand, nodded toward the piles of materials before the Thomases and me. "It's time to put on your aprons; we will start right away."

Guy stood at the rear of the table, a cutting board in front of him and an array of knives by his right hand. "Since we are divided today, Chef Bertrand has consented to conduct the class both in English and in French, so everyone will understand what is happening." As he spoke, he pulled carrots from a large bowl of vegetables and began chopping them. "When you are ready, please open your folders; you will find the menu for the day and the methods for preparing the dishes."

"Study them while we complete the initial preparations," Bertrand added. "I will answer your questions as we go."

Craig Thomas pulled an apron over his head, mussing his wavy hair. "Don't expect me to wear one of these at home," he joked. "I'll never be able to face my mates down at the pub."

Jill settled her sweater across the back of her chair and waited to tie his apron before drawing her own over her dress. She looped the strings around her waist and tied them in the front. I did the same.

His apron on, René hunched over the papers and reviewed his notes. Mme Poutine tried to read them over his shoulder. She leaned into his arm to get a better view and whispered something, which made him start. He looked up at her with one eyebrow raised, and she moved away gracefully. I wondered if she'd been successful in her spying.

I opened my folder and pulled out the pages with the menu and recipes for that day's class. They had been written in French on one side of the paper and in English on the other. With only the faintest guilt, I scanned the English side. We were to prepare chestnut blini, sautéed wild mushrooms, saddle of rabbit, and charlotte for dessert. I reread the menu with dismay. Saddle of rabbit. Of course, rabbit was a popular dish in France — I knew that — but somehow it never occurred to me that game meats would be the focus of a cooking class.

I've always considered myself to have a relatively sophisticated palate, but admittedly, I tend to avoid more exotic fare. There have been exceptions. I love escargots, especially the way Jean-Michel makes the snails at L'Absinthe. I've sampled sushi in Japan, although raw fish is not something I ever order at home. At a famous restaurant in Mexico City I made a point of tasting the classic dish, turkey mole. The sauce is chocolate, but not the kind you pour on ice cream. And I doubt I'll ever serve it on Thanksgiving in Cabot Cove. I do draw the line on some foreign foods, however. In Scotland, I managed to spend a delightful time at the table without ever having to eat haggis, the national dish. Just the thought of organ meats combined with suet, onions, and oatmeal, the whole mixture stuffed into a lamb's stomach, is enough to dull my appetite.

And now rabbit. I always envisioned that word with *bunny* in front of it. Disappointed that I couldn't look forward to lunch with enthusiasm, I promised myself that I would concentrate on the techniques demonstrated and use them at home on something more to my liking.

"Let's begin by going over our ingredients on the table," Chef Bertrand said, his eyes resting on René, who seemed to be writing down every word. "*Voici les coings.* Here are the . . ." He was pointing to a wooden bowl, which held large yellow apple-shaped fruits. "What are they called in English, Guy?"

"Quince."

"We will make them for dessert. You may substitute apple if quince is not available but probably will have to add some starch to thicken the sauce. Quince is very high in pectin, so no thickener is necessary for them." He picked up a large kitchen knife, and tapped the flat side on a bag. "This is the chestnut flour for the blinis, pancakes, I think you call them. We will make them to be a side dish like a vegetable, along with the *champignon des bois,* the forest mushrooms." He rapped on the edge of a tray on which several types of mushrooms were heaped, yellow chanterelles, white shiitakes, tan morels, and brown cèpes. "Over here I have wine, olive oil, mustard, honey." The jars and bottles made musical clinks with each strike of his knife.

91

Frowning at the door, he said, "Ah, at long last, our final pupil has arrived."

Guy opened the door for the sixth student, his tall body blocking my view. All I could see was the arm of a navy ski jacket holding up a large black backpack. There was a mumbled exchange as Guy took the backpack and turned to make the introductions.

"This is Miss Cartright," he announced.

Mallory grinned at me and took her seat, greeting Mme Poutine and M. Bonassé in French, and leaning across the table to shake hands with the Thomases. "Nice to meet you. I'm so sorry I'm late," she said.

Recovering from my surprise, I said, "How are you, Mallory?"

"Fine, thank you."

"Changed your mind about Marseilles?"

"Kind of."

"Oh, you know each other. How nice," Jill said, looking back and forth between us.

The chef cleared his throat, and Mallory looked abashed.

"Before this interruption, I was explaining the ingredients we will use today," he said pointedly.

"Please continue. My apologies for being late. I got lost. . . ." She trailed off under a scowl from the chef.

"You see the vegetables in front of Guy?" he went on, ignoring her. "These he prepares for the marinade. We cut up an onion, two shallots, carrots, whatever we have. Show them how we do the garlic."

Guy frowned at the peremptory tone, but took a head of garlic and pressed down on it with the heel of his palm.

"We leave the skin on. It is less bitter that way," the chef continued, looking at René. "Did you write that down? We wouldn't want you to miss anything."

Bonassé ignored the irony in the chef's voice, and looked up from his notes, his face composed without expression. "The garlic with the skin is less bitter," he repeated.

Bertrand pressed his lips together and continued his lesson. "It doesn't matter if the skin stays on now; later we will strain all these out of our sauce. We sauté the vegetables first, and then add wine and spices." He picked up a large sprig of thyme, and gazed at each of us in turn. "We boil it and pour it over the rabbit."

"Rabbit! Eeuw!" Mallory's face flamed as all eyes turned to her. "Oh, I'm sorry. I just wasn't expecting . . ."

Chef Bertrand growled, "Young lady, if you cannot contain yourself, I will ask you to leave. This is a class for adults, not tardy schoolchildren."

Mallory sank down in her chair, her eyes glued to her lap. "Sorry," she mumbled. I was embarrassed for her, and my heart ached when I saw a tear trail down her cheek. The chef was right to be annoyed, but I was sure he would never have spoken so harshly to the rest of us, no matter how disruptive we were.

"Chef Bertrand," I called out, hoping to pull attention away from Mallory. "Please tell us about your knife. Is it your favorite? What is the brand?"

Bertrand seemed pleased at the question. He smiled down at the knife he still held and raised it so we could see its shape from the side. "This is my own special design. There are only two in the world. I had them made for me twenty years ago. No, they are not something you can buy. See the form of the handle? This is so it fits in my palm comfortably. And this angle keeps my finger from sliding up onto the blade. Notice how the sides taper into the edge. This makes it easier to slide between the bones when you are cutting meat. I will pass it around, but be careful. It is very sharp." He gripped the top of the blade and gave the knife, handle first, to Craig Thomas.

"Nasty-looking weapon," Craig said, hefting the knife up and down to feel its weight. "Here you go, love. Take care." He put the knife down in front of Jill.

I took it after her. On the blade, near the molded black handle, was the mark of the maker, and the phrase *FABRIQUÉ POUR EMIL BERTRAND* — "made for Emil Bertrand" — in curving script. The knife was heavy, naturally turning sharp side down when I let the handle roll in my palm. I gave the knife to Guy, who handed it to Mallory, giving her a wink and a smile. She immediately offered it to René, not taking any time to examine it. Mme Poutine returned the knife to its owner.

"While Guy and I prepare the marinade, you may start on our dessert," the chef said. "We need you to peel the quince and cut it into wedges. Do not throw away the skin or the core. We will cook these, too, and make jelly later."

Guy placed an empty plate in the center of the table — "for the skins" — and handed each of us a small wooden cutting board.

The quince was more difficult to peel and cut than I had expected; the fruit is harder than an apple. Guy collected the wedges, poured sugar and water over them, and reached around Bertrand to place the pot on the stove, quickly moving out of the chef's way. They worked smoothly as a team, years of cooking side by side resulting in a fluid pace, where each knew his steps and the timing of the ballet, although it was clear who the principal dancer was. While the chef sautéed the vegetables, Guy distributed ramekins and butter and brioche bread, and instructed us how to line the dishes with the bread to form the outer crust of the quince charlottes.

While we followed Guy's directions, Chef Bertrand completed the marinade, pouring wine over the sautéed vegetables, and dropping different herbs into the boiling mixture. He took a spoon from a stack of them, tasted the sauce, threw the spoon in the sink, and picked up another to scoop up a hunk of butter, which he stirred into the pot. Guy cleaned up after him, and carried a tray of soiled dishes and utensils out of the room.

"Attention, s'il vous plaît," Bertrand said. "May I have your attention, please." We all looked up from our task. He had a bag in front of him and was spooning flour into a bowl he'd placed on a scale. "This is chestnut flour. We use two hundred fifty grams for three eggs," he said, stirring the eggs into the flour. He wiped off the spoon with his finger and switched to a whisk.

He looked over at René, who was bent over his paper scribbling rapidly. "Monsieur Bonassé, all I see is the top of your head," he said. "How do you expect to learn if you spend all your time writing everything down?"

The young man looked up impassively. "How else am I to learn except by writing it down?"

"You watch," Bertrand exploded. "That's the whole point of taking a class with a master chef. You watch to learn. Otherwise, why bother to be here? You can stay at home in your Paris apartment and read cookbooks."

"Very well." The younger man carefully put down his pen and crossed his arms over his notes. "I am watching," he said coolly.

"We will cook the blini now," Bertrand announced. He turned his back to the class as he fussed with a pan on the stove.

Mme Poutine got up from her seat and stood next to the chef while he cooked our blini. Since I knew she'd taken his class many times, I assumed what she did was permissible for everyone, and I joined the two of them at the stove. I stood behind Bertrand and heard her whisper in rapid-fire French, "René is rating you, I'm sure."

"Calm yourself," he said in a low voice. "You are always imagining things."

"Emil, I saw his notes," she murmured, offended. "It was an evaluation."

"Ridiculous!"

"I am only concerned with what is good for you. You do not appreciate me anymore, now that you have a younger admirer."

"Your jealousy does not become you. Save it for your husband," he said.

He sensed my presence, turned, and said in English, "Ah, Madame Fletcher, you see how the pan is ready now?" He poured olive oil onto a flat round griddle with a long handle, swirled the pan around, and dropped in a hunk of butter that sizzled.

Mme Poutine glared at me and walked away.

"I apologize if I interrupted a personal conversation," I said.

"Not at all," he replied mildly. "I am at your disposal. What would you like to know?"

I would have liked to know more about their discussion, but asked instead, "What kind of stove is this?"

"It's an old wood stove," he replied, ladling circles of the blini batter onto the hot griddle. "It is just for show, really. In my own kitchen I cook with gas. All my equipment is new." He pulled the griddle to the side to reveal a series of concentric rings around a small hole through which the flames were visible. Using an iron tong, he hooked one of the rings and removed it, enlarging the opening, and exposing the griddle to more flame as he slid it back on the burner. "This is a kitchen from years ago, very charming, but perhaps a bit artificial. However, a good chef adapts to the circumstances. I can cook on anything." He used a fork to flip the blinis, which were now browned on one side. "You are a good cook at home?"

"I hope so," I replied, "but I can always be better."

"*Bon!* I like this attitude. You are very intelligent, and much more." He gazed languidly into my eyes and then dropped his glance to my mouth and then up again. I had a feeling this expression of interest was more for Mme Poutine's benefit than for mine, and I didn't care to be used that way.

"I'd better finish preparing my charlotte," I said, returning to my seat. I took another ramekin and began to butter it.

Craig took my place at the chef's side. "So let me see how you do this," he said. "Can't have the women hogging all your time."

Bertrand set the blinis aside just as Guy brought in the makings of the main dish. "*Voilà!* Now we will really show our skill," the chef announced.

The three rabbit bodies were not recognizable as anything other than small animals, but my stomach lurched at the sight of the meat covered in blood. The heat in the kitchen carried the scent around the room.

"These are very fresh," Bertrand said as he picked up the first rabbit, rinsed it under the faucet of the sink to his right, and laid it on a cutting board. He explained his actions as he cut out the "saddle," separating the meat from the bone with his razor-edged knife. He worked rapidly, blood staining his fingers, which he wiped on the front of his apron. He tied the meat with string and laid it in a pan. Taking up his heavy knife, he chopped the skeleton in half, the crunch of the bones as the blade split them loud in the silent room. He threw the two halves into the pot with the boiled wine and vegetables.

"Everything gets used," he said, smiling, and picked up the second rabbit.

Mallory, her face very white, slipped off her stool and left the room. On the pretext of seeing if she was all right, I followed her, glad to breathe in the dank air of the courtyard and escape the coppery smell of blood.

"He's horrible," she whispered when I'd closed the door behind us. "A little rabbit, to end up like that. It was awful. He's a horrible man. Someone should . . ." She stopped in midsentence and hurried down the step, then stood in the middle of the room and wrapped her arms around her body.

"Let's go get some fresh air," I said, putting my arm around her.

We took the elevator upstairs and pushed through the hotel's glass front door. The rain had stopped but it was still overcast — and cold. I realized I'd left my jacket and handbag in the classroom, and so had Mallory, along with her backpack.

She was shivering, but now I wasn't sure if it was caused by her reaction to the butchering demonstration or the chilly temperature outside.

"I'm okay," she said, breaking away from me and pacing in a small circle in front of the building.

"It wasn't a pretty sight, I agree. We aren't used to seeing what happens to our meat before we cook it, are we?"

"Meat? I'm not eating that." She waved a trembling finger in the direction of the door.

"No one says you have to. Are you a vegetarian?"

She shook her head. "I wasn't before, but I could be now. What a horrible man."

She stepped into the narrow, deserted street and walked across it and back, rubbing her arms. Some color had returned to her cheeks.

"Mallory?"

"I know. I know." She continued pacing. "What did I expect from a cooking class?"

"No. That wasn't what I was going to ask."

"Oh." She halted in the middle of the road and turned back to me. "What?"

"I think you know."

She looked down at the cobblestone street, and toyed with the end of her braid before raising her eyes to meet mine. "Why did I leave Marseilles? What am I doing here? Why did I decide to take this class?"

"One at a time will be fine," I said, watching her closely as various emotions flitted briefly across her face.

"You're missing your class," she said, as if it had suddenly occurred to her. She clapped her hands and started walking toward the door, tossing her braid over her shoulder. "I didn't mean to interrupt it for you."

"Come on, Mallory. Talk to me."

"Nothing terrible happened in Marseilles, if that's what you're thinking," she said, stopping in front of me. "I just got bored. No one at the hostel was very friendly, and there's only so much to do there in the cold. You can't go to the beach or even sit outside in a café all day. And how much bouillabaisse can you eat?" She released a short bark that was almost a laugh. "I was thinking I would go to Cannes, but I don't know anyone there either, so I decided to come here instead. There's more to do, and you were the one who said I could call." She finished with a pout, as if I'd reneged on a promise.

"But you didn't call."

"Well, I would have," she said, pulling her braid over her shoulder and gripping the thick plait as if it were a lifeline, "but you told me you were going to be in town today, and I was coming to Avignon anyway. I met this guy who was on his way here, and he said he knew a great hostel."

"Is that where you're staying?"

"Yes. It's a couple of blocks from the station. An easy walk. Only took me fifteen minutes. And it's very cheap."

"But this class is not. If you're worried about money, why did you sign up for the class?"

She put her hand on the handle of the hotel door. "I have enough money, and I have a cash card. Actually, I'd only planned to come and ask after you, but the girl at the desk said someone hadn't shown up, and I could join the class if I wanted. She didn't charge me anything. I thought it would be fun," she said, disgusted. "I didn't think it would be like an *abattoir*." She used the French word for *slaughterhouse*. "And I thought I would surprise you," she finished softly.

"Well, you certainly did that," I said, shaking my head.

Abruptly she pushed the door open and held it for me. "We have to go back in. You must be freezing. I know I am. I'm sorry to have been so selfish, keeping you out in this weather."

As we reentered the lobby, Claire came around the front desk.

"Is everything all right with the class?" she asked.

"Yes. Fine," I said. "We were just taking a

little break, but it's too cold to stay outside."

"We serve coffee and tea in the atrium. If you want, I can have something brought up for you."

I looked at Mallory, who'd paused by a table and seemed to be casually browsing a newspaper left there for guests. "I think we're ready to return to the class, but thank you. We'll stop for tea later on."

We took the elevator downstairs and walked through the arch. At that moment the door to the classroom opened, and Guy emerged carrying the roasting pan with the saddles of rabbit neatly tied up in string. The other students followed him out. Chef Bertrand remained in the school kitchen, stirring a pot on the stove.

"We're going to put the meat in the oven, and take a short tour of the hotel kitchen," he said. "Are you up for it?"

Mallory nodded, and we joined the others.

The hotel kitchen, half as wide as it was long, was empty. "They don't serve luncheon in the winter," Guy explained, opening the top oven in a stack of three gas ovens and sliding in the roasting pan, "although Room Service can put together something for guests who don't want to go out." He knocked on a door. "This is the office, where the chefs plan menus, order supplies."

The narrow room had a small desk at the end, piled with papers, under which could be seen the curled cord of a telephone and the side of a laptop computer. Sitting at the desk was a handsome man in chef's whites who looked up from his book.

"Ah, Guy. Is this your class?" the man asked.

"Oui."

The office was cramped and messy. A battered file cabinet leaned against one wall. On the other was a long row of bookshelves filled with cookbooks, more piles of paper, and various kitchen implements, some still in their packaging. The untidy office was diametrically opposed to the kitchen with gleaming stainless-steel cabinets and counters.

Guy introduced Daniel Aubertin, the hotel restaurant's chef and director of the cooking school. "Daniel will give you a short tour of the kitchen," he told us, "while I keep an eye on the rabbits."

Daniel rose from his seat and treated us to a captivating smile, shaking hands with each student as he exited the office, and seeming pleased to meet us. Curly haired and clean shaven, he had the dark good looks of a movie idol and the confident, slightly bored manner of a man who has done this many times before. *The kitchen tour must be a standard part of the class,* I thought, as he walked backward down the aisle, speaking in English to accommodate the foreigners, and pointing out the four separate work areas used for preparing fish, meats, cold dishes, and desserts.

"For garnishing," he said, pointing at a rolling cart at the end of one counter near the door. Its top was covered with bowls, bottles, and canisters, the little containers filled with different sauces, spices, herbs, seeds, crumbs, chopped nuts, dried fruits, olives, miniature pastries, wafers, and other items used to garnish the food and decorate the plate.

"What time do you have to start cooking for the dinner guests?" René asked, his pen poised above a small notebook.

"The chef and his staff plan the menu after the market in the morning and then go their separate ways. The dinner chef returns at about four-thirty. That would be me. The pastry chef comes in a little later. And the kitchen closes at midnight."

"How do you choose the menu?" Jill asked.

"The full menu changes each season," he replied. "At the hotel restaurant here, certain specialties we will make every day, but half the menu depends upon what we find in the market in the morning." He went to a large double-door locker and opened it. We crowded around the opening to peek inside. The shelves were filled with a variety of fruits and vegetables bought that day. Several crates of squash were stacked on the floor. Daniel walked in the locker and picked up a squash. "These were plentiful in the market this morning. From this, we will make a wonderful cream soup. It's one of our signature dishes. It will also be caramelized to accompany the roast lamb. Later we will add it to our vegetable terrine. Perhaps we will also dry thin slices in the oven with salt and pepper for tomorrow's garnish. Everything we serve is fresh. We must use what we buy imaginatively and efficiently or the customer will become bored, and our business will fail."

"How do you know how many customers you'll have?" Jill asked.

"They take reservations, of course," Mme Poutine told her crisply.

"Yes, of course," Daniel said, nodding at her. "But reservations tell only half the story," he added, looking at Jill. "The rest you learn by being in business. We keep an eye on the weather. Here, for instance, rain will keep the hotel guests in house, and if occupancy is high, that is good for the restaurant. If it is not . . ." He shrugged. "We read the newspaper to know what groups are in town and likely to fill our seats. We know what festivals are on the calendar each year, and keep a log of how they affect our tables. We plan, we track, and we market ourselves; a good review can generate reservations for months at a time. But you must always be prepared for fewer guests as well as more guests than you expect. We cannot waste food or we lose money. And we must have enough or our diners will be disappointed."

"I never realized how complicated it was," Jill whispered to me.

"We've had fresh rolls and bread every morning," Craig put in. "Do you make them, or is there a bakery service that supplies the bread?"

Daniel put his hand over his heart and feigned an attack. "My baker would be stricken to hear you," he said. "Everything you eat here is made here. Come, I'll show our little secret." He led us to a steel cabinet with glass doors, near where Guy stood opposite the ovens. "This wonderful machine helps make the bread," Daniel said. "One puts in the shaped rolls and breads. The machine lowers the temperature to keep the dough from rising; it can stay that way for hours. In the morning, it is timed to turn on automatically, warm up the dough for the last rise, and bake the bread and rolls just in time for breakfast, and again in the afternoon in time for dinner. *C'est magnifique, n'est-ce pas?*"

"Bravo!" said Craig. "I'd like to get one of those for home."

"So would I," his wife deadpanned.

Guy looked at his watch. "*Merci,* Daniel. The rabbit should be ready now. We don't want to overcook it."

"No, we probably want it all bloody and rare," Mallory muttered under her breath.

We trooped back to the dining room with Guy leading the way, the hot roasting pan on a folded towel in front of him like a crown on a pillow. Chef Bertrand was waiting in the kitchen. "Now we will see how well we have done today," he said. He had eight plates set out on the table and proceeded to fill them with sliced rabbit, chestnut blini, and sautéed wild mushrooms. Over the meat, he poured a sauce made from the

107

strained marinade. While Guy took the quince charlottes to the hotel kitchen to bake, we removed our aprons, picked up our plates, and carried them to the medieval dining room next door, lining up at that table in the same places we'd occupied in the school kitchen. Several bottles of red wine had been set out, along with a basket of sliced bread. René began filling our glasses.

Bertrand, minus his toque and bloody apron, but still in a white jacket, joined us in the dining room, carrying in a platter with the remains of the rabbit, blini, and mushrooms, which he set on the table. He picked up his wineglass. *"Bon appétit!"*

"Bon appétit!" we chorused back.

The meal was consumed along ethnic lines. The two Americans and the British couple reached for the bread, and pushed the meat around the plate, nibbling on blini and mushrooms that had escaped the sauce. The four French ate everything on their plates, and sopped up the leftover sauce with the bread. The quince charlottes, however, were a complete success. Covered with a sauce made from frozen berries — "red fruits," Bertrand called them — they disappeared off everyone's plate, and afterward were followed by tiny cups of very strong coffee.

Conversation during the meal followed a similar pattern. Mme Poutine attempted to engage René Bonassé in a discussion of Paris theater, angling her body toward him and pointedly away from Bertrand. The young man listened politely, but had little to say. Bertrand spent the meal sorting through a stack of papers he'd drawn from a breast pocket. The Thomases, making up for earlier neglect, drew Mallory out and quizzed her on all she had seen in France, and gave her a list of must-sees in London, which she said she planned to visit next.

At the end of the meal, the chef walked around the table, stopping to share a word or two, complimenting us on how well we did. He ended up behind René Bonassé. He rested his hands on the young man's shoulders and addressed all of us. "*Merci, mesdames et messieurs.* Thank you for coming to the cooking school. Today's lesson shows you the basic marinade, and the creation of the sauce from the marinade. Also the charlotte. You can vary the filling and the sauce. Perhaps even use a simple bread and fill it with vegetables. It is a flexible recipe." He gave René's shoulder a slap, returned to the head of the table, and leafed through his papers, then pulled out one and squinted at it. He raised his reading glasses, which made his blue eyes look very large. "Tomorrow we will make the famous fish soup of Marseilles, the bouillabaisse." He looked at all our faces to see the pleasure his announcement had given. "To prepare for this class, I will require you to return here in one hour for your assignment. Each of you will be responsible for contributing an ingredient. We will discuss where they are available and what markets to visit. Right now, however, Guy and I will handle the cleanup." He looked at his watch. "You have one hour, and then back here, please. You may leave your folders and belongings where they are. They serve coffee and tea in the atrium upstairs."

We abandoned the table as a group and ambled toward the elevator, basking in the glow of self-satisfaction from having assisted in the creation of a Provençal dinner, our mood only slightly improved by the addition of a few glasses of wine. Behind us, the clatter of dishes as our plates were gathered up was punctuated by a stern "Guy!" from Bertrand. "Where are those papers I asked for?"

The elevator was too small to hold the six of us. The Thomases said they would take the stairs and meet us. "Be happy to treat you to a spot of tea," Craig offered. "We'll save you seats, as we'll probably be there ahead of you. This old lift is as slow as a hound that's lost the scent."

Only one table in the atrium was occupied; a couple of smartly dressed men frowned over some documents. We found a table with enough chairs for everyone, but René Bonassé excused himself to make a phone call, not indicating whether or not he would return. Mme Poutine dispensed with the niceties altogether and walked straight past us to the front desk.

"Ah, don't you find the French so warm and friendly," Craig said, settling into an upholstered armchair, while Jill and I sat together on a sofa. Mallory remained standing, shifting her weight from side to side.

"Bertrand was telling Guy off as soon as we left," Craig said. "We could hear his scolding echoing up the stairwell."

"I'm sorry to hear it," I said. "Guy seems like such a nice man."

"Well, I don't see how he could be a fan of the big guy. There probably aren't many. What an arrogant one that Bertrand is."

Jill made a face at Craig, and glanced at Mallory. "Claire at the desk is lovely," she said.

Craig took the hint. "Yes, she is," he said. "I stand corrected."

Mallory hopped on one foot and then the other, saying, "The French are only nice to the people they know. If they don't know you, they usually don't make the effort." She ran her hand across the back of the sofa, and craned her neck to look up at the skylight several floors above us.

She's a restless teen, I thought, *and has been cooped up too long this morning.* I wondered, not for the first time, what happened in Marseilles to make her seek me out. Did some incident spook her? Or was it just loneliness that brought her to Avignon? Where were her parents? Shouldn't she be in school?

"Would you mind if I took a walk?" she said, polishing her glasses with the tail of her yellow shirt. "I'm feeling antsy."

"Go ahead," I said. "But don't forget your

backpack is still downstairs."

"Don't worry. I'll be back in time for tomorrow's assignment, as instructed." She saluted like a soldier, clicked her heels, and walked off.

We watched her stride across the atrium to the front door of the hotel, braid bouncing on her back, long legs encased in jeans, and arms hugging her blue ski jacket.

"She's charming," Jill said. "How do you know her?"

"We met on the train coming down," I replied. "I'm worried about her. She's so young, and seems to have nowhere to go."

"Then you don't know her parents?"

"I really don't know anything about her except that she says she's been in France since August."

"Let Jill have a go at her," Craig said, scanning the tea menu. "She's a real archeologist when it comes to digging secrets out of the close-mouthed. She's exposed all of mine, haven't you, love?"

Jill ignored him and said to me, "I can see why you're concerned. She may be a runaway. So many children run away from home or school. Perhaps she had a fight with her parents. Why don't you ask her?"

"I don't want to scare her off," I said. "I've been hoping she would come to me, and I think she has. I'm going to invite her to the house I'm staying at in the country."

"That's a good idea," Jill said.

"Yes, but I've taken a room at the hotel for tonight. I thought it would be easier than going back and forth from St. Marc. That reminds me — I need to confirm with Claire that my room will be ready soon. The usual check-in isn't until three, but she said she'd try to accommodate me earlier."

"Go ahead," Jill urged. "What kind of tea would you like? We'll order for you."

"Any one is fine," I said, getting up. "English breakfast is my favorite."

Claire was not at her post, but the office door behind the front desk was ajar. I couldn't see inside, but I could hear Mme Poutine arguing with her.

"You're a fool, Claire. Emil is simply playing with you."

"He loves me and he needs me. And I'm free to be with him."

"You bore him. He told me. And it's only a matter of time before he will cast you aside. I'm only trying to warn you."

"He never said that. You're jealous, that's all."

"Why should I be jealous? He is not important to me."

"No? You were lovers once. You probably want him back. Why else would you follow him from class to class?"

"You are misinformed," came the icy reply. "I have known Emil many years, yes. All the chefs have their loyal followings. I have my reputation as a hostess to uphold. But you, your reputation is in tatters, and for what? He throws you a little smile, chucks your chin, tells you how beautiful you are, and you fall into his arms. I'm telling you, he has another fool, just as young, just as pretty, at the Hotel de la Mirande."

"You're lying." Claire's voice was tearful.

"We'll see. Just don't cry to me when he tosses you aside."

Claire burst from the office, a hand over her mouth, skirted the desk, ran across the atrium, and disappeared around a corner. A moment later Mme Poutine emerged, her face impassive, pulling on the cuffs of her jacket. She walked to the other side of the desk and stopped in front of me. "You have a bad habit of listening in on others' conversations, Madame Fletcher," she said coldly.

"And you have a bad habit of standing where you can be overheard, Madame Poutine."

She followed the direction Claire had taken, but stopped at the table with the two men and sat down. I returned to my seat with the Thomases.

"I take it she won't be joining us," Craig said, stirring a lump of sugar into his tea.

"What happened?" Jill asked. "Claire went flying by us in tears."

"Now, don't be nosy, darling."

"Jessica will say if she doesn't want to tell us, won't you?"

"Apparently Claire has a crush on Bertrand, and Madame Poutine was warning her off," I said.

"Poor Claire," Jill said. "She's no match for that sophisticated woman."

"However, their confrontation has left the front desk unattended," Craig added, "so you'll have to wait to get your room."

"You're welcome to use ours if you'd like to freshen up," Jill offered.

"That's very kind," I said, pouring milk into my tea, "but I'm sure she'll be back shortly. I'll wait."

As it happened, Claire didn't return. But we didn't miss her. The Thomases and I chatted about our lives back home and what had brought us to France. Like me, they were childless but with a large family of nieces and nephews. They were both retired and attempting to make up for all the travel that they'd put off when they'd been focused on their careers. This was their third "cookery course," as they called it. As we talked, we marveled at all the things we had in common, and how we felt as though we'd known each other for years. Theirs was a warm, relaxed relationship that easily accommodated others. I invited them to visit me in Cabot Cove if their travels brought them to the States, and they insisted I should stop off in England, particularly at Sheffield, on my way home from France.

Jill and I were laughing so hard over some story Craig had told that we barely noticed when Mme Poutine approached our table, stumbling into the back of the sofa on which we sat. Craig stood up, immediately sensing something wrong, and guided her to his seat. Her platinum hair hung down in her face. She was very pale, and visibly shaking.

"What's wrong?" I asked, sobering instantly. I leaned over to take her hand. Something had given her a shock. I had a terrible feeling that Claire had done some harm to herself. "Is it Claire?" I asked.

She nodded her head and attempted to talk, but her throat was so dry, it came out as a whisper.

"We can't hear you, dear," Jill said. "Try to tell us again what's wrong."

"Here, take some tea," I said, putting my cup in her hands and holding it with her as she took a sip.

Mme Poutine looked up at me gratefully, tears filling her eyes and flowing down her perfectly made-up cheeks. "It's Emil," she said, her voice hoarse.

"What about him?"

"Claire has killed him."

Chapter Five

"Jessica, where are you going?" Jill called out.

After Mme Poutine's shocking statement Craig had run to the phone at the front desk to call for an ambulance and the police. I'd decided to see for myself if Chef Bertrand were indeed dead or if his paramour was exaggerating.

"He may have suffered a heart attack," I said. "Perhaps there's still time to help."

"No. No. He is dead." Mme Poutine moaned, dropping her head into her hands and sobbing.

I rushed across the atrium, hoping he was still breathing. As I reached the entrance to the stairwell, the elevator door opened across the hall, and René Bonassé stepped out. I ran past him into the elevator and took it to the lower floor. The table where we'd eaten lunch had been partially cleared, but the large serving plate was still there, the sauce congealed around the leftover rabbit. There was no sound from the hotel kitchen and no sign of the sous chef, but the lights in the cooking classroom still blazed. I could see Mallory's backpack leaning against the wall, and while I'd taken my handbag with me, I'd left my jacket, which still hung on the back of my chair. The brilliance of the classroom only emphasized the murky shadows of the interior medieval courtyard that had been our dining room. I looked around. It took a moment for my eyes to find Bertrand.

He was dead. There was no doubt. His body was slumped against the arched door in the wall to the right, the papers he had been consulting earlier scattered about him on the floor. A red stain above his heart was spreading down the front of his white shirt. His eyes were open, the vivid blue fading, and his mouth gaped, forming an O, the expression of surprise that must have greeted his murderer. Apart from the papers on the floor there was no sign of a struggle. No overturned chair. No obvious defense wounds on his hands. No clothing askew. The only blood was a few drops spattered on the stone near the wall but away from the body.

I knelt down and placed two fingers on his neck where a pulse should have been, and felt only cool skin. In his right hand he clutched a piece of stationery. I angled my head to read the name at the top. It said, P. FRANC, *AGENT IMMOBILIER* — real estate agent. Bertrand's fist had crumpled the paper. I knew not to disturb the scene and left the letter where the police would find it. I glanced over the other sheets on the floor. Most of them were recipes, lists of ingredients, and menus. A slight breeze ruffled them. I stood.

The door in the archway on the opposite wall was partly open. A sliver of light could be seen along the jamb, and the undulating sound of the Klaxon horns of emergency vehicles leaked into the room. Reluctant to leave my fingerprints, I pulled a handkerchief from my bag and used it to draw open the heavy wooden door. It led to a small paved area outside. From the doorway I scanned the ground for evidence, something the killer might have dropped if he or she had departed this way. A short flight of stairs connected to the street level. I went outside, climbed the stairs, and found myself halfway up a steep hill. The street was deserted. I couldn't see over the top of the hill; not even a car crossed the intersection at its base. If someone had escaped through this door, they were gone now.

The sirens were deafening. I retraced my steps and reached for the door. Using the handkerchief again, I reentered the hotel, drawing the door closed behind me. My eyes had difficulty adjusting to the gloom, but I knew one thing: I was no longer alone.

"Bonjour, madame," said a voice filled with irony. "May I ask what you are doing here?"

"Oh, my," I said. "You certainly gave me a start."

"I could say the same of you," he said in near-perfect English.

The speaker was a debonair man in a gray suit. A black trench coat was slung over one arm. His auburn hair was streaked with gray and he wore it slicked back from his forehead, which emphasized his high-bridged, prominent nose and the piercing look in his hard brown eyes. A colleague in a tweed jacket was leaning over Bertrand, his fingers probing the same area of the chef's neck where mine had been earlier.

I put out my hand. "I'm Jessica Fletcher," I said. "I was one of Chef Bertrand's students this morning."

"You are American?" he asked, ignoring my hand.

"Yes. I'm staying at the home of a friend who lives in St. Marc. I came to Avignon this morning to take Monsieur Bertrand's cooking class." I nodded toward the kitchen classroom.

"What are you doing down here?" he asked. It wasn't a friendly question.

"I was having tea with some of the other students when Madame Poutine — she was also in our class — accosted us. She was distraught, and crying that the chef had been killed. I thought perhaps she'd been mistaken in what she'd seen. I rushed down here hoping he might be alive, in need of medical help. But, as you see, she was right."

"You are a doctor?"

"Heavens, no!"

"A nurse, perhaps?"

"No. I have no medical education."

"Yet you came down here to offer medical help."

"I know that sounds odd," I said, "but if he'd had a heart attack or choked on something, I thought I could lend assistance until an ambulance arrived."

"And, of course, you are trained to lend assistance. No?"

"In a way, yes," I said, relieved I could answer

in the affirmative. "I've taken several first-aid courses, and CPR; that's cardiopulmonary resuscitation."

"I know what CPR is."

"Well, I wasn't sure if it was the same in French."

"And what were you doing outside, if I may ask?"

"Certainly," I said. "I noticed that the door was ajar and went to see where it led. I thought perhaps the killer was making his escape."

"And was this killer 'making his escape'?"

"No. No one was outside."

"You don't seem at all disturbed to be confronted by a dead man. Women are usually — how do you say? — delicate. They scream or faint at the sight of a corpse."

"That's not —"

He interrupted me. "They don't look so calmly around, notice the door is a bit open, and go investigate. *Vous gardez votre sang-froid.* You are very cool." He raised an eyebrow and glared at me. "But what if the killer *had* been around, Madame Fletcher? Would you have known what to do if you were confronted with a gun?"

"Oh, he wasn't . . ." I stopped midsentence.

"You were about to say?"

I sighed. "I was about to say that I don't think Monsieur Bertrand was shot. And I also don't think that the killer would hang around outside, waiting to be discovered."

"And why is it, madame, that you don't believe the victim was shot? Do you see another murder weapon?"

"No, but I also don't see any shell casing. And there wasn't a shell casing outside the door, or anything that could be a murder weapon. I checked. You'll see that for yourself, I'm sure. From the hole in his shirt, it looks to me like Chef Bertrand was stabbed, although since I didn't examine him, I can't say what the instrument might have been."

"You intrigue me, madame," he said. "You are not, by any chance, a homicide detective?" His sarcasm was palpable.

"No, but I have made a study of the subject for some time."

"And why is that?"

"I study murders because I write murder mysteries. That's how I make my living, Detective . . . I'm sorry, I don't believe you gave me your name."

"The rank is Captain, madame. I am Captain LeClerq."

"Captain LeClerq, while you and I are conversing, the killer could be getting away. Chef Bertrand was alive an hour ago. The person responsible for his death may still be in the hotel. We should be looking for the murder weapon. We're giving the killer too much time to dispose of the evidence."

"*We?*" His eyebrows rose. "You seem to think, madame, that Lieutenant Thierry and I are inadequate to the task. That we require your assistance."

"I didn't mean to imply —"

"Please allow us to do our job," he said coldly. "The Commissariat Centrale d'Avignon is well equipped to investigate all crimes. We can do more than arrest the pickpockets and petty thieves who arrive each summer along with the tourists."

"I'm sure that's true," I said, sorry I'd gotten into this argument. I heard my name being called.

Mallory raced through the archway from the hall, and drew to a halt at the sight of the two policemen. "Mrs. Fletcher, are you all right?" She was panting, her eyes huge behind her wire-rimmed glasses.

"Yes, dear. I'm fine."

"I heard upstairs" — she was trying to catch her breath — "that there had been a murder." She shook her head. "You weren't around." A deep breath. "I got worried. And they wouldn't let me downstairs to look for you," she finished in a rush.

"Then how did you get here?" LeClerq asked.

Mallory flushed. "There's a set of stairs from the hotel's dining room." She pointed behind her. "It goes to the other end of the hotel kitchen."

Just then the elevator door opened and two men entered the room. One was carrying a small case, the other a camera with a flash unit.

"It's getting a bit crowded in this place," Captain LeClerq grumbled. "Perhaps you would be good enough to wait upstairs with the others so we may finish our work down here?"

Thierry had positioned his body to block Mallory's view of the chef, but now he moved aside to allow the newcomers to conduct their part of the investigation. Mallory gasped when she glimpsed the lifeless body of Emil Bertrand. "Oh, my gosh. Is it him?"

"I think Captain LeClerq is right," I said, taking Mallory's arm and turning her around. "We should wait for him upstairs. Why don't you show me where this other staircase is?"

We walked down the hall to the hotel kitchen, Mallory excitedly burbling about how she searched for me upstairs and begged the officer guarding the stairwell to let her try the lower floor. I recognized the signs of adrenaline release. It would take a while for her to come down from its intensity. I took her arm as we walked and patted her hand. "You can see I'm just fine," I said. "Thank you for worrying about me."

"Who do you think killed him? I can't believe it. I've never seen a dead body before. Do you think the police are going to question us?" Her whole body was trembling.

"Shhh," I said. "Try to calm down."

As we passed the door to the office used by the hotel chef, I heard a sound, as if something had fallen off a desk or shelf. I put my ear to the wooden panel and my hand on the knob. Someone was inside. I twisted the knob and the door opened. Guy was on his knees, gathering a sheaf of papers and folders that had slid off the overloaded desk.

"Hello," he said, pressing the folders to his chest. "Daniel's desk is such a mess. Is it already time to start again?"

"Where have you been, Guy?" I asked, wondering if he was trying to shield the front of his uniform from view.

He looked confused. "I went to the restaurant to get materials for tomorrow's class, and then I . . . then I came back. There's a lot of work to do to prepare for these classes. Why do you ask?"

"How did you manage to get in here without running into the police upstairs?"

"There are police upstairs?" A few papers slipped out of his grasp and fell to the floor. He made a grab for them.

"Oh, Guy, the most terrible thing," Mallory began. I squeezed her arm, and she stopped abruptly.

"How long have you been here?" I asked, watching his face closely. I sensed someone behind me and whirled around.

"You're doing my job again, Mrs. Fletcher." The fierce eyes of Captain LeClerq bored into mine. "Why don't you take this young lady upstairs, and leave the questioning to me?"

"Of course, Captain."

Mallory and I left Guy's office and walked

through the silent kitchen to the other set of stairs.

"Guy doesn't know, does he?" Mallory whispered.

"I don't know," I said. "But Captain LeClerq will tell him."

"Do you think they'll let me get my backpack from the classroom?" she asked, pulling her braid over her shoulder. I recognized the gesture. Mallory fiddled with her hair whenever she was nervous or insecure.

"I'm sure they'll let you retrieve it later," I said. "Unless the police are planning to camp out downstairs and use your sleeping bag."

Mallory gasped. "They wouldn't!"

"I'm only teasing," I said.

Once back on the main floor, we traversed the dining room.

A small staff was starting to set the tables for dinner. I checked my watch. Daniel would be coming back in another hour to start cooking. I wondered if the news had gotten out to the local media. If France was anything like the States, the hotel would be overrun with reporters as soon as the police withdrew, and probably even before.

We returned to the atrium, where the room was buzzing with rumors of the murder. Hotel guests returning from their day's activities or coming downstairs from their rooms in response to the sirens had seen the emergency vehicles and heard whispers of what had occurred. Every table was occupied, and in the lounge next door, a noisy group crowded around the bar. Mallory went to get herself a Coke, and I found Craig and Jill Thomas, who were still sitting where I'd left them. René Bonassé had rejoined them. He'd changed into a slate blue knit turtleneck and gray jacket, the colors accentuating his light eyes against his dark skin. His expression was fixed in a frown, and he chewed on the side of his cheek as he listened to Craig tell a story. Mme Poutine was nowhere in sight.

"Oh, Jessica, thank goodness Mallory found you," said Jill. "We were really starting to fret."

"I'm just fine," I said, "but I'm afraid our instructor will not be revealing the secrets of his bouillabaisse to us tomorrow."

"Then she was right," Jill said, despondent. "I'd hoped she was just overwrought. The French are so high-strung. Oh, excuse me, René. I meant Madame Poutine was so high-strung."

"I thought she was rather a cold fish myself," Craig said, an opinion I shared.

"She had that appearance, I admit," Jill said. "But look how distraught she was."

"Understandable, considering the situation. Not every day one discovers a murder," Craig said, putting his arm around his wife's shoulder.

"Did she say anything more after I left?" I asked.

"I'm not sure," Jill said. "You heard her say Claire killed him."

"Did she say how she knew that?"

"She was close to hysterical and babbling in French, and we don't really speak well enough to understand her. René came back right after you went downstairs. He spoke with her. She told him she saw Claire leaning over Bertrand's body, and when she cried out, Claire ran out the door. René wanted to go downstairs after you, but we persuaded him to wait with Madame Poutine until the authorities arrived."

"Where is she now?"

"When the police came, she collapsed altogether, and they took her off in an ambulance. Poor thing."

"If there's a 'poor thing,' it's the chef, love," Craig told his wife. "At least Madame Poutine is still alive."

"Do you know her well?" I asked René.

He seemed taken aback that I addressed him. "No, madame," he replied.

"But you'd been in the class with her before."

"We are here to learn from a master chef," he said, "not to make friends. Madame Poutine was a student in the last class I attended, yes, and she was at this one. As you saw, there is not a lot of time to spend on conversation in these classes. Under the circumstances, I doubt I will meet her again, or you, for that matter."

His voice carried a world-weary note, as if the death of the chef were nothing more than an inconvenience, but his fingers trembled when he passed his hand over his dark, close-cropped hair. I decided not to question him further, for now. People respond so differently to murder, I thought. Some withdraw, feeling depressed or sad. Others are shocked or angry or frightened. Still others become hysterical. It is rare for someone to have no reaction at all. René's shaky hand betrayed some response, but it wasn't clear to me what he was feeling. *Yes,* I decided, *put away your doubts, Monsieur Bonassé. You will definitely meet me again. I'm sure we can find some things to talk about.*

Mallory came back from the bar, walking slowly and trying not to spill her full glass. "Everyone in there is talking about the murder," she said. "I heard someone say his restaurant will probably lose its star now." She took a sip of her soda and sat on the sofa.

René glared down at Mallory but, catching me looking at him, schooled his features into an impassive expression and looked away.

"Has anyone seen Claire since the police arrived?" I asked.

"I saw her," said Mallory. "She was getting in the back of a patrol car when I returned from my walk."

"Oh, dear," I said. "I hope they're not too hard on her."

"Why would they be?" she asked.

Jill looked at me. "Do you think Madame Poutine was right? After all, she didn't actually see Claire do it."

"Claire would never hurt anyone," Mallory

said vehemently, although the statement was aimed at me.

"I agree," Craig said. "But it's not a stretch of the imagination to see Madame Poutine putting a spotlight on her rival."

"Was Claire really her rival?" Jill asked. "I can't see her having an affair with Bertrand. She's so much younger than he is — or was. What do you think, Jessica?"

"I think Claire thought she was in love with him," I said. "I don't really know anything more than that."

"I hope you will all excuse me," René said stiffly. "I am going to return to my room." He turned to Craig. "Would you kindly inform the police where I can be found, if they ask?" He strolled off toward the stairs.

"Odd chap," Craig muttered.

An hour later, Captain LeClerq's lieutenant came to take our names and the addresses where we were staying. I asked him to bring up Mallory's backpack and my jacket, if that was permissible. We were tired and ready to go home.

"I believe the men have finished their search of that room," he said. "They're going to bring the body out now. After the ambulance leaves, I can ask the captain if you can sign for your things, and we should be able to release them."

"How long will that take?" I asked.

He scratched his chin and shrugged. "Police work takes time, madame. The captain doesn't like to be rushed. Since your things have been examined, he probably won't mind if I set them aside for you. Maybe another hour. Maybe two."

Chapter Six

"Did you hear the scratching last night?"

"What scratching?"

"There was scratching at the door."

"It was probably the wind blowing a branch against the side of the house," I said. "I've heard it before."

"And what about the howling?"

"I think it must be a dog. There aren't any wolves. I've asked."

"So you've heard the howling before, too."

I was in the bathroom, elbow-deep in soapy water, rinsing out some of my things. Martine's farmhouse had many amenities but a washer and dryer were not among them. There was a sharp rap on the front door, loud enough for me to hear upstairs.

"I'll get it," Mallory said, popping up from the edge of the tub where she'd been perched, keeping me company. She was terribly pale and had spent half the morning braiding and unbraiding her hair. I worried that yesterday's murder was weighing heavily on her mind. I intended to talk with her about it and insist she call her parents. Just hearing a familiar voice could be very soothing. Whatever had occurred to prompt her to run away could surely be put behind her now. It was time to face the telephone and call home.

A minute later she was back at the bathroom door. "Mrs. Fletcher, the police are here." She chewed on her lower lip nervously.

"Would you tell them I'll be right down, please? See if they'd like some tea."

Mallory and I had returned to St. Marc late in the evening following the murder. I'd decided not to stay overnight at the hotel after all, and had called off my dinner reservation at Christian Étienne, the well-known Avignon restaurant owned by a friend of Jean-Michel Bergougnoux, the chef at L'Absinthe in New York. The young man who took over the front desk at the Hotel Melissande for the absent Claire was very understanding about my cancellation, but I could see he was worried that the bad news would cause other guests to leave or change their destinations. The Thomases, I knew, would be staying, and so would René Bonassé. Captain LeClerq had asked all those who had been in the chef's class to remain in Avignon or nearby until the investigation was concluded and he told us we were free to leave.

I'd insisted that Mallory come back with me, and she'd readily agreed. Fortunately, Mme Roulandet at the bakery was able to reach Marcel, who came to collect us. Mallory and I were so wrapped up in what had occurred, and Marcel peppered us with so many questions — he'd had to breach the police barrier to pick us up at the front of the hotel — that we'd barely noticed the ride back to the country, and were grateful to get there quickly.

After a light supper, Mallory had fallen into bed — into a living room couch, to be more precise — still dressed in her clothes. I'd offered her Martine's room, but she'd declined to sleep there.

"I'm imposing as it is," she'd said, stifling a yawn. "I'd feel worse to be in someone's private room when she doesn't even know I'm in her house."

Mallory's sensitivity impressed me, even though I was sure Martine would have had no objections to allowing the teenager to sleep in her bed.

We'd drowsed in the living room, sitting across from each other on the colorful sofas. The peacefulness of the wood fire in the hearth was lulling after such an emotional day, and she'd fallen asleep sitting up. I covered her with a blanket and quilt, and stared down at her troubled face. Was I doing the right thing taking her in?

Now the police were here for a follow-up interview. I pulled the plug in the sink, then dried my hands.

Captain LeClerq, in another elegant suit, this one dark blue, and a yellow-flowered silk tie, was examining one of Martine's paintings when I entered the living room. Fingers linked behind his back, coat thrown carelessly over one shoulder, he leaned back to allow himself a wider view, then stretched forward, squinting to take in some detail of the artwork.

"She is very talented, your friend," he said in English. "Where is she? I would like to offer my compliments."

"Your compliments will have to wait a month, I'm afraid," I said, taking a seat next to Mallory on the sofa. "Martine is in America right now. She's staying at my house in Maine."

"Interesting."

"I expect her back in a few weeks," I added. "I'll be sure to tell her how much you like her work."

"*Merci,*" he said, walking to the fireplace and resting his arm on the mantel.

I could see he was formulating his questions for us, but I headed him off. "How is Madame Poutine?" I asked. "I heard she was taken away in an ambulance."

"*Seulement une crise de nerfs,*" he replied. "Only a case of nerves."

"I wonder," I said, almost to myself.

"It is not so surprising," he said. "A bit of a trauma for her; the Poutines and Bertrand were old friends."

"Is that what she told you?"

"Yes," he said, smiling. "And her husband said the same when he came to collect her. But we are getting away from our —"

"And Claire?" Mallory interrupted. "Is she okay?"

"Yes," I added. "How is Claire today? I understand you took her in for questioning yesterday."

"That is correct," he replied patiently. "We have taken her into custody. She cannot account for her time, and we are holding her under suspicion of murder."

"Captain —" I started.

"No more," he interrupted. "I am the one to ask the questions. This is a murder investigation, not a discussion. We must address the facts, not your opinion." He nodded at Thierry, who'd taken a chair in a corner of the living room next to Mallory's backpack, where he could observe us sitting on the sofa. The lieutenant removed a narrow notebook from his breast pocket and waited while LeClerq paced in front of the fireplace.

"Tell me, Madame Fletcher, how long did you know Chef Bertrand?"

"I met him last week," I said. "When I arrived in Avignon, I stayed one night at the Melissande before coming out to St. Marc. I was introduced to him the next morning when I asked Claire to confirm my registration for the cooking class."

"And you, Mademoiselle Cartright?"

Mallory was sitting on the sofa looking sick. She'd pulled the rubber band off the end of her braid and was concentrating on unraveling a knot in the elastic. She jumped when the captain directed his question at her. "I . . . I . . . I never met him before yesterday," she stammered.

"And Claire, Madame Fletcher. Had you met

her for the first time last week as well?"

"Yes."

"And you, mademoiselle?"

"Yes."

"Yes, what?" he asked.

Mallory glanced up, confused. "Yes, I only just met her."

"That is interesting, mademoiselle, because one of the bellmen reported that he saw you talking together, and that you appeared to be old friends."

"No. That's not true," Mallory said, looking at me. "I mean, I liked her right away, but this is the first time I've been to Avignon." Mallory's glasses had slipped down her nose. She pushed them up with the hand that wasn't fisted around the end of her braid.

"So you just met her for the very first time yesterday?" he pressed.

"Yes." Her eyes were still on mine.

"Do you think you could look at *me* when you answer my questions?"

"Captain, that tone isn't necessary," I said.

He put a hand up to stop me, still staring intently at Mallory. "Silence, madame. You will have your turn."

Mallory raised her eyes. She was close to tears and her lips trembled.

I took her hand and held it. Speaking to the policeman, I said, "Captain LeClerq, Mallory wasn't even in the building when Bertrand was killed. You're trying to intimidate her for no reason."

137

"My apologies, madame, but I must follow up on all leads." He addressed Mallory again, but his voice was less harsh.

"Tell me where you went at the end of the class."

Mallory cleared her throat and sat up straighter. "We all came upstairs together," she recited. "We were supposed to meet back in the classroom in an hour. I'd been sitting all morning, so I asked Mrs. Fletcher if she minded if I took a walk." Her eyes sought mine again, and I nodded.

"Where did you go?"

"I don't know the name of the streets," she said, raising her hazel eyes to LeClerq's, "but I ended up in the square with the merry-go-round."

"What is this 'merry-go-round'?" LeClerq asked, irritated.

"She means a carousel, Captain," I explained.

"Ah, Place de l'Horloge."

"That's it," Mallory said, brightening.

"Who saw you there?"

"I don't know," she said slowly, pondering the question. "No one, I guess. I didn't talk to anybody." She looked worried again. "I was just watching the children riding the carousel."

"May I see your passport, please?"

"Really, Captain," I said. "You can't believe that Mallory had anything to do with Bertrand's murder."

"Madame Fletcher, you are interfering with

138

my investigation." He looked at Mallory and put his hand out, palm up.

Mallory looked at me, eyes pleading.

"You'd better give it to him," I said softly.

She went to her backpack, unzipped an outside pocket, withdrew her blue American passport, and placed it in LeClerq's hand. She stood before him, smiling uneasily. "You know," she said, "it's a couple of years old, and I've grown."

LeClerq scrutinized her photograph, his eyes moving up and down and up, from Mallory's face to her passport and back again. "I can see that it's you," he said, flipping the pages to check her date-of-entry stamp. "You are due to leave the country soon. Did you know this?"

She nodded.

"Where do you live in the States?"

"Cincinnati."

"Mallory, you told me you lived in Portland," I said.

"Did I?" She frowned, her eyes roaming the room to avoid the stares of the three adults. "Well, we did live there, but my father got a new job — he's a record promoter and he has clients all over the country. We can always get tickets to the best concerts, my brother and I — so we moved to Cincinnati. I liked Portland better, actually." She watched Thierry, who was writing furiously in his notebook, and her expression softened, her frown smoothed away.

It was obvious to me that she was improvising. I hoped LeClerq hadn't come to the same conclusion. But why would she lie about something so unimportant? Now I was uncertain which city, if either, was where her family lived.

"Would you like to see my passport, too, Captain?" I asked, hoping to draw his attention away from Mallory.

"Oui, madame."

I went to the kitchen, where I'd left my bag, brought back my passport, and handed it to him.

LeClerq didn't bother to look at it. He put both passports in his breast pocket. "I'm afraid I must confiscate these temporarily."

"Why?" Mallory was shaken.

"This is a murder investigation," he said, beckoning Thierry that it was time to go. "For the time being, I must be sure you do not leave the country. I will be back."

"But I have to go home soon," she said, putting her hand on his sleeve. "It's almost three months."

"I am aware," he said, shrugging off her hand. He strode to the door and waited while Thierry walked out ahead of him and climbed into the driver's seat of their police vehicle.

I followed them outside.

He hesitated at the passenger door, looked back at me, anger simmering beneath his brittle veneer, and said icily, "One of you is lying, madame. You may want to think about that until we return."

Chapter Seven

"Mallory, I want you to call your parents and tell them where you are."

"I did that already when I was upstairs," she said, holding up her cell phone and then zipping it into a pocket of her ski jacket, which was hung over the back of her chair. "And I hope it's okay that I left them your telephone number here."

"Of course it is. I'd like to speak with them if they call."

We were sitting at the kitchen table drinking tea and sharing a slice of one of Mme Roulandet's delicious cakes. The baker had begun warming to me, and had actually gone so far as to recommend I try this particular *gateau* the last time I visited her shop. Whatever the peculiarities of her personality, she had a deft hand with her pastries, several of which I'd put in the freezer against times when I couldn't get into town. The cake had a ribbon of sweetened almond paste through it and powdered sugar and ground almonds on top. I vowed I would ask her for the recipe before I left the country, although I didn't hold out much hope she'd accommodate me.

After the policemen had left, Mallory had dragged her backpack upstairs and taken a bath. She'd washed out a few of her things, as well, and hung them alongside mine on a line outside the side door off the kitchen. This was our first chance to talk since the interview, and I wanted to get some things clear.

"My parents are so grateful that you're letting me stay here, Mrs. Fletcher. My mother said to tell you she'll put you in her prayers."

"Please thank her for me," I said. "Did you tell them what's happened?"

"No," she said, taking a deep breath. "They'd be horrified at the idea that I was anywhere near a murder. Since I can't leave the country anyway, it would just upset them even more."

"I don't approve of your lying to your parents."

"I didn't lie, Mrs. Fletcher. I just didn't tell them everything."

"You've been away from home a long time, Mallory," I said, taking the cups to the sink. "Don't you have to be in school?"

"I have a semester off for travel," she said. "It's part of a cultural exchange program. I have to do a big report when I get back in order to get credit. I'm really not looking forward to it. I'm a terrible writer. I have no imagination at all. Would you like some help with that?"

"No, thank you," I said, turning on the water. "It won't take a moment. Where do you go to school? How old are you?"

"I'm eighteen. I go to Hamden Junior College in Kentucky. That's another reason why my family moved. They wanted to be closer to my college. We go everywhere together on weekends."

"That's very nice," I said, leaving the cups to drain on the side of the sink. "When do you have to be back in school?"

"Oh, not till after Christmas," she said.

"Then why did LeClerq say you were due to leave the country soon? It's only November."

"It's the three-month rule," she said, grinning. "It's silly, when you think about it. Americans don't need a visa to visit France, but we're only allowed into the country for three months at a time. After that you have to leave, even if it's only for five minutes. You can go to any border, get your passport stamped in another country, have a cup of coffee, and go right back into France. I have friends who say they've stayed here for years that way."

"I see," I said. "You told me you took a course at the Sorbonne. Did the school arrange housing for you, or were you on your own the whole time?"

"I stayed with a French family," she said, doodling with her finger on the tabletop. "But they didn't like me. I think the older brother had a crush on me, and they were —"

Her reply was interrupted by a knock on the door.

"Wow, we've got a lot of visitors this morning," she said, jumping up to get the door. "Come on in," I heard her say, and she led an old woman into the kitchen. Our visitor carried a basket containing a half dozen shriveled potatoes and a bunch of carrots, their dried-out stems and leaves indicating they'd been pulled some time ago.

She introduced herself as Mme Arlenne. Hers was the house at the end of our driveway, across the paved road. I'd seen her peeking through her window at me once when I'd pedaled the bike past her house on my way to St. Marc, and I'd waved. Her response had been to let the lace curtain drop back into place. This was the first time we'd met formally.

She was a tiny lady in a long gray jacket several sizes too large for her. Bright black eyes, like two raisins in a soft bun, took in every detail in the kitchen as she removed a paisley scarf covering her gray hair. When I offered her tea, she grinned, exposing some gaps where her eyeteeth once were. She appeared to be in her late eighties, but I couldn't be sure. The drying effect of the wind and sun in Provence made many of its inhabitants look older than their true ages. Her Provençal accent was difficult for me to understand. Mallory, however, was able to negotiate it easily.

"She wants to know why the police were here this morning," Mallory told me cheerfully, probably relieved that my interrogation of her had had such a timely interruption. While I put the kettle on, she rattled away in French, speaking so quickly I couldn't keep up with what she was telling our guest.

Madame Arlenne oohed and ahhed at various places in the narrative, and when Mallory mentioned the police, she frowned in disgust, pursed her lips, and blew out a puff of air — obviously not a fan of the local constabulary.

I cut another slice of the almond cake and poured our neighbor a cup of tea. Sitting down at the table again, I watched while she ate and drank and took in Mallory's animated account of the murdered chef. Madame Arlenne could have learned of the crime from the news. It was probably Marcel who had connected it with us. Now with inside details to impart, she would be the center of attention for the next week, I was sure, as the tale made the rounds of the local residents of St. Marc. I'd love to be her shadow, I thought, to hear the story embellished as it moved from mouth to ear to mouth.

The phone rang. I excused myself and went to the living room to answer it.

"Jessica, how are you?"

"Martine, how nice to hear from you. I have one of your neighbors here."

"Who would that be?"

"Madame Arlenne. She just brought over a basket of potatoes and carrots."

"If she's giving them away, they must be past their prime," Martine said, laughing. "She's the local busybody. I'm sure she just wants to find out what you're up to. Make something up. She'll be very happy."

"I don't have to fabricate anything," I said, and related the facts about the murder of the chef.

"Poor soul. And he'd just gotten his star."

"Did you know him?"

"Only by reputation. The awarding of a Michelin star is big news in Provence. It was in the local paper."

"Do you know anything else about him?"

"Not really. There was some scandal about him several years ago, I seem to recall. I can't remember now what it was. If you really want to know about him, ask Daniel Aubertin, the chef at the Melissande. He runs the cooking school, too, and knows everyone in the business."

"I met him yesterday," I said. "I'll call the hotel when we hang up."

"If he's not in today, you can probably catch him at the truffle market tomorrow morning."

"Oh?"

"Yes. Friday is market day in Carpentras, and November is also the beginning of the truffle season. He'd never miss that. It's worth seeing anyway, even if he's not there. Truffles are big business in Provence and it's a colorful scene."

"Speaking of truffles, have you given anyone permission to hunt for them on your property?"

"Only Philippe Telloir. He pays me with a portion of whatever he finds and sells the rest at the market. Last year we ate very well on his harvests. He had an excellent dog, but I understand it was stolen. Has he recovered it, do you know?"

"I don't believe so," I said, deciding to keep the news of Martine's trespasser to myself. There was nothing she could do and no point in upsetting her. "By the way, did Marcel come on time to pick you up in Avignon?"

"Yes, he did," I said, "but you didn't warn me about the way he drives."

I heard Martine's tinkling laugh on the other end of the line. "I'm sorry, Jessica. I forgot to mention that in France, everyone behind a wheel imagines they're competing in Le Mans," she said, referring to the country's annual sports-car race. "It's amazing, but somehow they seem to avoid each other's fenders, for the most part, anyway."

"Amazing," I said dryly.

She laughed again. "Well, see if you can get to Carpentras sometime. The market there is many times the size of ours in St. Marc. You can buy everything you want."

"Where would I find the truffle market?"

"Look for the Brasserie Le Club at the Place Aristide Briand," she said. "You can ask anyone in Carpentras. They'll know."

"I'll keep it in mind," I said.

"Sounds like you're going to have a busman's holiday, if you're looking into a murder."

"There's more," I added, and told her about my new houseguest, and the confiscation of our passports.

She made sympathetic noises over the inconvenience and assured me an extra guest was no problem. "Of course I don't mind if your friend uses my room," she said. "Why don't you empty the top drawer or two in my bureau for her. You can just put those things in a bag and leave them in the studio or the garage."

"That reminds me," I said, "I found a treasure in your garage."

"You can't mean my wreck of a car."

"No, I mean your bicycle. I cleaned it up and I'm using it. I assume that's all right."

Martine laughed again. "I didn't even remember I had a bicycle. Of course, use anything you find. My house is your house, and your house, by the way, is just perfect for me. Your neighbors have been plying me with casseroles and baked goods. I've hardly touched what you left me in the freezer."

We chatted a while longer, swapping experiences in each other's countries. Martine was delighted with her stay in Cabot Cove. She and her sister Elise had taken a trip down to Kittery, where the discount stores are, and she'd stocked up on items she couldn't find in France. I told her how I solved the mystery of the *sac à pain,* the bread bag hanging in the kitchen, and said I planned to bring some home as gifts for my friends. She said Seth Hazlitt had called to see how she was getting along, and asked after me. I described my introduction to the crusty Mme Roulandet, and how helpful M. Telloir had been. She praised the view from the town dock and swore she'd gained five pounds eating blueberry pancakes at Mara's luncheonette.

I hung up, slightly homesick, and not a little guilty that I'd left Mallory alone to entertain

Mme Arlenne. The two of them were still talking when I returned to the kitchen. Mme Arlenne had emptied her basket onto the kitchen table, and was pulling on her jacket. I thanked her for bringing the vegetables and apologized for taking so much time on the telephone, but neither of them seemed to mind.

"Martine offered you the use of her bedroom, if you want it," I said after Mme Arlenne had left. "I can empty a few of her drawers so you'll have a place for your things."

"That's awfully nice of her," Mallory said, smiling at me. "You're being so kind to me, Mrs. Fletcher, and I must be such a bother. I can go back to the hostel in Avignon, you know. I don't mind waiting there till Captain LeClerq returns my passport. I'm sure it'll only be a few days."

"Nonsense," I said. "You're welcome here. I enjoy your company. And I'm sure if your parents knew the truth about why you can't leave, they'd be more comfortable knowing you had a nice place to stay and someone looking after you."

"Oh, I know you're right, Mrs. Fletcher," she said earnestly. "I can't thank you enough for them, and for me."

"Why don't you go upstairs and unpack," I said. "I've got a call to make. I'll join you in a moment, and we'll find something to store Martine's things in."

I went back to the living room and dialed the hotel. When a man answered the phone, I asked for Daniel Aubertin.

"*Certainement, madame,*" replied the man. "*Un moment.*" There was a long pause; then he came back on the line. "I'm so sorry, madame, but he isn't taking calls."

"He's there, but he won't pick up the phone?"

"Unfortunately, he is very busy right now."

"I understand," I said. "I'd like to make an appointment to see him when it's more convenient. Can you find out when would be a good time?"

"I will try."

After another long pause, the chef himself came on the line. He was not happy. "Madame, why do you need an appointment?" he barked. "What is this about?"

"We met yesterday," I said. "I was in Chef Bertrand's class."

"I am very sorry for your experience, madame," he said, softening. "If you want your money back, I will talk with Guy and arrange this."

"I hadn't even thought of —"

"Of course, we will have classes again next week. And these are with Christian Étienne. You are welcome to take them, even though we charge a bit more for him."

"No. No. That's not why I'm calling," I said.

"It's a very good bargain."

"I'm sure it is, but —"

"Then why do you insist to speak with me?" The edge was back in his voice.

"I'd like to talk with you about Monsieur

Bertrand," I said quickly, hoping to get in a full sentence before he interrupted me again. It worked. He was silent. "I understand you know everyone in the restaurant business in Provence," I continued. "I just have a few questions and —"

"Absolutely not!"

"But I won't take up very much of your time."

"You will take up none of my time," he spat. "I have already spoken to the police. Those imbeciles! They removed every knife from my kitchen. I have to cancel dinner. How am I expected to run a restaurant without knives? The only person I wish to speak with is my cutlery supplier. That is all I have to say about this incident."

"Yes, but Monsieur Bertrand was your colleague. Surely you would want to help anyone who could assist in finding his killer."

"I have no responsibility in this matter."

"I wasn't accusing you, but —"

He interrupted me again. "You interfere with a police matter. This is not something for amateurs."

"If you'll just listen —"

"*Non!* I don't listen."

"But he was —"

"I am hanging up, madame. I am finished with you. If you call again, I will report you to the *commissariat.*" He slammed the phone down.

"Another temperamental chef," I said to myself, and replaced the receiver on the telephone. If he thought he was "finished" with me, he had another think coming. When people don't want to talk with me, it only fortifies my resolve. *I'll find a way to change his mind*, I thought. I turned back toward the kitchen and saw Mallory dart away from the door. She'd been eavesdropping.

"I thought you went up to unpack," I said, entering the room.

"I wanted to put these away for you." She busied herself with the carrots and potatoes.

"Don't worry about them," I said, shooing her out of the kitchen. "I'll take care of them. You go unpack."

Mallory hurried upstairs, and I tried to shake off a feeling of discomfort. More than a week had passed since I'd arrived in Provence, and I could see the time slipping by too quickly. Instead of relaxing, I found myself getting ready to embark on another investigation. But I knew I couldn't rest until I learned more about Bertrand and why someone would want to kill him. Martine had said there was a scandal in his past. Could that have been the motive for murder? Could a jealous spouse or lover have caught up with Bertrand? Or a rival for the coveted Michelin star? Why did Daniel refuse to talk with me about him? Where was he when Bertrand was killed?

And the murder was only half the problem. Now I had a teenager in the house, an adolescent who, all her lovely manners aside, did not always tell the truth. How much of what I knew about her was fact, and how much fantasy? Could I trust her? This wasn't my own home, after all. Was I inviting trouble by encouraging her to stay at Martine's?

I piled the dried-out potatoes and carrots in a bowl and left them on the counter — they'd probably be good for soup — and went outside. The air was crisp but not cold, and reminded me I was due for another walk in the woods. I pulled open the garage door to hunt for a paper or plastic bag. The gray cat pushed her head through the hole under the stairs and meowed at me.

"Hello, kitty," I said, kneeling down so I could reach behind her ears, her favorite place for scratches. She accompanied me as I circled around the bicycle and waded through the machinery and cast-off furniture to the back of the garage. A large shopping bag stood against the wall. Inside were unopened cans of acrylic paint. As I stacked them on the floor, it suddenly occurred to me that I'd never seen Martine's studio. *She must have a special place to paint,* I thought. I eyed the rickety stairs to my right, wondering if they led to her workroom.

"That's where you are," Mallory's voice said from behind me. "I wondered where you'd gone to."

"I've found something to hold Martine's clothes," I said, lifting up the empty shopping bag, and angling to avoid the sharp edge of an old scythe that was lying against a box.

"I'll take it," she said, reaching for the bag and putting a hand out to steady me as I stepped gingerly over a pile of wooden planks. "You've got another visitor, and this one's brought eggs."

"Monsieur Telloir," I called out as I exited the garage, brushing cobwebs off my sleeve. "You're just the man I want to see."

Chapter Eight

We got on the road at seven. M. Telloir had declined a cup of coffee and a slice of Mme Roulandet's cake; he was impatient to start out. It was a chilly morning, but high, wispy clouds promised a sunny day. Dressed in a warm sweater, long woolen skirt, and low-heeled shoes, I locked the door to the farmhouse behind me. I'd decided not to invite Mallory to join us — she seemed perfectly content with that — and had left her sleeping in Martine's bed. It was going to be hard enough to find Daniel and get him aside for a private conversation without the added worry of keeping an eye on a teenager.

On reflection, it seemed silly to worry about a girl who'd been traveling around France on her own for months. But now that she was, nominally at least, under my care, I felt I owed her parents the courtesy of keeping track of her. I was eager to speak with them when they called, and contemplated calling them myself if I could figure a way to pry their number out of Mallory without her getting upset and leaving in a huff. I couldn't imagine what the Cartrights had been thinking when they agreed to allow Mallory to wander abroad by herself.

While I'd never had children of my own, I did have young nieces and nephews and cousins, and knew that none of their parents would have considered for a second allowing a teenager to wander in Europe, not only unescorted but without an adult informed of her whereabouts. But maybe I was old-fashioned. In Paris I'd seen groups of teenagers who seemed to be touring together without a grown-up leader. Perhaps today's teenagers were more mature than they'd been years ago; maybe their parents trusted them to behave appropriately, and that trust was rewarded. Mallory certainly was polite, and, truth to tell, I hadn't seen her act irresponsibly. It was possible she'd been calling her parents every step along the way. Still, no matter how trustworthy a young person was, there were many untrustworthy adults ready to prey on a youngster without adult supervision.

Mallory had said she was eighteen, technically an adult herself in many parts of the world. But I suspected she wasn't being honest about her age. That was another concern altogether. "Oh, stop it, Jessica," I told myself. "She'll be fine back at the farmhouse, and you have things to do."

I'd given M. Telloir only the barest facts yesterday when I'd asked to accompany him to Carpentras, but he was well informed by the time he drove up in his old red Peugeot. Marcel and Mme Arlenne had been very busy making sure all of St. Marc was up to date on the *on-dit*.

"Too bad about the chef," he said, when I'd settled myself in the passenger seat.

"Yes, it was," I replied.

"And your passport."

"I'll get it back soon, I'm sure."

"Did they find the weapon that killed 'im?"

"Not that I've heard."

" 'E had a good restaurant."

"Have you eaten there?"

"*Non! Trop cher.* Too expensive."

He let out the clutch and we bumped along on the dirt drive as he turned around the big tree in front of the house and started toward the main road. The car had an earthy, moldy odor to it, the air inside damp, and the windows clouded with condensation. I loosened the top button of my jacket, and wondered what could have happened to create such a strong smell. Perhaps the car had had a leak and the upholstery was mildewed. I cracked the window to let in a little fresh air.

"*Non!* You must leave the windows closed," he cried out in agitation, gesturing frantically.

I jumped at the outburst. "Why? What's the matter?"

"*Pour les rabasses,*" he said, cocking his head toward the backseat.

I turned around to see a wet towel draped over a lumpy canvas bag on the seat.

"What're *rabasses?*" I asked.

"*Rabasses?* Truffles. It is the Provençal word for truffles."

"You have truffles in there?"

"*Oui!*"

"That's what I smell?"

"*Oui!*"

157

"Why do you want them wet?" I asked.

"Not wet, just 'umid. I try to keep them like the soil they were found in. If they dry out, *c'est terrible*." He made a fist and shook it.

"I see," I said. "That would spoil the flavor."

"No, no," he said, disgusted. "Do you know what they call them? Black diamonds."

"Black diamonds," I echoed.

"Yes. And like diamonds, one sells the truffles according to the weight."

"Oh!" Now I understood. If the truffles dried out, they'd lose weight, and M. Telloir would receive less money for them. At several hundred dollars per kilo — more, by the time they reached Paris — his truffles were a precious crop indeed, and every lost ounce was costly.

He drove slowly down the dirt lane before stopping at the end of the drive across from Mme Arlenne's house. He looked both ways, then pulled out into the lane of traffic even though a car was speeding toward us. There was a blare of horns as the infuriated driver jammed on his brakes and swerved around the Peugeot. M. Telloir honked back in irritation.

We rode in silence. I tried to ignore M. Telloir's driving and concentrated instead on taking shallow breaths until I became accustomed to the pungent aroma of the truffles. It was a smell I would not soon forget.

The road wound away from the village and merged with a larger one, snaking down the hill toward the highway. Here and there were lines of tall cypress trees that defined a farm's border or served as windbreaks for the occasional stone houses that hugged the thoroughfare. We passed fields of grapes, their bare vines twined around lines of string or propped up by wooden supports. M. Telloir pointed to a grove of olive trees. Their trunks were gnarled and their branches reached out, nearly touching those of the neighboring trees.

"It's good Martine, she keeps 'er trees."

"They're beautiful, aren't they?"

He smiled. "Beautiful, yes, but what is of importance, they give fruit," he said. "Today, too many farmers, they are cutting them down." He made a slashing move with his arm.

"Why would they do that?"

He shrugged and raised both his hands in a gesture of bafflement. "Why? They cut them to plant the grapes instead," he said. "There is more money to be made with grapes. But they will learn it is not so easy. Martine's trees, they're old and don't require much. Grapes are more work."

"Martine told me you pick the olives for her," I said. "What do you do with them? Do you cook with them yourself?"

He shook his head. "*Non.* I bring them to the market, or if there is a big 'arvest, I sell them to the mill, where they press them for olive oil. We share the profits."

"I don't think I've ever tasted olive oil from Provence."

"The best olive oil comes from Provence," he said, tapping the steering wheel vehemently.

"The only olive oil I've ever seen is from Italy."

He grunted and a frown creased his brow.

"But of course, all the Mediterranean countries make olive oil," I said, half to myself, hoping I hadn't offended him. "And Provence is on the Mediterranean, too. I'll have to make sure I bring home some olive oil. Perhaps you'd recommend one for me when we're at the market?"

Mollified, he launched into a discussion of the merits of different olive varieties and the best blend for oils. I listened but looked away from him, focusing on the scenery so I couldn't see him gesturing with both hands off the steering wheel at what must have been seventy miles an hour.

Shortly before eight, we arrived in Carpentras. The city was much larger than I'd expected, and I was glad M. Telloir knew the way. He followed the broad avenues that led to the center of town, and then turned off into a warren of small streets. They reminded me of the narrow lanes of Avignon, built for mules, not cars. Finding a place to park was a difficult assignment, especially with the competition from vehicles owned by merchants who'd arrived before us to set up for market day. Eventually, M. Telloir crammed the car between two others in a space in front of a notice posted on a pole that threatened dire consequences to all who left their cars there. Once in the space, however, he had to back up again to let me exit the car. How he managed to squeeze himself out, along with the damp sack of truffles, I'm not sure, but at eight a.m. we presented ourselves at Le Club on Place Aristide Briand along with close to a hundred others milling about in front of and inside the bar.

A combination brasserie and pizzeria, according to a sign that ran along the awning, Le Club was jammed with people apparently unaffected by the overpowering mixture of truffles and cigarette smoke that permeated the air. My eyes watered, and I tried to maneuver myself to stand near the door, hoping for a little air as people entered and left. A group of men had gathered around the bar in the back, some drinking coffee, others sipping beer, wine, or brandy. M. Telloir had elbowed his way to the counter and emerged ten minutes later with two cups of the strongest coffee I have ever attempted to drink. A few of the tables in the front were available. We took a seat near the door and watched the parade of farmers and tradesmen, housewives and students, sophisticates and peasants, all of whom had come to sell their *Tuber melanosporum*. On the table next to us, someone had laid a portable scale for use when the bidding got serious. A dangerous instrument, it had a sharp hook at the end of a chain attached to a long metal bar. A movable lead cylinder allowed its user to determine the weight by sliding it along the calibrated bar till the two sides balanced.

The sight of a chef in his gleaming white coat and tall toque making his way through the throng started a buzz among the patrons. As if by signal, they moved back to open a path for him. He disappeared in the back by the bar.

"Who is that?" I asked.

"Claude 'Arvé. 'E has a three-star restaurant in Cannes. They buy over four hundred kilos of truffles every year."

"Do you know Daniel Aubertin from the Hotel Melissande?"

"Only by reputation, but it's possible I know 'is face."

"He's the one I need to see."

"If 'e cooks, 'e will be 'ere."

Outside the window was a man in a long green coat, the sleeves and capped top edged in gold. He held a brightly colored flag with a red symbol in the center. I noticed several others dressed in the same livery.

"Is the market about to start now?" I asked.

"They wait for more to come." He poked his chin in the direction of a stout man in a shabby blue jacket with two sets of zippered pockets. "See Jean-Paul there? 'E is a *courtier,* a broker. 'E is not so large. The pockets, they are filled with cash. 'E buys for a consortium in Paris."

Standing next to Jean-Paul was a beefy young man in black leather. Probably his bodyguard, I thought.

"*Et voilà* Albert Belot, next to the lady in the red jacket."

"Who is he?"

"Gave up farming and planted 'is land with oak trees to grow the truffles. Everyone, they think 'e's crazy. Did not make money for years. But 'e's crazy like a fox. Those trees, they make the truffles. 'E's rich now."

Albert, who was dressed similarly to the other men in the room in a nondescript jacket and gray wool cap, clutched a blue-and-rose-patterned cloth bag, heavy with the prized tubers. It was hard to tell the professionals from the amateurs, except perhaps by the size of their bundles. Wrapped in ski jackets, field jackets, wool corduroy, and tweed coats; in rubber boots, sneakers, and sturdy heels; wearing caps, berets, or bare-headed, they brought their truffles to market in plastic bags, canvas sacks, leather purses, or bulging pockets, all equal in their eagerness to place their treasures before the men who would judge them — the chefs and the truffle brokers.

In a booth diagonally across from ours were two men with their dogs, mangy creatures with dirty coats and unkempt whiskers. The same could be said of their owners. The animals lay peacefully under the table while the men hunched over coffees, each with one hand roped to his dog and the other resting on his sack of truffles. Their presence reminded me of why M. Telloir had come to Carpentras.

"Where will you find the man selling the dog?" I asked.

" 'E will be 'ere later, at the end of the market."

"Do you know what kind of dog it is?"

"Doesn't matter, if 'e has the good nose," he said, tapping the tip of his own. "Some say the Labrador, 'e is *un bon chien truffier,* a good truffle dog. 'E can smell them from fifty meters. But a big dog like that, 'e takes up too much room in the bed. *Moi, je préfère le petit chien.* I prefer the little dog."

"The dog sleeps with you?"

"It's harder to steal the dog if 'e lies next to the master."

When I thought the addition of one more person would split the walls of Le Club, a cry went up and the restaurant began to empty. It was nine o'clock — we'd been there for an hour. The wait was worth it, I thought, when the pageant began with the assembly of members of the black-caped Confrérie de la Truffe and green-coated Confrérie des Vignerons, the brotherhoods of the truffle and the winegrowers. The crowd in the brasserie spilled out onto the sidewalk, where a U-shaped setup of empty wooden tables was arranged against the building. In their distinctive hats, medals dangling from their necks, multihued banners held aloft, the brotherhoods, which I was happy to see included a few sisters, took their places in a line behind the tables and sang the official ode to the truffle, their voices enthusiastic if not always on key.

The anthem was followed by a fanfare from trumpeters in red-and-green berets and crimson jackets with white ruff collars, their uniforms and long horns harking back to medieval days.

"Do they do this every week?" I asked, delighted with the festivities.

"Non," M. Telloir replied. "Today is opening day, so we make a fuss."

The formal ceremonies over, the market began in true. The crowd that had waited so patiently in the bar now fought for space at the tables, where they could plunk down their bags and entice a chef or broker, or even a well-heeled private customer, to judge their wares. M. Telloir pushed me before him to the front of the line, shouldering aside others less aggressive. When we reached the table, he gently laid his truffle sack on the table and waited for a visit by one of the brokers. Chef Harvé was one of four chefs in white uniform who made the rounds of the sellers, poking their heads into sacks and breathing heavily to allow the scent of the truffles to fill their sinuses. I tried to see the faces of the others, but two of them had their backs to me.

A man came over to us, reached into the sack, and pulled out one of M. Telloir's prized pieces. It was about the size of a plum and looked to me like a clod of dirt. The broker squeezed the truffle, turned it over in his hand, dug his thumbnail into its side, and then sniffed it, holding it first under one nostril and then the other. He dropped the truffle back in the bag, wrote a number on a small pad of paper in his palm, tore off the top sheet, and stuffed it in M. Telloir's hand, then moved on to the lady next to us.

"*Poufft!* They're worth more than that," M. Telloir exclaimed, crushing the offer and stuffing it in his pocket. "Chef 'Arvé will do better for me."

"What was he doing to your truffle?" I asked.

"They look to see if it is hard and black inside," he replied. "It is necessary to check. There are many who are not above using black ink to change the color, or poking pellets inside to make the truffles weigh more."

I looked with new eyes at the men and women vying for the attention of the experts. Were there swindlers among their ranks? Naively, it hadn't occurred to me that such a situation could exist in a country market in Provence. But sadly, con artists will surface anytime a profit can be made.

"Daniel! *Venez ici!* Over here," a man called from a table on the other side.

One of the chefs at a table opposite us raised his hand and went to greet his next truffle seller, his back to me.

"Is that Daniel Aubertin from the Hotel Melissande?" I asked the lady next to me.

"*Oui,*" she replied. She draped a damp cloth on top of her basket, then left to bring her chit to the brasserie to collect payment. Two people took her place.

I turned to M. Telloir. "That's the man I came to find," I whispered to him, pointing to Daniel across the way. M. Telloir grunted, but his attention was focused on Chef Harvé, who was working his way toward us, checking each bag on our side of the table. M. Telloir opened the top of his sack to expose the clutch of truffles he was selling and watched intently as the chef plucked the largest one and cut a nick in it with a wood-handled knife. "I'll be back in a little while," I said.

Once I was away from M. Telloir's side, it was not easy to navigate the crowd. People pressed in from behind trying to reach the tables. It was each for himself. There was no line and no orderly procession. I waded out to the edge of the throng and jumped up and down, trying to get a glimpse of Daniel. It would be just my luck to have him stroll back to M. Telloir's side of the U when I'd reached the other. I could see the tops of four toques over the heads of the people in front of me. Taking a chance that one of the two on the left was Daniel's, I circled around the crowd and joined the people trying to reach the buyers. By the time I made it to a table, M. Telloir was gone from our space on the other side. Daniel was off to my right, not too many people away. He was several years younger than Guy, I realized, about thirty years old, young for a master chef, I thought. Notwithstanding the chilly temperature, a sheen of perspiration covered his brow. I rested my handbag on the rough wood and waited.

"Daniel, me now," a boy next to me shouted.

"I'm coming. A little patience."

The youngster removed a handful of truffles from his pocket and held them out to the chef.

"So much noise for this," Daniel said, winking at him. He picked up a few pieces from the child's hand and held them under his nostrils, breathing in slowly. *"Bon!"* he said, and wrote a number on a paper and dropped it on top of the truffles.

"Merci, Daniel. Next week I'll have more; you'll see."

"Yeah, yeah. You've said that before."

"It's too cold for the flies; that's the problem," the boy said, pushing away from the table.

"Say hello to your papa."

At last Daniel reached me. He pulled my handbag in front of him and opened it, surprised to see not truffles, but the usual items a woman carries with her. "I don't know how to bid for this," he said, laughing.

"Oh, no," I said, grabbing my bag. "I just want to talk with you." I put out my hand. "We met yesterday. I'm Jessica Fl—"

"I see reporters after the market, not now," he said, and moved on to the woman next to me. A big man stepped between us and shoved his bag at the chef.

"Excuse me," I said to the man who'd pushed me aside, but I couldn't see over his shoulder. I called out to Daniel. "I'm not a reporter. I just want to talk to you." But I'd lost my place at the table and wasn't sure he'd heard me. Two more people squeezed in front of me, pushing me farther to the back of the mob. I couldn't see the table anymore, nor where the chef might be. I was jammed in the middle of the impatient truffle sellers who were not about to yield their space. It was impossible to stand still. People kept pushing past me, and eventually I was carried back to the street, grateful to escape the pack.

I straightened my coat, checked the contents of my bag, and zipped it up again. I walked along the edge of the group and peered through the window of Le Club to see if I could spot M. Telloir. At one table, the lady in the red jacket was weighing a net bag of truffles. Beside her, an elegantly dressed woman with a silk scarf tied carelessly at her neck counted out bills for the exchange, and talked to someone on her cell phone. I opened the door and stepped inside. The odor was still strong but not as overpowering as it had been earlier. Perhaps my nose was becoming accustomed to the scent. M. Telloir was nowhere to be seen, but two men dickered over a bag of truffles in a corner, with a small group watching and waiting their turn. Finally one wrote something on the palm of his hand and showed it to the other, who nodded solemnly. The buyer spat in his palm and rubbed it on his thigh. He opened a cardboard box and removed a stack of bills, turning his back on the observers while he counted out the payment. He folded the bills and gave them to the seller, who emptied his bag into a bushel basket at the buyer's feet. The next man handed his slip of paper to the buyer and the scene repeated itself.

While the business dealings took place around me, I sat in an empty seat and waited, assuming M. Telloir would look for me there if he couldn't find me in the throng. I was able to monitor the activity at the tables through the windows, and follow the movement of the four toques. When the crowd on the sidewalk began to thin, I went outside again. Daniel was talking to the man M. Telloir had pointed out to me earlier, the one with the orchard of oak trees. The chef had removed his toque and held it under his arm while he wiped a handkerchief over his brow. The man M. Telloir had called Albert was speaking in low tones, his eyes glancing around furtively. He touched the chef on his arm and walked away, turning at the corner. Daniel watched him, then leaned down to pick up a heavy bag.

"There you are," M. Telloir said, taking my arm. "It's time for the man with the truffle dog. Would you like to come? Or do you prefer to wait 'ere?"

"I'd love to see the dog," I said, "but I have to speak . . ." I looked around for Daniel, but he'd disappeared. "Oh, no, where did he go?" I searched the remaining faces, thinking he might have donned a coat that covered his white uniform. But no handsome, curly-haired man was nearby. "I'll meet you here," I said to M. Telloir, and ran toward the corner where I'd last seen Albert. I looked up the cobbled street and thought I caught sight of someone in white entering an alley between two buildings. I hurried to follow, hoping it was Daniel. When I reached the passageway, I peered around the corner. A man holding a heavy bag was pulling on a brown coat over his white jacket. He had dark hair — I couldn't see if it was curly — and was walking quickly. Twenty yards ahead of him, another man carrying a bag and wearing a dun-colored jacket and gray cap turned left. When the chef turned left as well, I entered the alley. It was a short footpath between two streets with ivy-covered stone walls on either side, probably enclosing gardens. The branches of trees reached over the walls, the sun was shining, and birds were singing. It would be a pleasant walk if I hadn't been so intent on not losing my quarry. At the end of the passageway, a young couple entered the alley holding hands. They smiled at me, and I smiled back as we passed. When I reached the street, I glanced back at them to be sure no one was watching me and casually turned left, as the chef and the man he followed had done. I saw them halfway down the street on the other side, standing at the rear of a car. Their backs were to me. I walked slowly, staying on my side of the road but keeping them in sight.

Albert opened the trunk and pulled out a

bushel basket. I stepped into a doorway and pretended to examine the contents of a shop window. Through the corner of glass, I could see the men as they emptied Albert's bag into the bushel basket and spread the blue-and-rose-colored sack on top. Daniel then emptied his bag over the cloth. A pile of potatoes fell out, obviously meant to camouflage the real contents of the bushel basket.

"Madame, may I help you?" a woman's voice asked.

I looked at the woman and back at the window I'd been hiding behind. On display were several coils of wire and electrical appliances I'd never seen before.

"Non, merci," I said, smiling with a shrug, and stepped back out into the street. Albert was pulling out of his parking space, and Daniel was walking away with the heavy bushel basket of what were purported to be potatoes. I crossed the street and followed Daniel until he reached his car, a blue Renault wagon. Quickly, he pushed the basket into the back of the car and opened the driver door. Luckily for me, he didn't use a key, which meant his car was unlocked. I ran to the passenger door, pulled it open, and jumped inside as he started the engine. His face paled when he saw me.

"You are from the government, yes?" He pulled a wad of bills from his pocket and held them out to me. "Take what you want," he said. "This is my business. A chef cannot make his name without truffles."

"I'm not from the government," I said, "so put your money away."

His fear turned to anger as he stuffed the wad back into his pocket.

"If you're a reporter, I don't speak to you. Get out of my car."

"I'm not a reporter. I'm Jessica Fletcher," I said calmly. "I spoke to you on the phone yesterday —"

"I spoke to a hundred people yesterday. I don't recall your name."

"It's not important," I said, pulling the seat belt around me and clicking it into place.

"What are you doing?"

"I'm not getting out of the car until you talk to me. I want to ask you some questions about Emil Bertrand."

"I wasn't even in the hotel when he died," he argued. "I was at Héllas, having lunch with a supplier. You can ask the *maître d'hôtel*." He looked at his watch. "I was there from noon to three."

"That's good to know."

He eyed me suspiciously. "You're not a reporter."

I shook my head.

"You're not from the police?"

"How many Americans work in the Police Judiciaire?"

He relaxed back in his seat and turned off the engine. "None, of course."

"Did you know Emil Bertrand well?"

Daniel stared at the dashboard, thinking back. Myriad emotions flitted across his face. *"Non,"* he said. "No one knew him well."

Chapter Nine

It was barely daylight when I steered the bicycle out of the garage and leaned it against the tree. My feline friend was also up early and came to greet me, pushing her head and side against my calf, leaving a smear of gray fur on my navy sweatpants. I gave her a scratch behind the ears and prodded her back toward the barn. I'd dressed in layers and needed all of them against the chill that froze my breath in little clouds. I hadn't been able to reach the baker, Mme Roulandet, yesterday; M. Telloir and I, along with the newest addition to his household, had arrived home after she'd closed for the day. When I'd tried to call again this morning, there was no answer. Either she was late getting in, or was ignoring the ringing while she fired up the huge ovens in preparation for her first customers.

I needed a ride into Avignon. M. Telloir would be occupied training his new dog, a disheveled terrier with a cocoa-colored coat, who took every opportunity to lie down on the ground, back legs splayed, looking more like a miniature shag rug than a valuable hunter of "black diamonds." Mallory had fallen in love instantly, and M. Telloir had promised to bring "Magie" with him this morning for a test run behind the house. I thought it would be "magic" indeed if the dog proved to be a good truffle hunter, but kept my opinion to myself. We were to benefit from any truffles the dog turned up on Martine's property. Of course, based on all the little mounds of earth I'd seen on my last walk, there might not be any truffles left to find.

Since M. Telloir wasn't available, Marcel was my second choice as chauffeur — that is, if Mme Roulandet was able to raise him. Otherwise I'd have to put the trip off until Monday. Captain LeClerq hadn't returned our passports yet. If he was on duty, it was the perfect excuse to inquire about them and also to ask how the case was going. Too, if Claire was still in custody, I could check off another name on my list of people to interview. But even if I struck out at the police station, I had other stops on my itinerary. I planned a visit to Bertrand's restaurant to speak with his staff, and to call at the Melissande to see Guy and get Mme Poutine's address. Then there was the real estate office on the paper the chef had been clutching when he died. I pedaled down the driveway, mentally ticking off the errands I could accomplish with a ride into Avignon. Where was Héllas? I wondered. It was the restaurant where Daniel said he was having lunch when someone drove a knife into Emil Bertrand.

After all my trouble pursuing him and following him into his car, Daniel had not proven to be very helpful.

"Tell me about Bertrand," I'd said. "Did he

have any enemies?"

"He was a great chef," he told me, "known for the classic dishes, but prepared with imagination."

"Yes, but what was he like as a man?"

"He was a man, nothing so different. You met him. What did you think of him?"

I ignored his diversion. "Tell me," I said, "how would you describe him?"

"He runs a good kitchen. He is a good teacher. He is a smart businessman, too, buys his own building, invests in the future. I learn a lot from him."

He spoke of Bertrand as if he were still alive. It had disconcerted me at first, but I soon realized it was the French way of speaking, to use the present tense. I tried another tack. "Did he get along with his students?"

"Everyone is always pleased with his classes. I hire all the best chefs in the region."

"You never had any complaints? He never made anyone angry?"

"*Non.*"

"I heard there was a scandal associated with him. Can you tell me about it?"

"I know of no scandal."

"Was he a ladies' man?"

"What is this 'ladies' man'?"

"It means he flirts with women. Maybe he has a lover, or more than one."

He laughed. "You have described a great many men in France, madame."

"Do you know who his female friends were?"

"I only pay attention to *my* female friends."

"What about Claire in the hotel? Was she his lover?"

"She is young and easily impressed."

"You're not answering my question."

"I am not in bed with them. I do not know who he sleeps with."

"What do you know about Mme Poutine?"

"She is Emil's student. She attends all his classes."

"Isn't that unusual?"

"Not at all," he replied. "All the good chefs have their followings, people who want to learn everything a master chef is willing to teach them. Some go from chef to chef; others stay with just one."

"Did they have a personal relationship?"

"It's possible. I don't notice these things. In France, a man may have many mistresses. It is not unusual."

"And a woman having an affair outside her marriage?"

He shrugged. "It can happen."

"How long did you know him?"

"Oh, ten years or so."

"How did you meet?" I asked.

"We all know each other in Avignon. It's a small community, after all."

"Where did he work before he opened his restaurant?"

"He travels the world. Tokyo. New York. Rio de Janeiro."

"Did he ever talk about the other places he worked?"

"Only the ones with famous chefs."

"Why only those?"

"A chef makes his reputation by working with the masters who come before him. You don't need me for this. Go to his restaurant. They have his life on the back of the menu."

"I'll do that, thank you."

"Are we finished now?"

"Just a few more questions," I said, trying to think of how to break through his reserve. "Bertrand was very successful, wasn't he? He had a Michelin star."

"*Oui*. He had a star."

There was just the hint of something in his eyes that put me on alert. Earning a Michelin star is the goal of every chef around the world. Bertrand had been awarded one. Daniel had not. Of course, Daniel was still young, only in his thirties. Was he jealous of the older man's success?

"Do you agree that he deserved the star?"

"I don't dispute the findings of *The Red Guide*," he said. "They are, after all, the experts." Whatever I'd seen was fleeting. He had put on a bored expression, and was not about to reveal himself to me.

"Did Bertrand have family?" I persisted.

"Maybe a wife and child, once."

"But you're not sure of that?"

"It is only a rumor."

"You never spoke with him about his family."

"We only talk about cooking and the restaurant business."

"Then how do you know about a wife?"

He shrugged. "Someone in the restaurant may have told me."

"But not Bertrand?"

"No. He never discusses his private life."

"And your relationship with him? Was it good?"

"Oh, yes, we are old friends. We talk of going into business together."

I rode down the hill; the crunching noise of the tires on the dirt road was loud in the early-morning stillness. Even the birds were still asleep. A faint breeze rustled the leaves on the olive trees, and the air smelled clean. I inhaled deeply and let out a stream of vapor into the cold. I'd awakened early again. I couldn't shut off my imagination, couldn't ignore the lure of the puzzle that a murder presents. As the wheels turned so did my mind. Perhaps I could talk to the Thomases again at the hotel. And René Bonassé. Had he been rating Bertrand the morning of the killing? And if so, why? For what organization? When would Bertrand's funeral take place? Would Mme Poutine be there? Would her husband?

I stopped at the bottom of the drive. Mine was the only vehicle on the road at that hour. I turned left toward St. Marc, and as my eyes

180

roved over the peaceful landscape, I let go of the murder and let the beauty of the French countryside wash over me. *This is what I came to France for,* I told myself. *An early-morning ride. A beautiful view. A new culture to experience.*

There were only a few homesteads between Mme Arlenne's house and the village. The land rolled away into fields that must have captured the palette in the summer, but now were exploring what it meant to be brown. Ocher, russet, taupe, fawn, sienna, bronze, rust. In the patchy bark of the trees, the stubble of crops cut down, the exposed roots on the hard ground, in bushes and branches and brush, every shade of brown was represented. Ahead of me a road crew was digging by the side of the road, their blue uniforms cheerful against the not-quite-monochromatic landscape. I waved as I pedaled by.

"*Bonjour. Bonjour,*" they called to me, and I returned the greeting.

For the first time I began to feel at home in France. The experience of riding a bicycle on a country road, my muscle memory engaged, making each move automatic. The vibrations of the road under my hands and feet, the hum of the wheels, the slap of the wind at my face as it colored my cheeks. These sensations were comforting, known to me, and now I enjoyed them in a new country, on a route I'd traveled before and that was becoming familiar.

The road curved sharply to the right, past a

stand of dark cypress trees and just before the turnoff to town. I rode around the arc and had to swerve wide to avoid hitting a green car stranded in the right lane. A woman was walking on the shoulder, kicking at the dirt in obvious frustration. It was Mme Roulandet.

"Is this your car?" I asked, braking the bike and pointing behind me.

She scowled at me. "And who else's car would it be?"

"If you leave it in the road, it'll be the junk-yard's," I said. "The next automobile along will crash into it."

"There have been no automobiles," she said, furious. "I want there to *be* an automobile, but no one comes, except you."

"What happened?"

"Stupid machine! The engine, she won't start."

"Let me help you," I said, looking back toward the dead sedan.

"Do you have a phone with you?"

"No," I said. "I'm sorry. Mine only works in the States." I walked the bike back to her car. "Do you have a sign or a light or something we can put in the road to alert any oncoming driver there's a problem ahead?" I asked.

She shook her head, but opened the trunk. We peered inside. It was filled with crates of fruits, bunches of herbs, sacks of flour and sugar, baskets of eggs — she must have just come from the market — but nothing I saw could serve as a flare or warning sign. "I'll be right back," I said, climbing on the bike and pedaling back the way I'd come.

She was standing on the shoulder when I returned with three strapping members of the road crew trotting behind me. A rapid-fire exchange ensued, from which I gathered that the men would push the car off the road, but their crew chief had the only phone, and he wasn't due back for several hours.

I circled back on my bike to head off any traffic that might unknowingly round the curve and threaten the lives of our good Samaritans. Fortunately, the road was still deserted, but might not be for long as a thin slice of the sun edged over the horizon. Mme Roulandet was going to be behind schedule. Her customers might have to do without their baguettes today.

Minutes later, the road crew reappeared from around the curve, laughing and talking, happy for the break in the routine of their digging. I thanked them and caught up to the baker, who'd started walking down the road again toward the village, this time at least with her car safely parked on the shoulder. When I reached her, I hopped off the bike.

"Do you have someone to help you at the bakery?" I asked.

"Only in the summer when the tourists come," she replied. "If I am early, I can manage to do it all. But today . . ." She trailed off, a worried look on her face.

"Do you ride a bicycle?" I asked. "You can take mine to ride to the farmhouse. It will be a lot faster for you."

"No," she said. "The legs, they are not good." She smiled wryly. "But thank you. That is very kind of you to offer."

"It's ironic," I said. "I was riding into town to see you."

"Yes?"

"Yes. You didn't answer your phone, and now I know why."

"*Poufft!* So many calls I will miss this morning, and no one to bake the bread." She sighed. "Why did you want to see me?"

"I need a ride." We both laughed. "I want to go into Avignon, and I was going to ask you to call Marcel to see if he can drive me today."

"Alas, Marcel, he drives his cousin to Marseilles today. Perhaps tomorrow?"

"Oh, dear. I was hoping to go today."

"*Quel dommage!* What a pity."

We walked along quietly. I, enjoying the crisp, clear morning, and she, fretting about the business missed. Then she brought up a new topic.

"I hear from a bird that you and your houseguest were in Avignon at the hotel where Bertrand was killed," she said.

I smiled. "Mme Arlenne knows how to fly around."

"A story like that is too good to keep under your basket. It's worth at least a glass of pastis in the brasserie. There will be many to buy her a drink for the next month, especially if your little friend gives her more to work with. Even if she doesn't, Mme Arlenne knows how to embroider a good story."

"I'm sure she does," I said. "Did you know him at all, Chef Bertrand?"

"Oh, yes. I'm thinking all the good bakers knew him. He was not above stealing a recipe or two if he thought it would do him some good."

"Martine told me there was a scandal associated with Bertrand. Did it have to do with stealing recipes?"

"There was a story, some years back," she said, standing still while she searched her memory for the tale. "I'm not sure I can remember. I forget so much these days."

"Ah, where is Mme Arlenne when we need her?"

Mme Roulandet had a big laugh for a small woman. "She would certainly remember," she said.

The sound of an engine far behind us broke into our conversation. We turned and waited until a truck came rocketing around the curve where Mme Roulandet's car had been only moments ago. Four arms went up in the air as we signaled the driver to stop. With brakes squealing, the pickup shuddered to a halt on the shoulder of the road.

The driver was a young man with a shock of black hair slicked back from his forehead. He stuck his head out the window and yelled back at us, "Marie! What has happened?"

"Ah, Antoine, the automobile, she stops," Mme Roulandet replied, hurrying to his door. "Can you give us a ride to the village? I will call the mechanic."

"Absolument!" He jumped from the truck and lifted my bike into the bed, resting it against a folded tarpaulin.

Mme Roulandet and I scrambled up into the cab, and minutes later the two of us and my bicycle were deposited in front of the bakery. She unlocked the shop and picked up several pieces of paper that had been slipped under the door. "Come, come," she said. "You deserve a special treat this morning."

"No, first call the mechanic," I said, "and then tell me how I can help you here."

Mme Roulandet frowned, but picked up the telephone and called the garage, explaining where her car was located and asking them to bring her the supplies in the trunk before they towed the vehicle for servicing. Several customers poked their heads in the bakery and waved to her. She bustled to the door, explained the problem, and said she would reopen soon. Then she locked the door again.

I unbuckled the little bag I wore at my waist and looked around to see what needed to be done. Since I had no idea about the prices of her baked goods, I would be no help to Mme Roulandet as a salesperson. Instead, I pulled an apron off a peg near the cash register, put it on, and went into the little café. The chairs were piled on top of the tables to leave the floor clear for cleaning, so that would be my first job. I found a broom and started sweeping while the baker pulled bowls of dough from the refrigerator and set them in a just-warm oven for rising. I swept out the shop while she consulted the orders that had been faxed and phoned in. I pulled down the chairs, arranged them around the tables, and wiped off the tabletops while she shaped the croissants, placed a tray of rolls into an oven, and cut out circles of cookie dough. I brushed the crumbs from the display shelves and washed the canister for the baguettes while she started a new batch of dough, iced a cake, and put away the supplies from her trunk that the garage had delivered. All the while, she kept shouting at me to stop, but I can be very stubborn when my mind is set on something. An hour later, with the alluring aroma of baking bread and cookies making my mouth water, she unlocked the bakery door and admitted her first customer.

"This is Madame Fletcher," she said, introducing me to an elderly lady with a scarf tied under her chin. "She is visiting from America and staying in the house of Martine Devries."

As villagers entered, placed their orders, and left with their purchases, Mme Roulandet introduced me to them, explaining my presence, and crediting me with saving her day. In between sales, she answered the constantly ringing phone, punched down her bread dough, formed her baguettes, placed a damp towel over the loaves, baked her first batch, and slid trays of the second batch onto a warm shelf. At eleven o'clock, when the crush of customers finally subsided, she poured us two cups of coffee, which we drank standing up.

"Madame, you have been my savior today," she said. "I will not forget it."

"It was my pleasure," I said sincerely. It had been fun to see how her bakery operated and to experience the myriad complicated steps it takes to get started in the morning. The hours had flown, and while my feet were tired, I was feeling exhilarated, grateful to have played a small part in the daily life of a French village.

"If there is anything I can do for you, Madame Fletcher, you have only to ask it."

"There is one thing," I said.

"It is yours."

"I'd like you to call me Jessica."

"And I am Marie," she replied.

I put out my hand. "It's a pleasure to make your acquaintance."

She grinned, wiped her hand on her apron, and replied, shaking my hand, "The pleasure is all mine."

The phone rang again, and Marie smiled at me while she spoke to someone called Robert on the other end of the line. "*Oui,* she is here now. I will tell her."

"Was that someone I know?" I asked when she hung up.

"You will," she said, putting some warm rolls in a bag and handing it to me, along with a box of my favorite almond cake. "Robert is my brother. He is coming now to pick you up."

"Pick me up?"

"Yes," she said. "You want to go to Avignon today."

Chapter Ten

Claire's gray eyes were puffy and bloodshot, her shiny black curls lank and dull. She shuffled to the metal chair in the visitor's room of the Commissariat Centrale d'Avignon and sank onto the hard seat. Chin on her chest, she leaned forward, her thin arms hanging down between her knees and her shoulders curved as if the chair had weights pulling all parts of her body toward the concrete floor.

"Hello, Claire," I said. "I'm sorry to see you here."

She nodded, keeping her eyes downcast.

"Are you all right?"

Her shoulders rose slightly and fell again.

"You're not surprised to see me here, are you?"

This time she shook her head slowly from side to side.

"Why not?"

Gradually she raised her head and slumped back in the chair. "Emil said you write about murder," she whispered, her voice hoarse.

"I do write about murder," I said, "but what I write are stories, not true crime."

"I wish this was one of your stories." She lifted her arms and ran both hands through her hair. "I would like to read about it in my own bed at home, where no one screams at night and no one watches me through a window and no one asks the same questions over and over."

"What do they ask you?"

" 'Claire,' " she mimicked in a harsh tone, her eyes squinting and her mouth turned down, " 'did you kill Emil Bertrand?' "

"And what do you reply?"

"*Non.* I tell all of them *'non'* — the captain, the magistrate, the lawyer — but they don't believe me."

"Where were you when he was killed?"

"Did they ask you to ask me these questions again?"

"No."

She was quiet for a while, her eyes staring at the gray wall over my shoulder.

"Claire?"

"I don't know who did it. I didn't see anything."

"Sometimes," I said, "you see things you don't even realize. Why don't you tell me what happened."

She heaved a great sigh, and her head dropped down on her chest again.

"I know," I said. "It's awful to keep repeating the same things over and over. But do it one more time for me, please. Maybe together we can learn something."

A single tear ran down her cheek and dripped off her jaw onto her lap. She didn't bother to wipe her face. "All right," she said wearily. "What do you want to know?"

"First tell me what Madame Poutine was saying to you in the office."

"She tells me what she always tells me," she said, her voice quavering, "that Emil is unfaithful, that he does not love me, that he has many lovers."

"Why do you think she told you that?"

"Because she is jealous?"

"I'm asking *you*. Is that what you think?"

"Yes. I think she wants him for herself."

"Were they ever lovers?"

"Yes."

"Are you sure?"

She nodded her head vigorously. "He wouldn't talk about her. He was very discreet. I asked him; he wouldn't say. But I knew."

"Did you live with Emil?"

"No. No. I have my own apartment on Rue Saint-Joseph."

"And Emil?"

"He lived near the restaurant on Rue Racine."

"But you were lovers?"

"He loved me. I know he did."

"Yes. He loved you," I said, smiling at her. "After Madame Poutine spoke with you, where did you go?"

"I was very upset."

"I know."

"I went to the back room behind the stairs. It's for storage. No one goes there. I could cry in private."

"Did anyone see you go into the room?"

"I don't know. I didn't see anyone."

"No one came in while you were there?"

"No."

"No one at all?"

She shook her head.

"Then what happened?"

"I hear Emil in an argument. I recognize his voice, but I cannot hear what they say. The boxes are in front of the window."

"There's a window in the storage room?"

A nod.

"One that overlooks the cooking school," I guessed.

Another nod.

I recalled the first time I'd seen the windows in that ancient courtyard, when Guy had taken me downstairs to give me a tour. The room had chilled me, and I remembered feeling that it wasn't just the temperature of the air that had given me goose bumps.

"Claire, did you see who killed Emil?"

"No. I told you, the boxes —"

"Did you *hear* the person who killed him?"

"Maybe. I don't know."

"Was it a man or a woman?"

"I'm not sure."

"Did you recognize the other voice?"

"No. I —"

"What? What did you hear?"

"They were fighting. That's all I could tell. I hear Emil yelling that it's his decision what happens to the restaurant. Then the voices were low again."

"Could you make out any other words?"

"Something about 'partners' and 'Paris.' I wasn't really listening at first."

"How many voices did you hear?"

"Two, but maybe someone different the second time."

"The second time?"

"The arguing stopped for a while, and then someone came back in and they argued again."

"What happened then?"

"I thought I heard a moan and a crash, like a chair falling over. But I wasn't really paying attention to the argument. I just wanted them to stop so I could run downstairs and find Emil. I wanted to tell him what Madame Poutine had said. I wanted him to tell me she was wrong."

"And when you went downstairs?"

"He was . . . dead."

"How did you know?"

She moaned and began rocking back and forth in her chair. "I didn't know. He was lying there. I saw the knife in his chest."

"What did you do?"

Her breath hitched and she began to sob. "I pu . . . I pulled out the knife and . . . and . . . and threw it on the floor." Her shoulders were heaving, her whole body convulsed.

"Why, Claire? Why did you remove the knife?"

"I don't know," she wailed. "I . . . I . . . I thought if I pulled it out, he would be okay. There wasn't a lot of blood." She looked at me, her eyes pleading for understanding.

"There never is with a single stab wound."

"I thought that must mean he could . . . could heal. He would get better and I would take care of him and we would be together forever." Her arms were wrapped tightly around her body as she rocked on the chair. Slowly her eyelids lowered. "I kissed him," she whispered hoarsely. "I kissed him . . . and . . . and then I took his shoulders and shook him. I yelled at him to breathe." Her own breath hitched convulsively.

"And then? Keep going, Claire. Just a little bit more."

"And then I . . . I . . . I heard Madame Poutine scream and I ran out the door."

Chapter Eleven

The matron, a squat woman with hard eyes, came to take Claire away. When Claire saw her jailer, her body seemed to fold in on itself again, the mantle of fatigue settling once more on her narrow shoulders, the light of interest gone from her eyes.

She'd been questioned on Wednesday afternoon. On Thursday the police had taken her in again, and this time they'd kept her. In France, the first twenty-four to forty-eight hours of custody are called *garde à vue,* which means to "keep an eye on" someone while an investigation is proceeding. On Friday morning Claire had been brought before a magistrate who determined that sufficient evidence existed to charge her. When I saw her, she was under *détention préventive,* and because of the nature of the crime she was accused of, she would remain in jail until her trial.

I'd been with Claire for twenty minutes, all that was allowed, and promised to return another time. I was concerned that the conditions in the jail would have an impact on her health. She appeared much thinner than I remembered. She was worried about what would happen to her, of course, but she was also in mourning for the man she loved and who, she was certain, had returned her affection.

Her story sounded convincing. Of course, many murderers lied convincingly. If she'd killed Bertrand, it had probably not been a premeditated act. It could have been an act of passion; people thwarted in love have been known to react violently. Whether or not she had wielded the weapon, however, Claire held the key to the identity of the murderer. Of this I was certain.

She claimed to have overheard an argument between Bertrand and one or possibly two others. The Thomases had heard Bertrand reprimanding Guy when they'd climbed the stairs leading from the cooking school to the lobby. Could that argument have escalated enough for the sous chef to kill his former boss and mentor? Or had another man assaulted Bertrand, perhaps the husband of a lover, or a jealous competitor? There was much to investigate, and the day was already half gone.

I walked quickly down the corridor, past the security desk, toward the front entrance of the police station. My mind was occupied with what to do next when a voice interrupted my thoughts.

"Madame Fletcher, what brings you here?"

"Captain LeClerq. I was just on my way out."

"I can see that," he said. He pulled on one end of a maroon cashmere scarf thrown casually around his neck over the jacket of his suit. "Were you looking for me?"

"I was hoping to retrieve our passports," I replied, "if you no longer need them."

He looked at me carefully, waiting for more, and when I simply returned his stare, he said, "If you will guarantee not to leave Provence — you and the young lady — for the next week or so, until I give you permission, I have no objection to returning your passports."

"You have my word. May I get them now?"

"Of course. Please accompany me to my office." He guided me to a stairwell and we climbed one flight to the next floor.

The police station was a post–World War II building set outside the city's ancient walls. It had the same institutional decor that can be found in similar establishments the world over, walls a drab beige, scuffed and dingy, gray concrete floor. I followed LeClerq to a windowless room crammed with a desk, file cabinet, computer table, and two chairs. He squeezed behind his desk and indicated the other chair for me, tugged off his muffler, folded it carefully, and placed it in a drawer. He was meticulous about his appearance, and I presumed he'd be just as scrupulous following up on the details of a case. He removed a set of keys from his jacket pocket and unlocked his file cabinet. It was filled with folders neatly organized in hanging files. He removed one, laid it on the desk, and opened the cover to reveal a pair of passports on top of other papers.

"Madame Fletcher," he started, as he picked up one passport and checked the photograph.

"There is an attraction, I'm sure, for you to follow the investigations of the police, especially for one so interested in crime. But I feel I must caution you not to interfere with our handling of this case."

"I have no intention of interfering," I said.

"Then we understand each other?"

"But I could be helpful to you."

"Please do not misunderstand, madame, but we do not need your help."

"Are you making progress in finding the killer?"

"We believe we have the killer in custody."

"It's possible, of course, but she's not very strong, and it takes a lot of muscle to force a knife through fabric and flesh."

He winced at my description and began to tap his fingers impatiently on his desk. "When one is in the throes of murderous passion, madame, one often finds a strength unknown before."

"That's true," I said. "Intense emotion releases hormones that can increase your body's muscle power. I'm aware of the effect."

"So, you see?" He put out his hands, palms up, as if I'd proved his case.

"And you think that's what happened with Claire?"

He shrugged.

"At the hotel, Madame Poutine told Claire that Bertrand was unfaithful."

"We know this."

"When Claire ran away she was crying. She

wasn't angry; she was sad, hurt."

"Your point?"

"My point is that crying is cathartic, Captain. It releases the tensions of grief, and could have made her less prone to violence, not more."

"Grief can easily turn to rage," he said, tapping his fingers again. "I do not find it profitable to psychoanalyze the criminal mind. It is the action we address."

"And a motive."

"Are we finished, madame?"

"What about Bertrand? He was a volatile man. He could have made many enemies."

"Now, madame —"

"Have you looked into his business practices?"

"Madame, I lose patience."

"I hope you haven't concluded your investigation. It doesn't sound to me as if you have very much to go on."

"To you, it may look that way. You have a very active imagination. It must serve you well in your profession."

"You're patronizing me, Captain. What other evidence do you have against Claire? Madame Poutine didn't actually see her kill him, did she? Have you found the murder weapon? Were her fingerprints on it?"

I had reached the end of Captain LeClerq's tether. "I cannot comment on specifics of the case," he said in clipped tones. He laid the passports on his desk, returned the folder to the drawer, and pressed his fingers on the handle, sliding it closed very carefully. I had the impression he was restraining himself to keep from slamming the drawer shut.

"I understand," I said.

"I hope you do." He slid the two passports into a white envelope, handed them to me across the desk, and stood. "I believe these are what you came for."

"Thank you."

"Now, I have a great deal to do, madame." He came around the desk and placed a hand on the back of my chair. "You must excuse me. I will be happy to show you out."

"That's not necessary," I said, putting the envelope in my bag.

"Oh, but it is."

He escorted me to the front entrance, nodding at other staff members as he passed them in the hallway and on the stairs. We shook hands at the door.

"You have said you will not interfere, madame, and I expect you to keep your word," he said. "I wish you a pleasant and uneventful stay for the rest of your time in Provence."

It was threatening to rain when I crossed the ring road, what in medieval days had been a moat, and passed through one of more than a dozen *portes,* or gates, that pierce the fourteenth-century ramparts surrounding the old city of Avignon. With a good pair of shoes I could walk anywhere within the walls. But in the rain that prospect was less appealing. I consulted my map. Luck was with me. Bertrand's restaurant, L'Homme Qui Court, the Running Man, was not far from the Hotel Melissande, and both were near Héllas, the restaurant where Daniel claimed to have met with his supplier on Wednesday. I found the main street, Rue de la République, and walked north toward the Palace of the Popes. The street was crowded with Saturday shoppers. Groups of teenagers flirted with each other as they hopped in and out of stores catering to a young clientele. Skateboarders hugged the curb and occasionally jumped onto the sidewalk in an effort to impress their peers. They were more successful in startling their elders.

I thought about my conversation with LeClerq. He hadn't challenged my assertion that the murder weapon was a knife. Did he know I'd learned that information in my visit to Claire? His presence in the hallway when I was leaving certainly was fortuitous. I was disappointed that he wasn't willing to listen to my thoughts on other possibilities in the case. But I'd encountered resistance by the police before. I understood their pride in their profession and their hesitation to work with "amateurs," even if those amateurs could contribute valuable information. But there were practicalities to consider here. The investigation shouldn't stop just because the police had made an arrest. What if they were wrong, as I believed they were? I'd have to talk with LeClerq again, and see if I could persuade him to listen to me. After all, I intended to continue looking into the murder anyway. Together we could make faster progress.

Walking swiftly, I reached the farthest end of the Rue de la République where it opened onto the Place de l'Horloge, or Clock Square, named for the gothic clock tower above the town hall. A row of cafés lined one side of the plaza, the outdoor tables occupied despite the damp weather. Tall plane trees, their leaves still green, softened the cityscape. In front of the Opéra Theatre, next to the town hall, was a beautiful antique carousel, its fanciful appearance out of place among the elegant stone facades of the municipal buildings. Beneath the blue-and-white tent top, colorful painted panels depicting country life were framed by scalloped rows of lightbulbs. Children skipped around the carousel, but the attraction was closed. The lights were off; no music played. Those who tried to climb aboard were shooed off by a burly guard in a navy blue uniform. He pointed to a placard leaning against one of the white horses that read, *Fermé pour Travaux,* "closed for repairs."

"When will it be open?" I heard a father ask. "It's been out all week."

"Come back tomorrow. The man comes to fix it in the morning."

"We go back home tomorrow." The man picked up his daughter. "She wants to ride the horse. Can I take a picture? We'll only be a minute."

The guard looked exasperated — I imagined this wasn't the first such request — but he unhooked a chain across two poles and allowed the pair to climb on the carousel deck. The father sat his little girl on the red saddle and coaxed her to grasp the horse's wooden mane. "Just hold on. You won't fall. I'm right here." When he took his hand off her back, the child's face screwed up and her bottom lip quivered. She looked over her shoulder for him and would have tumbled off if he hadn't grabbed her quickly.

"Would you like me to take the picture for you?" I offered. "That way you can both be in it."

"Would you do that?" His face lit up. "She's a bit nervous being so far off the ground." He handed me his camera and showed me the buttons to push.

I stepped back a few feet and focused on the child, who was clinging to her father's arm. "Okay, now smile." I clicked off two shots, and returned the camera to its owner.

"*Merci, madame.* We are very grateful." He pulled his daughter from the carousel horse, climbed down, and went off to tip the guard, who was talking to a tall man in a trench coat. The little one waved shyly to me from her father's arms. I waved back, and was rewarded with a big smile.

On the other side of the town hall, I turned left onto a small street, which led to the Rue Racine. Bertrand's restaurant was located in an old yellow stone building, set back on the street, allowing for a small patio in front. A pair of iron-filigree tables flanked the door. Above the entrance was an iron silhouette of a man running, his legs far apart in a wide stride. The figure wore a long coat and held on to his top hat as he ran. I tried the door and it was unlocked. Inside, the restaurant was open for business. A stylish brunette in her forties greeted me. She was a darker version of Mme Poutine, perfectly coifed, and with the same stony expression.

"Do you have a reservation?"

"No," I replied. "I wasn't sure you would be open."

"We are open, but only for lunch and with a limited menu today," she said. "We have lost our chef, but the kitchen staff does very well with the new chef. I promise you won't be disappointed."

She took my coat, led me past a small but active bar into the dining room, and pulled out a table near the front of the room to allow me to slide into the banquette. It was late for lunch — most of the diners were eating dessert — but I hadn't had anything since the roll and coffee I'd consumed at the bakery. The hostess handed me the menu, wished me *bon appétit*, and returned to her post.

The restaurant was masculine, elegant and stark, not unlike Bertrand himself. Heavy white linen cloths covered the tables. Dark wood banquettes ran down both long walls and were fitted with thick cushions covered in a tapestry fabric. The chairs that were drawn up to the tables along the banquettes, and to another row of tables down the center of the room, had seats in the same fabric. Stone walls were bare except for arched niches containing alabaster urns spotlighted by halogen lamps suspended from wires.

I read the selections on the handwritten menu, which was clipped to a coated card. A short history of the restaurant and a biography of Emil Bertrand, *Maître Cuisinier de France*, Master Chef of France, were on the back of the card. I read them carefully.

"Are you ready to order, madame?" the waiter asked when he came back. He was a young man with precise posture and artfully spiked brown hair, intended to be chic rather than rebellious.

"No, but I'm sure you can recommend something."

He stood a little taller. "I will be pleased to do so. We have several traditional Provençal dishes. Do you like seafood?"

"Very much."

"Then I recommend the skate with *raïto*. *Raïto* is a sauce with red wine, tomatoes, olives, capers, and garlic. Or the mussels with lemon, white wine, and garlic. Both are excellent. They are served with a medallion of carmelized vegetables."

"What kind of fish is skate?"

"It's the fish that flies on the bottom of the

ocean." He put his arms out and tilted from side to side.

I laughed. "It must be like a stingray or manta ray."

"Yes. Yes. That's the word. We use the meat from the wing. It's delicious."

"After your demonstration, I think I'll have to try the skate, please."

"Would you like a salad as well?"

"May I decide later?"

"Of course. Some wine with your meal?"

"What do you suggest?"

"A Cotes du Rhône will complement the dish perfectly. And we have it by the glass, if you prefer."

I gave him my sunniest smile. "You echo my thoughts exactly."

"*Merci, madame.*" He grinned. "We try very hard to please."

"Tell me, are the dishes on the menu specialties of Chef Bertrand's?"

"Alas, Monsieur Bertrand is no longer here to run the kitchen. A terrible tragedy. We follow as closely as we can his directions. Today, the dishes, they are his. But the new chef, he will choose the next menu."

"What will happen to the restaurant now? Will it be sold?"

"No, I don't believe so. The partner, he takes over. He is putting the new chef in charge, and we will see how well he does. We have a Michelin star, you know. It is hoped we can earn it again."

"I didn't realize Monsieur Bertrand had a partner."

"Not in the kitchen, of course, and not to hire the staff, but to pay the bills and take care of other business matters. The chef, he makes all the decisions. It is his name that is connected to the restaurant."

"Gaspard," the hostess interrupted, tapping the waiter on his shoulder. "Monsieur Peyraud would like his bill, please." She smiled at me. *"Pardon, madame."*

"Bien sûr," the young man said. "Of course. I will take care of it right away." He bent toward me. "Madame, your pardon, please."

"Of course. My apologies for holding you up."

"Not at all."

Gaspard went off to bring M. Peyraud his check, and I observed the other patrons in the restaurant. Most appeared to be businesspeople; they were dressed in suits. There were two tables of tourists, easily distinguished by their less formal attire. One young couple was German, and the others — a mother, father, and teenager — were American. I could tell by their accents, their voices carrying in the quiet dining room. The waiter returned shortly with a saucer holding two disks of red-skinned potato topped with a créme fraîche, and sprinkled with a combination of chopped mint and chives.

"A small sample of the chef's imagination," he said, setting the plate in front of me. "It is to encourage the appetite." He stood by while I tasted it. "The chef, he is practicing for the summer tourists," he said. "It is refreshing. No?"

"It's refreshing, yes," I said. "And delicious."

"*Bon!* I will tell him you like it."

"Do you know the name of Bertrand's partner in this restaurant?" I asked as he placed an empty glass at my place.

"I should," he said. "He signs the checks. But I do not remember. I can find out for you, if you like."

"Yes. I'd appreciate that."

"Are you in the market to buy a restaurant in Provence, madame?"

"Are you making me an offer?"

"I am a wonderful cook myself. And I am handsome, too. You could do worse."

"I don't think I'm ready to invest," I said, laughing, "but it might be fun to explore the opportunity."

"I'll see what I can find out for you."

When Gaspard returned with my entrée, he slid a folded slip of paper next to my plate. "Here is the partner, and his place of business," he whispered.

"Is everything all right with your dinner, madame?" the hostess said, coming to the table, a concerned look on her face.

I palmed the paper and slipped it into my pocket. "Everything is wonderful," I said. "I'm enjoying the restaurant very much. And Gaspard is an excellent waiter."

"Yes." She smiled tightly. "I hope he will give

as much attention to all our guests."

"I am a wicked boy," he said after she'd left. He uncorked a bottle of wine and filled my glass. "Perhaps she is in love with me, too." He winked at me. "All the girls are."

"I don't doubt it for a minute."

My meal was delicious, as promised. Gaspard talked me into a salad, and wouldn't let me skip the cheese course, but I managed to resist when it came to dessert. The restaurant was nearly empty when he served me coffee. Only one table of businesspeople remained other than myself.

"May I get you anything else?"

I looked up. "Just a check, please, Gaspard. And thank you for everything."

"My pleasure," he said. "I will get it for you right away."

I sat back and sighed, experiencing the sensation of well-being following a satisfying meal. I also promised myself a long walk to counter some of the calories. How did Frenchwomen stay so slim? I wondered, accustomed as they were to having major meals for both lunch and dinner. Fortunately, weight had never been a problem for me — probably because I don't drive. Having to rely on two pedals or two feet to get from place to place was a good way to work off the sins of overindulgence. Many a time it had saved me after I'd yielded to the special doughnuts at Charlene Sassi's bakery, or to Mara's blueberry pancakes at the luncheonette on the town dock in Cabot Cove. Of course, at home I rarely cooked big meals, unless I had guests for dinner. Even then, by the time I served what I'd been preparing all day, I'd often lost my appetite for it.

I pulled the note Gaspard had given me from my pocket and unfolded it. My peaceful musings disappeared instantly when I read the name of Emil Bertrand's silent partner — P. Franc. That was the name that had been on the letter Bertrand was clutching when he died. Did that paper have any significance in his death? Was his partner aware that Bertrand was talking to others about joining the business? Guy had hopes for a partnership. Daniel said Bertrand had talked to him about going into business together. But did he know Bertrand already had a partner? Had Emil been planning to cut his partner out? Or were they planning together to expand the business?

A burst of laughter from the table of businessmen drew my attention. The chef had come out of the kitchen to join them. Dressed all in white, he stood with his back to me; I couldn't see his face.

"More investors?" I asked when Gaspard placed a leather folder in front of me.

"One can only hope," he said. "A chef who is well financed can make himself famous, even without a star."

"How would he do that?" I asked, placing my credit card in the folder.

"He can go on television, write books, open

other restaurants. If he is famous, people will assume he is good, and make his restaurants a big success. And, of course, the more successful he is, the better for his staff."

"I see," I said. "Well, I wish you luck with your new chef."

"Merci, madame." He took my card to the cash register at the bar. I watched idly as he chatted with a man sitting on the end seat while he waited for the barmaid to process the bill. The sound of laughter drew my attention back to the chef and his clients. I tried to eavesdrop, but their voices were too low to hear clearly. The chef leaned his lanky frame over the table to shake hands with the men on the other side. As he turned, I caught sight of his profile. Wait a minute. Was that . . . ?

"Here is your card, madame. It has been a pleasure serving you."

"The chef, your new chef," I said, standing and trying to see around Gaspard.

"Yes?" He turned around, but the chef had left.

"I know him."

"Yes? He leaves for his other job now."

"His other job?" I sank back in my seat.

"He cooks for another restaurant at night."

"The Hotel Melissande, right?"

"Ah, *oui,* you do know him."

Chapter Twelve

"I wonder if you could help me. I'm looking for this address." I showed the elderly gentleman the paper Gaspard had given me. It was late in the afternoon, the skies were darkening, and there were few people on the street. A cold wind had entered the city. It whipped around the sharp corners and turned what had been a light rain into a horizontal attack.

I'd already visited Héllas, the restaurant where Daniel had said he'd been meeting a supplier during the time Emil Bertrand was killed. Henri, the maître d', thought he recollected seeing Daniel there on Wednesday, but maybe it was Tuesday, no, definitely Wednesday, or at least probably Wednesday. The book would be no help; the restaurant didn't take reservations for lunch. But either way, he couldn't be sure if the young chef was there from noon to three, as Daniel maintained. "We are so busy, madame," he told me. "I cannot keep watch on all my customers. Did he leave and come back? I didn't see this, but it is possible."

The address Gaspard had given me for Emil Bertrand's partner in the restaurant business was in a section of town I'd never been in before. I'd followed my map but had become disoriented by the twisting, narrow alleys — were they streets? — that angled off other streets, by the intersections with two or three unlabeled possibilities, by passageways that proved to be dead ends.

"*Oui*. Avignon, she is confusing," the old man said. "I will try, but I don't have my glasses with me." He squinted at the paper in my hand.

"Would you like to use mine?" I slipped the cord that held my reading glasses over my head and offered them to him.

He took the glasses, positioned the lenses in front of Gaspard's neat handwriting, and read the address out loud. "Ah, *oui*. This is not too far, but you must go back there, and take the second left, not the first." He pointed with a pudgy finger in the direction from which I'd come. "It is a small street but it will take you to a larger one. There you turn right, and then left at the next intersection. It should be down that street."

I thanked him and headed toward the street he'd indicated, debating whether I should abandon the search and come back another day. It was getting darker by the moment. I'd long since given up using my little umbrella; the wind had turned it inside out several times. I'd put on a scarf instead and dropped the disappointing contraption in my coat pocket.

I turned left at the second intersection, as instructed. It was more an alleyway than a street — I doubted it was wide enough to accommodate a car — and it was deserted; there wasn't another pedestrian in sight. At least the wind was calmer here. I walked quickly toward a store window halfway down the block, its fluorescent glow a comforting beacon as the daylight died away. When I neared the window, the light went out. A man emerged from the shop door, locked it behind him, and scurried past me in the opposite direction. I listened to the fading sound of his shoes on the cobblestones as he lengthened the distance between us. But then there was another set of footsteps behind me. They weren't vanishing; they were getting closer. I increased my pace and the footsteps sped up. Was someone following me? Or was it my imagination again, spurred by the drama of being lost and alone in a gloomy, unfamiliar city?

I reached the end of the alley and rounded the corner. The street was larger, as promised, but just as quiet as the previous one. I jogged to the next corner and glanced back to see a tall man in a trench coat standing at the intersection from which I'd just come. A hat hid his face. He hadn't been there less than a minute ago. I turned left, hoping to find the company of fellow pedestrians. A couple under an umbrella was leaning against a car about twenty yards ahead, completely absorbed in each other. Relieved, I walked past them, searched for the right address, and spotted it on the other side of the street.

The wooden door creaked when I pushed it open and entered a small vestibule. I peered at the names on the mailboxes but didn't find a listing for P. Franc. The interior door was also unlocked. It was glass but had been painted over, preventing anyone from seeing into the poorly lighted hallway. There were doors to three offices, one of which stood open, and just past them an emergency exit marked by a red light. At the end of the hall was an elevator. I poked my head into the open office; the lights were on but there was no one inside. Perhaps they'd gone on an errand, never thinking a stranger would walk in uninvited. I checked the names painted on the frosted-glass windows of the other doors; nothing sounded familiar and no lights shone through the glass. I knocked anyway and tried the doorknobs, but they were locked. Either the offices weren't open on Saturday or they had closed early. Should I wait in the open office until someone returned? Or should I see if I could find Franc's name on the second floor?

There was no knob on this side of the emergency exit. I rang for the elevator. It opened immediately and I took it to the second floor. One dim ceiling fixture, fitted with a red bulb, hung between a stairwell door and the elevator. At the far end of the corridor, twilight leaked in through a smudged window. The rest of the hall was in shadows. I walked slowly, trying to make out the names on the darkened glass panes of the doors. At the last one, nearest the window, I found what I was looking for. The sign said *AGENT IMMOBILIER*, real estate agent, and underneath the gold letters were two names. The first was the one I was seeking: P. FRANC. But the second name was a surprise: M. POUTINE. Was this Mme Poutine's husband?

A sound outside drew me to the window; I looked down on the wet pavement. A man in a trench coat crossed the street. Was it the same man I'd seen on the corner? I heard the creak of the outer door downstairs as he entered the building. Why was he following me? What did he want? Whoever he was, I had no desire to confront him in an empty building with no one around to sound the alarm.

How could I get out? The elevator was not an option. I rushed back down the hall, praying the stairwell door wasn't locked. I twisted the knob and leaned with my shoulder. It opened. I closed the door quietly and crept down the stairs, wary of making any noise that would give away my location. The door on the first floor had an emergency push bar to allow people to leave, but not to permit access from the other side.

I put my ear to the door and listened. The whine of the elevator made me jump. I heard the elevator door open and close on the first floor. The engine whined again, and I waited for the sound of the door opening on the second floor before I pressed on the bar and escaped into the hall. All the office doors were closed now, and I fled the building, knowing the squeal of the front door would alert my pursuer. I hugged the buildings as I hurried down the street, hoping he wouldn't be able to see the direction in which I was heading if he looked out the window. Bright lights at the intersection ahead promised a bigger thoroughfare, and I gratefully turned the corner onto a street with traffic and stores.

"Madame Fletcher. It is good to see you again, but I don't think the authorities would be happy for you to be here."

"I'm sure you're right, Guy, so I won't tell them if you won't."

"I am closing my lips with a lock," he said with a sad smile. "Would you like to go in?"

I leaned against the side of the arched entry and scrutinized the medieval dining room where Emil Bertrand was killed. "Yes," I said. "You won't mind?"

"There is no need to keep away. The police have finished their forensic work in here. We start our classes again next week."

"Oh, that's good," I said, stepping down into the room. "Will you be teaching?"

"As a matter of fact, I will," he said, brushing off the front of his white apron, which was stained with the ingredients of tonight's dinner. "Daniel has asked me to be director of the school."

"Congratulations," I said.

We gravitated toward the school kitchen. Guy opened the door and flicked on the overhead lights. I took the seat I'd sat in as a student. The room was immaculate. There was no sign of the last meal prepared here. The butcher-block table had been scrubbed; no rabbit blood stained its surface. In fact, it was empty except for a stack of folders next to a pile of starched white aprons. Guy walked around checking materials. He straightened the folders and turned the aprons so all the strings were on the same side. He adjusted the angle of one of the tall olive jars lined up on the shelf jutting out from the oven hood, making sure its "hermine" was precisely centered. He counted the number of knife handles jutting from a pottery pitcher.

"I take it the police returned all your knives," I said.

"How do you know about that?" Guy asked.

"Daniel told me," I said. "I met him at the truffle market in Carpentras."

"*Oui,* they did."

"Do you ever go to the truffle market?"

"*Non.* It is for the master chefs, not the sous chefs. Of course, I *could* go, if they gave me the money to buy. I know what a good truffle should be."

"Of course you do," I said. "You're a chef with many years' experience."

He smoothed his mustache with his thumb and forefinger. "*C'est vrai.* That's true." He removed his glasses, letting them dangle by their cord, and leaned against the wall, his arms and feet crossed.

"I hope Daniel appreciates that," I said.

A puff of air escaped his lips. "*Poufft!* No one ever gives me credit," he said. "Daniel, he says I have great administrative skills. He thinks I don't know he isn't complimenting my cooking."

"He doesn't realize how observant you are."

He nodded in agreement.

"You said once that Daniel hires chefs for the school even if he doesn't like them," I said.

"True."

"I got the impression you were talking about Chef Bertrand."

He nodded again.

"Why didn't he like Emil?"

He pushed himself away from the wall and put his glasses back on. "The old man, he thinks Daniel is challenging him. He never likes that Daniel gets the hotel position, even though he didn't want it himself."

"And Daniel held that against him?"

"No, no. That wasn't it at all." He slid his fingers under his eyeglasses and rubbed his eyes.

"Then why?"

He blinked several times and squinted as if he were trying to see the story. "Daniel, he thinks Emil kept him from getting a star," he said.

"How could he do that?" I asked.

"Oh, it's a long tale, and maybe it's not true about the star."

"I heard there was a scandal about Emil some years back. Is this what they're talking about?"

"*Oui, oui.* I am sure it is."

"You have to tell me what happened. You can't leave me in suspense."

"All right. I will tell you. But the story has been embellished so many times, it may not be true."

"Okay. I'll take it with a grain of salt."

Guy started to giggle.

"Did I say something funny?" I asked.

He tried to hold it in, but his laughter broke out anyway. I watched, perplexed, as he bent his long body in half, hands holding his knees, and laughed till the tears rolled down his cheeks. *All the tension of the last week must be catching up to him,* I thought. Finally he wiped his eyes, and blew his nose in a big white handkerchief. "You will see in a minute," he said with a grin. He cleaned his spectacles with a corner of his apron and pulled the sidepieces over his ears. The lenses magnified his eyes so that the one that turned in was now even more noticeable.

"Now you really have me curious," I said, smiling at him.

"It's called 'L'Affair du Sel,' " he said, stifling another giggle.

I laughed, too. "The Salt Affair?" I translated.

"*Oui. C'est ça.* That's it."

"So tell me."

He pulled out another of the tall stools and sat. He sighed, still smiling. "As an instructor, Emil, he is permitted to use the hotel kitchen for his food supplies for the classes. You understand?"

I nodded.

"It was said he put salt in the sugar box."

"Uh-oh!"

"You can see what will happen, yes?"

"How bad was it?"

"Daniel, he has a table of important guests. He ruins his famous dessert, which takes many hours to make."

"Oh, my goodness! Did he serve it to them?"

"He didn't mean to. He sees something is not right, tastes the dish, and puts it aside. He is furious. He screams for the sous chef to get another dessert from the locker, and he goes to call who he thinks is the culprit. While he is out of the kitchen, the waiter finds the famous dessert unattended and brings it to the table with great fanfare."

"What happened?"

"The guests take one spoonful of the dessert and spit into their napkins. The meal is ruined. They forget the delicious dishes that preceded this one and complain to the management that the chef is trying to poison them. News of the disaster flies all over the dining room, and people at other tables start to feel sick."

"The power of suggestion," I said.

"Very much so. One lady faints. Another throws up at the table. People are running from the room without paying for their meals. Ambulances arrive and cart the people off to the hospital. The reporters cover the story and Daniel is made a laughingstock. He was very lucky not to get fired."

"And did Bertrand do that? Did he switch the salt and sugar?"

Guy shrugged. "He denies this, of course, but Daniel accuses him."

"How could he be sure it was Bertrand who made the switch? And if Bertrand did do it, how can Daniel be certain it was deliberate? Couldn't that have happened accidentally?"

"Emil was the instructor for that day. So he had the right to use the kitchen. He was furious at Daniel. Daniel had been sous chef under him, and he was offended that his student would be so ungrateful. He said that the famous dessert was just not good, and that Daniel made up a story to explain his failure. They didn't speak for years."

"And Daniel thinks that incident kept him from earning a star."

He shrugged. "He could not know. The Michelin inspectors, they never reveal themselves. But he suspected they were here that night. He still has not been given a star, and he is a very fine chef. It is a pebble in his shoe."

"I'm sure it is."

"I must get back to the kitchen. I have taken too much time away. Do you want to stay more?"

"No. I'll go, too," I said, getting up and pushing the stool back into place.

Guy turned off the overhead lights, and we walked across the ancient courtyard.

"If you're going to be director of the cooking school, does that mean you won't be cooking for L'Homme Qui Court anymore?" I asked.

He appeared uncomfortable with the question. "It doesn't look as if I will be offered the partnership I was expecting."

"Oh, I'm sorry," I said. "Do you know who the new chef will be?"

He cleared his throat. "It will be a little time, I believe, before the decision is made," he said. "I am being considered, along with others. Emil had a star, you see. His partners want someone who will make certain they keep it."

"Who are his partners?"

"Emil would be angry at what they do." He waved his hand in front of his face. "I have talked of nothing but Emil this week. I don't want to talk of this anymore," he said. "Tell me, how is your little friend? Is she still in Avignon?"

"Yes," I replied. "Mallory is staying with me."

"I'm glad she has an adult to look after her. You will say hello for me, eh?"

"Yes, I will." I hesitated, finally asking, "Have you been to see Claire?"

"Ah, *pauvre petite*. Poor little one. Such a shame. I tried to tell her he was cheating on her."

"So you think she is guilty."

He shrugged. It was a particularly French expression of resignation, a gesture that said, "What can you do? This is what the world is like. There is nothing to be done."

"We rented a car to take rides into the country," Jill Thomas said, pouring a cup of tea for her husband. "It was beautiful weather and we wanted to take advantage."

"We would have tried to visit you in St. Marc, but the rental company didn't supply maps," Craig added. "Never heard of such a thing, not to have maps."

"The hotel gave us a map, but it was just for the city," Jill said. "We managed to make a nice day of it all the same."

"I was away all yesterday morning at the Carpentras market," I said. "You would have missed me anyway."

"What brought you here today?" Craig asked. "Going to base one of your crime novels on the mystery of the dead chef?"

"Craig, don't pry," Jill said.

"That's not such a terrible question," he said.

"I was hoping to bump into you two, of course. Do you know if René Bonassé is still at the hotel?"

"He's gone," Jill said. "Captain LeClerq left us a message that we were no longer needed for the investigation. I assume he did the same for René. He checked out this morning."

"Interesting. The captain took our passports — Mallory's and mine — on Thursday, but he gave them back today," I said.

"He must be convinced Claire is guilty," Jill said, "although I have difficulty believing it."

"*I* think Madame Poutine 'fingered her,' " Craig said. "Isn't that what your American 'cops' call it?"

"I see you're a fan of gangster movies," I told him. "I don't think Claire killed him either, but

Madame Poutine did accuse her. Whether that's Captain LeClerq's only evidence, I don't know."

"Jessica, would you like some tea? The waiter can bring an extra cup."

"I'd love some," I said. "But would you two excuse me for a moment? I just remembered a call I need to make."

The young man at the desk was the same clerk who'd replaced Claire after she was taken away by the police. He recognized me and greeted me warmly, evidently relieved to see that the chef's murder had not kept me from returning to the hotel.

"*Bonsoir, madame.* How may I help you?"

"I've signed up for one of your cooking classes next week," I told him. "A friend said he might be taking it, too. May I see if his name is in your book?"

Eager to assist me, he pulled out the heavy cooking school ledger and laid it on the counter. He flipped the pages to the date I indicated and turned the book around so I could read it. I pretended to look at the names in next week's class until a guest drew his attention away. I turned back to the page listing the students in the class I had taken. There were columns for names, addresses, and telephone numbers, and a place for signatures when the students signed in. Mme Poutine had not provided her address, but René had given his. The address was in Paris. I committed his telephone number to memory and went to the telephone booth, actually a table with phone books and a chair, in an alcove to the right of the front desk. I sat and jotted the number down on a pad next to the phone. I got out my calling card and dialed. A woman's voice answered.

"*Non.* Monsieur Bonassé is not here."

"Do you know where I can reach him? It's very important."

"*Oui.* He is visiting his aunt. She lives in Les Baux."

"Les Baux?"

The woman gave me the aunt's name and telephone number. I wrote them down, although, given a choice, I wouldn't announce myself with a call. Over the years I've found that face-to-face conversation yields much more data. Observing someone's facial expression and body language while listening to the tone and inflection of their voice usually results in learning a great deal more than they think they are telling you.

I thanked the woman on the phone, rang off, and took advantage of my location to consult the telephone books for a listing under the name Poutine. There was one for M. Poutine but not at the business address I'd visited. I wrote down the information and returned to the Thomases. "How is Mallory doing?" Jill asked when I reclaimed my seat.

"She's healthy enough," I said, "but she seems preoccupied." I stirred my tea, thinking about her baffling behavior. "She's been sleeping a lot.

She went to bed early on Thursday and was still wearing her pajamas when I returned from Carpentras on Friday afternoon. I got the impression she'd jumped out of bed when she heard the car pull up."

"Typical teenager," Craig said. "They like to sleep late."

"Maybe so," I said. "My experience is limited there. She did take an interest in Monsieur Telloir's new dog. And she made us a wonderful pasta dinner with little truffles he turned up." I'd been wrong about Magie, who was turning out to be a pretty fair truffle dog. M. Telloir had great hopes for him. "But today, again, she was in bed when I left at noon," I said. "I'm a little concerned."

"Nothing to fret about," Craig said. "I remember sleeping till teatime when I was a young bloke."

"Yes, but you didn't get to bed till very late," his wife pointed out. "You closed the pubs, as I recall."

"Don't frown. I've fond memories of those days."

"Being anywhere near a murder is very unsettling," Jill said to me. "I never saw Bertrand's body, but I had trouble sleeping Wednesday night. Mallory's young and impressionable. Perhaps the murder is on her mind."

"That's what I thought," I said. "I've tried to get her to talk about it several times, but she always cuts me off."

"It probably has nothing to do with the murder," Craig said. "She's young and lazy. She needs more stimulation, shouldn't be hanging about in the country." He put down his cup. "Say, we're going for a drive on Monday. Be happy to take you both along."

"That's a wonderful idea, Craig," Jill said. "Jessica, why don't you come with us? I'm sure Mallory would love it, and you'll enjoy it, too."

"I have so much to do —"

"I won't take no for an answer," she said. "There's plenty of room in the car. Do come with us."

"Where are you going?"

"Wherever you like," she said. "We thought we'd drive south to St.-Rémy-de-Provence and then continue on to Les Baux, but if you'd rather go up to Gordes or over to Arles or someplace else, we can alter our plans."

"Les Baux? I would be interested in going to Les Baux. I've heard of it, but I'm not sure where it is," I said.

"Just south of St.-Rémy," Craig said. "It's a village in the Alpilles mountains, built on the site of a tenth-century fortress. The ruins are still there."

"Boys love anything to do with war," Jill said, smiling at her husband. To me she said, "It's supposed to be absolutely charming, but overloaded with tourists in the summer. Our guidebook said to visit off-season, if you can. And we can."

"It's just one day," Craig said. "You'll get Mallory out of the house early, and we'll all tramp around the ruins."

"Oh, do come, Jessica," Jill urged. "We'll have fun. Can't be serious all the time."

I smiled. "You've talked me into it," I said.

"I'm so pleased," she said. "We'll pick you up the day after tomorrow. Be sure you and Mallory have both got good walking shoes and warm clothes on. How's ten? Is that a good time?"

"We'll be ready."

Chapter Thirteen

"Mallory? I'm going for a run. Would you like to come?"

Mallory buried her face in the pillow and curled her knees up toward her chest. She mumbled something unintelligible, pulled the covers over her shoulder, and was silent. From her muffled response, I understood she wasn't in the mood for a run or even a walk, and I wasn't up for an argument. I left her to sleep.

The sun was shining; in Provence in November you learn to take advantage of the sun when it shows its face, since there are many days when it doesn't. It was Sunday, and I'd decided I would take a run through the olive orchard to start the day. I marched down the drive in my jogging suit, swinging my arms across my chest and behind my back to warm up. Ahead, a pickup truck had pulled onto the grass at the edge of the orchard. When I came abreast of the truck, I was delighted to find M. Telloir and several others gathering the fruit. They had spread large plastic tarpaulins on the ground beneath a half dozen trees. Triangular ladders were braced against the gnarled trunks, and the pickers' legs and feet could be seen balancing on a rung. The rest of their bodies disappeared into the canopy of the tree. The only sounds were the gentle *plop-plop* of the olives as they fell onto the tarp, and the soughing of the leaves as the pickers combed their tools through the branches.

Magie ran to greet me, yapping excitedly, his tail wagging in a circle. I bent to pet his curly head.

"*Bonjour, madame,* 'ow are you today?" M. Telloir said.

"Well, thanks. And you?"

"As you can see, we pick."

"I see. How exciting."

"We were 'ere yesterday afternoon, and will pick again today. Next Saturday, I think, we will finish. The men, they work in town during the week. They can only pick on weekends. But it's nice to spend the day outdoors, no?"

"Especially when it's not too cold," I said. "Tell me, why don't you use a machine to pick the olives? Wouldn't that be faster?"

"There is no machine. There is only this." He held up a tool with widely spaced teeth that looked like a comb for a giant. "The trees, they are very delicate and the olives must be picked by 'and."

"What kind of olive trees does Martine have here?" I asked, remembering his lesson regarding blends of olive oil as we drove to Carpentras.

"She has *good* trees," he said. "These are mostly *aglandau,* but there are some *picholine* down at the other end of the orchard. We 'arvest them separately. The mill, 'e wants only olives from one kind of tree in the load."

232

"What makes these 'good' trees? Because they produce a lot of fruit?"

"*Peut-être*, perhaps. But also they are resistant to the drought and to the bugs, and they endure our harsh winters."

"You mean the weather will get worse?"

He laughed. "You haven't experienced the mistral yet. Wait till you feel the wind."

"I'm going to feel the wind in my face now," I said. "I'm going for my run."

"Ah, you Americans with your exercise," he said, shaking his head. "Spend a day picking olives and you will get very 'ealthy."

"I'm sure you're right," I said, smiling. "But not today. Today I run."

I took leave of M. Telloir and his pickers and, after more stretching exercises, jogged across the orchard between the rows of *aglandau* olive trees. The soil was firm beneath my sneakers, the smell of damp earth and clean air refreshing. I ran, hoping to clear my mind of the pieces of the murder puzzle, and to reclaim my purpose for being in France to begin with. As the kilometers fell away, I allowed the workout and the brilliance of the day to relax me, timing my breathing to the tempo of my feet as they hit the ground. At home, I often run on the beach. I strive for endurance, not speed, and the opportunity to enjoy nature at a comfortable pace.

I reached the end of the orchard and circled back via the paved road to Martine's drive, waving at Mme Arlenne's window in case she was watching. When I walked up the dirt road to the house, I saw the pickers had moved farther into the orchard, and baskets of olives sat under the trees where the tarps had been earlier. The pickup truck was gone, probably delivering the first load of olives to M. Telloir's barn to await shipment to the mill.

The gray cat was sitting in front of the garage when I arrived back at the house. This was my day for communing with nature, I thought. The cat and I had become fast friends. Each time I went to take the bike from the garage, she'd push her head through the hole in the wall under the stairs and come to greet me. She was a charming companion, and deserved a little extra attention. Once, I'd fed her a few scraps of leftovers, and that had sealed her devotion. There was a bit of cooked chicken in the refrigerator she might appreciate, but I preferred not to feed her on Martine's nice dishes. I'd seen some discarded tableware in the garage that would serve the purpose. I pulled open the large wooden door as far as it would go to allow light into the murky interior and rummaged around in boxes of crockery looking for suitable plates.

The cat followed me inside, gracefully leaping on top of tables and chairs and over equipment until she reached the corner. She ran halfway up the flight of stairs and sat, quietly licking her paw. Was Martine's studio up there? I'd wondered about that before, but hadn't yet explored the loft.

Well, as long as I was still in my running

clothes, a little extra dirt and dust wouldn't hurt. I put down a chipped bowl I'd found, and wove my way to the corner, around the collection of detritus that filled the garage. At the base of the staircase an industrious spider had woven cobwebs across the beams. I batted them away and climbed up, feeling my way to the door at the top. The knob was rough, probably rusty, but it turned easily. When I pushed open the door, daylight flooded the stairs.

I climbed the last few steps into Martine's studio. The underside of the peaked roof of the garage was her ceiling, and light streamed in from an enormous skylight that I'd never noticed from the outside. It gave her northern exposure, the quality of light most prized by artists.

Martine had two easels, and tables next to them to hold the myriad equipment she required when she was painting. On one table a can held palette knives and a variety of other metal tools. Brushes stood bristle-side up in an old beer stein. Her palette was a kidney-shaped pad of shiny paper with a thumbhole in the middle; the top sheet could be pulled off when there was no more room to mix paint on it. I perched on a stool in front of one of the easels and admired the painting Martine had left unfinished when she departed for Maine. She had a wonderful eye for color. Of course, I already knew that, from the paintings, fabrics, and furniture she'd chosen for her home. To someone so drawn to vivid tones, Provence in winter may have lost some of its appeal. Perhaps that was why she chose to travel at this time of year.

My eyes roamed over the rest of the studio. The room was large, but the angle of the roof cut off a lot of space. Martine had nailed up panels of plywood to serve as walls, but there were gaps between the boards, and I could see she used the triangular areas for storage. The room itself was a little neater than the garage downstairs, but it, too, was filled with clutter. Stacks of paintings leaned against one wall. On another, unpainted canvases were awaiting her inspiration. A large cabinet with open shelves holding cans and tubs of paint, balls of twine, and rolls of tape was covered with a rainbow of spatters and smears, an unintentional but interesting effect. In one corner, bolts of canvas stood on end, and boxes held slats of wood for stretchers. A toolbox sat nearby. I also noticed two bowls on the floor. The gray cat was nosing them, but she'd long ago licked them clean. Apparently I wasn't the first to befriend this animal.

I walked to where Martine's finished canvases were arrayed along the floor leaning against the wall, in places two or three paintings deep. I tipped one painting forward to look at the one behind it. To my right, I heard the cat scratching behind one of the plywood panels. Cats are born hunters. Domestication has barely changed that. She was probably on the trail of a mouse that had dared enter her territory. I moved to the next painting and studied the swirls of lavender and green suggesting the fields of herbs for which Provence is famous. Out of the corner of my eye, I saw the cat pawing something brown and white. I turned to watch her. She'd found a cloth Martine probably used to wipe her brushes. It was folded up in a tight bundle, but as the cat hit it with her paw, it started to come apart.

"What do you have there, kitty?"

The cat was pressing her nose into the cloth and pushing the bunched-up fabric across the floor. I followed, leaned down, and picked up the loose end of the cloth. It unrolled and something fell out of the center, clattering to the floor. I gasped. Spinning on its side was a large carving knife with a molded black handle. I put out my foot to halt its rotation. I knelt down. The blade was smeared, but I could make out the letters near the handle. They read: *FABRIQUÉ POUR EMIL BERTRAND.*

I picked up the fabric that had held the knife. It was a white T-shirt, or had been. The brown stains were dried blood. Was this the murder weapon? How did it get here?

I felt a shiver go through me. I knew how it got here.

A rasping noise drew my attention. Slowly I looked up. Still clad in her pajamas, her feet bare, Mallory stood in the door. Breathing heavily, she brushed stray wisps of hair off her forehead with trembling fingers. The expression in her eyes was bleak, her voice hard.

"I was afraid you would find that."

Chapter Fourteen

"I swear I didn't kill him. I know you won't believe me, but I swear I didn't."

"Mallory, this looks very bad."

"I know, I know. I should have said something when I found it, but I thought you wouldn't believe me. I can see you don't believe me. I knew it. I knew no one would." Her voice was shrill.

"Where did you get this knife?"

"Someone stuck it in my backpack. I found it when I unpacked on Thursday. It fell out when I took out my laundry." She started to gag at the memory. She put her hand over her mouth, turned, and ran downstairs.

I dropped the T-shirt over the knife and picked them both up. This was important evidence, and I hoped I hadn't contaminated it. I found an empty box in Martine's storage area, put the knife and shirt in it, and sealed it closed with tape from the large cabinet.

My heart was heavy. Mallory was so young and aimless. Was she deranged as well? Had Bertrand's nasty comments to her snapped something in her psyche? Had she, like the tormented children who bring guns to school, lashed out at a bully who'd humiliated her? Had I misjudged her so? Had I been harboring a murderer all along? Was my own life now in danger?

I carried the box downstairs, closed the garage

door, and walked back to the house, worried about this child and what I had to do next. The living room and kitchen were empty. I put the box on the mantel of the kitchen fireplace and walked to the staircase. I could hear Mallory crying in Martine's room, her sobs echoing in the stairwell. I wanted to comfort her. I wanted to yell at her. How could she hide something so important? How could she be so foolish?

Mallory had thrown herself across Martine's bed, and was clutching the pillow. She sat up when I entered the room and pulled the pillow across her chest as if to protect herself from my onslaught. Her nose and eyes were red, her cheeks wet with tears. She looked at me fearfully. "Wh . . . wh . . . what are you going to do?" she got out.

"What do you think I should do?"

She drew a big breath and hiccuped. "I . . . I . . . I don't know."

"I have to call LeClerq."

She hung her head and sobbed. Tears streamed down her cheeks.

"Why didn't you tell me as soon as you found it?"

She shook her head.

"Concealing evidence is a crime," I said. "Not to mention that it makes you look guilty. At least if you'd come forward right away, the police would have had less reason to suspect you. Now . . ." I trailed off. I took a box of tissues from Martine's dresser, placed it in Mallory's lap, and sat on the bed next to her. "Now I don't know what they'll do."

Mallory blew her nose, took another tissue, and pressed it against her swollen eyes. She put on her eyeglasses. "I didn't kill him," she said, her voice quavery. "You do believe me, don't you?"

"I don't know what to believe, Mallory."

"But I didn't," she whined. "Why don't you believe me?"

"I didn't say I don't believe you. But you've lied to me before, Mallory, so I'm reserving judgment."

She dropped the tissue and turned to me. "When? When did I lie?"

"You told me you lived in Portland, yet you told LeClerq you live in Cincinnati."

"I explained that."

"You told me you were eighteen."

"I am."

I raised an eyebrow and waited.

"So what? So what if I'm not eighteen? It's not that important." She jumped off the bed, letting the pillow fall to the floor, and began pacing the room.

"Telling the truth is important."

"What else? What else can you say I lied about?"

"You told LeClerq you were watching the children on the merry-go-round when you went for a walk."

"So?" She was getting angry now.

"So, the carousel has been closed for repairs for a week."

She stopped pacing and faced me. "You checked on me?" she said, her voice rising with hysteria.

"Not at all," I replied, standing. "I believed you. But I passed the carousel yesterday and heard a father asking the guard when it would be fixed. He said his daughter was disappointed that the carousel had been closed all week."

"Well, there were kids sitting on it then."

"That's not what you said. And it was cordoned off."

"So does that mean I killed Bertrand?" She was yelling now. "Does it? Does it make me a murderer because the merry-go-round was broken? Because there weren't any kids on it?" She started pacing again, then picked up the pillow and threw it on the bed.

"No, lying doesn't make you a murderer," I said, "but it does make you an unreliable source of the truth. And it could make you a suspect."

"You don't believe I didn't kill him. I knew it. No one ever believes me."

"You make it difficult for people to believe you when you lie. Sit down, Mallory."

"Why?" she yelled.

"Because I have some questions for you and I want you to tell me the truth." I pointed to the bed. "I want you to sit down calmly, and behave like the adult you claim to be."

She glared at me, but sat on the bed.

"Did you really call your parents? Or was that a lie, too?"

She pulled her braid over her shoulder and twisted it.

"The truth now," I said.

"No," she answered in a small voice.

"Why not?"

"The battery's dead in my phone."

"You could have asked to use Martine's phone."

"I didn't really want to talk to them."

"Are you running away?"

"They know where I am."

"The truth?"

"I took a course in Paris this summer — I told you about that on the train — and I . . . I just decided not to go back."

"Why not?"

She closed her eyes and shrugged, her anger having dissipated, leaving her looking tired and dejected.

"You *are* running away. Why?"

"I didn't want to go back to school."

"Why not?"

"They don't like me there."

"Who doesn't?"

"The other kids."

"Mallory, you're bright and charming. Why wouldn't they like you?"

She was silent.

"Did you get in trouble because of lying?" I asked.

"I didn't lie. I just didn't tell them everything."

"Tell me what happened."

She picked up the box of tissues that had fallen on the floor and pulled one out. She dabbed at her eyes under her glasses. "One of the girls had gotten some pot, you know, marijuana. A bunch of us wanted to try it. But we needed a place no one would come." She hesitated.

"Yes?"

"I knew where the key to the teachers' lounge was kept, so I took it." Her eyes were glued to her hands in her lap. "And the security guard caught us. Not me. I'd gone out to the bathroom. I heard him coming down the hall and I ran back to my room. The other girls, they got in trouble for doing drugs and also for breaking into the teachers' lounge."

"But you had let them into the room."

Her head bobbed up and down.

"So if you'd told the authorities the truth, you would have gotten into trouble yourself. They would have punished you for stealing the key."

Another nod.

"Your friends were certainly not innocent in all of this, but you let them get blamed for something you'd done."

"They hate me."

"Mallory, you can't keep running away from responsibility. You have to acknowledge the truth and accept the consequences. Lying has gotten to be a bad habit with you."

"I know."

"What did you mean when you said your parents know where you are?"

"When I didn't go back to school, they sent my uncle to Paris to look for me. He found out where I was staying. I don't know how he does it, but every time I move somewhere else, he finds me."

"Your cash card."

"Huh?"

"The bank keeps a record of each time you use it and where. Your parents are probably relaying to him the location of every ATM machine you stop at."

She snorted. "I wondered why the money hadn't run out yet."

"They must be adding money to your account."

"So they can keep track of me."

"So they can take care of you, make sure you have enough to live on. Mallory, don't you realize how worried they must be?"

"Maybe," she murmured.

"When did you find the knife?"

"I told you, when I unpacked."

"Was that before or after LeClerq and Thierry were here?"

She hung her head and mumbled something.

"I can't hear you," I said.

"Before," she said in a small voice, pulling the elastic off the end of her braid.

I threw up my hands. "Do you realize what an opportunity you wasted? He would have questioned you, yes, maybe even taken you in for further questioning, but by coming forward, you would have shown that you had nothing to hide."

"What will he do now?"

"I don't know, Mallory. But we must call him."

"Why?" She stretched the elastic over the tip of her braid and twisted it around and around, replacing what she'd removed only a moment ago.

"If we don't call him, I'm an accessory after the fact," I said. "I won't commit a crime for you, Mallory, even if I believe that you didn't kill Bertrand."

"I'm sorry," she said, pulling off her glasses and wiping her tears again.

"I know you are," I said, walking to the door.

"Are you going to call him now?"

"Yes, unless you want to do it yourself. That would be a good idea."

"No." She gasped. "I can't call him."

"All right. I'll do it." I paused in the doorway. "Why don't you wash your face and then come downstairs. We'll call your parents together. You're going to need a lawyer."

"Are you still mad at me, Mrs. Fletcher?" She gave me a pleading look.

I hesitated. "I'm very upset with you, Mallory, but I'll help you whatever way I can."

Downstairs, I picked up the phone in the living room and called LeClerq. There was a long wait, and then the captain came on the line. I explained the situation.

"We'll leave right away," he said.

"I want you to remember she's a frightened child."

"What have you done with the knife?"

"I'm asking you to handle her gently."

"We're not animals. We will do as we are trained to do. Now, what have you done with the knife?"

"I didn't touch it," I replied. "It's sealed in a box for you."

"You are not to leave."

"We're not going anywhere. We'll wait for your arrival."

"Where is she now?"

"Upstairs, washing up."

"Keep an eye on her."

"We're going to call her parents and make sure she has a lawyer."

"Yes, she will need one."

"Do you have to take her in?"

"I cannot see any other way."

I hung up and stared at the phone for a moment. *What a mess.* Here was a young woman, alone in a foreign country, about to be detained in jail. She must be terrified. I walked to the bottom of the stairs and called up, "Mallory, come down. Let's call your parents right now."

There was no answer. I couldn't hear the sound of water running. "Mallory? Mallory!" I raced up the stairs. She wouldn't harm herself, would she? I never should have left her alone. She was so distraught. I should have insisted she come downstairs with me. *Oh, Mallory, be all right.*

I flew into the bathroom. No Mallory. I ran into Martine's room. She wasn't there — and neither was her backpack. I heard the garage door slam back against the wall.

"Oh, no."

I dashed downstairs, flung open the front door, and ran outside. "Mallory!" I shouted. "Don't do it." Too late. She'd taken my bicycle and was pedaling furiously down the drive. There was no way I could catch her on foot.

Disgusted, angry, and sad, I went back to the living room and phoned LeClerq again. He'd already left. I hung up and sank down onto the couch, my head in my hands. *Poor child. Poor deluded child.* She was only going to make matters worse for herself. The police would find her, and there would be no sympathy, no careful handling. She was now a fugitive, wanted for questioning. Was she also the murderer?

Chapter Fifteen

"Gone? What do you mean, she is gone?" Captain LeClerq was practically apoplectic with rage. His eyes bulged, his face flamed, the veins on his temples stood out.

"It happened while I was talking to you on the phone," I said. "She sneaked out the kitchen door, ran to the garage, and took my bicycle. By the time I caught on, she was halfway down the driveway."

"Why didn't you go after her?"

"I couldn't catch up to her on foot."

"Don't you have a car?"

"I don't drive."

LeClerq exploded with what in translation would be a shower of four-letter words. "Whoever heard of an American who doesn't drive?" he shouted at the sky. "You're supposed to be obsessed with cars." This was directed at me.

I straightened my shoulders. "It's inconvenient," I said, "but not unheard of."

"Do you have any idea where she'll go? Who her friends are?"

"I know she spent a lot of time with the expatriate community in Paris. At least, that's what she told me. She might try to return there."

LeClerq nodded at Thierry, who scribbled a note on his pad.

"Can you describe what was she wearing?"

I looked down the drive and tried to envision Mallory riding away. Was she wearing her ski jacket? Yes. And she had her black backpack with her, too. If she hadn't thrown clothes over her pajamas before she left, she could easily pull off the road and get dressed later on. I described what I knew to the policemen.

"Thierry," LeClerq addressed his lieutenant, "put an alert out for her. Then drive around. See if you can find her. I want to talk with Madame Fletcher."

The officer drove off, one hand on the wheel, the other holding a two-way radio transmitter.

"I am praying you still have her passport," LeClerq said to me as we entered the house.

"Yes, I do." I led him into the living room.

"*Dieu merci!* Thank goodness. May I have it back, please?"

"It's upstairs," I said. "I'll get it for you." On my way through the kitchen, I hooked my handbag off the table and ran up the stairs. Relieved that I'd forgotten to give Mallory back her passport, I set the bag on my dresser and dug out the envelope LeClerq had given me the day before. I wrote Mallory's passport number on it, along with the issuing office, her place and date of birth — I knew it! She was only fifteen — and, just in case, the date of her entry into France. I returned to the living room as quickly as I could, pausing only to lift the box containing the knife off the mantel.

"Here's her passport," I said, handing him the

blue booklet. "The knife, and the shirt it was wrapped in, are in this box."

LeClerq pocketed Mallory's passport, took the box, and sat on the couch, resting it in his lap. He peeled away the tape, opened the flaps, and peered inside, but he didn't touch its contents. "Do you know if her fingerprints are on it or if she wiped them off?"

"I don't know," I said, "but if it's the same knife that Bertrand was using in our cooking class, it could have everyone's fingerprints on it. He passed it around to all the students."

LeClerq's eyes flew up to the ceiling as he closed the box and pressed the tape in place again. "And you expect me to believe she simply found it?" he asked.

"She said it fell out of her backpack when she pulled out her laundry."

"That's when she told you about it?"

"No. She was afraid I wouldn't believe her."

"What did she do with it then?"

Reluctantly, I told him. "She hid it in the studio."

"This is not the behavior of an innocent," he said.

"It's the behavior of a confused child," I said. "She's only fifteen. She panicked when she saw the knife because she was convinced no one would believe she hadn't killed Bertrand."

LeClerq raised his eyebrows. "You give her too much sympathy. There are many young people today, younger even than she, who do not hesitate to kill anyone who gets in their way. This is an epidemic, the young criminals. You see them on the streets, irresponsible, disrespectful. They want the government to carry them from the bed to the table to the chair. Work! Why should they work when everything is given to them? Life, it is without meaning unless it is *their* life."

"Surely there are many responsible, respectful young people as well," I said. "Don't let the bad behavior of a few color your view of them all."

"*Poufft!* You are too trusting. But she will not get away." He stood and looked out the window.

"Do you have a way to contact her parents?" I asked.

"We will leave that to Interpol," he said, referring to the international police agency. "First we have to find her, and we will." He turned back to me, eyes piercing, voice low. "If she returns here, you are to notify me immediately."

"I doubt she will."

He held up a hand. "But it is possible. I want your promise that you will notify me."

I nodded.

He shook his head. "What is your promise worth?" he muttered. "I ask you not to interfere in this case, but do you listen?"

I sat stiffly. "Would you have preferred if I hadn't called you when I discovered the knife?"

"*Non. Non,*" he backtracked. "You did the

correct thing. This time."

"This time?"

"I will have to turn her over to the SRPJ. They have jurisdiction over this case."

"The SRPJ?"

"Service Regional de Police Judiciaire. It is our criminal-investigation department for this region. It is based in Marseilles."

"Marseilles? But Claire —"

"She was transferred there. After your rendez-vous." His expression told me he was not happy that I'd neglected to inform him of my visit when I'd seen him yesterday.

The sound of an engine drew us both to the door. Thierry pulled up in front of the house, but he was the only person in the car. I sighed softly in relief. I wasn't looking forward to what would occur once they found Mallory.

"How could she disappear so quickly?" LeClerq muttered. On his way out, he gave me a card with his cellular number. I was to phone him if I heard from her.

"By the way, Captain, I forgot to mention this," I called after him. "I think I was being followed yesterday in Avignon."

He grunted. "Stay in the country, then," he said, and climbed into the car.

The house was unusually quiet when I closed the door. I listened carefully to what was different. Mallory hadn't been a noisy guest, but her lively presence had filled the house with . . . what? Conversation? No, we hadn't talked that

much. It was more the expectation of compan-
ionship, the understanding that another person
was there to share with if the mood struck. Although she'd lived here for only a few days, she'd
made the air vibrate differently, brought another
perspective to the view. Would I miss her? I'd
been irritated with her more times than not.
While she was here, I was concerned about her,
never really comfortable, knowing she fabricated
stories even when the truth was innocuous. That
wouldn't change until I knew she was safe. Even
if she was guilty, she still needed my help. She
needed her family. How could I contact them?

I retrieved my handbag from the bedroom and
sat down in the living room next to the phone.
My first call was to the bakery.

"*Allô. J'ecoute.*"

"Marie," I said. "It's Jessica Fletcher."

"Ah, Jessica, *bonjour.*"

"I didn't really expect to find you in the bakery
on Sunday afternoon. I was going to leave you a
message on your machine."

"It's all the fault of the tax inspectors."

"The tax inspectors?"

"The papers they require are impossible."

"I apologize for interrupting. Would you like
me to call back another time?"

"If they think I am going to tell them how
much bread I sell in a month, they are very
much mistaken. That is my business, not theirs,
the thieves."

Taken aback, I asked, "How can the government determine the taxes if it doesn't know how much you earn?"

"The government. *Poufft!* The government has plenty of money. They always want to take more from the poor."

I smiled to myself. I doubted if she'd appreciate my pointing out that she hardly qualified as poor.

"It's the politicians," she sputtered. "Always with their hands out."

"I can call another time," I said.

"They're out to get me."

"The politicians?"

"*Oui.* You work hard all your life, and the politicians, they steal your money. You must be very creative with writing the reports or they will trick you out of everything. You will have nothing left, not a sou."

"Should I call tomorrow?"

"*Non. Non.* We can speak now."

"I wanted to ask you a favor," I said quickly, hoping to avert another tirade.

"*Oui?*"

"Would you mind if I had some papers sent to me on your fax machine? If it's inconvenient, please tell me."

"This is fine. It is no trouble."

"Thanks so much," I said. "I really appreciate it."

She gave me her fax number and I hung up wondering what "creative" writing she planned with her forms. I looked at my watch, picked up the phone, and dialed again. With the six-hour time difference, it would be early morning in Cabot Cove.

Mort Metzger answered on the first ring. Our village sheriff was already on the job.

"Mrs. F! How're you doing over there? They treating you good?"

"I'm just fine, Mort."

"Never been to France myself, but I had an uncle was there during the big war."

"It's a beautiful country."

"Maureen's always going on about how she'd like to see Paris before she dies, but I tease her and tell her she's too young. Maybe for our next anniversary."

"That would be a lovely gift," I said. "How's everyone at home?"

"Well, I'm in here bringing breakfast to Jake Howard. Went on a toot last night, had to take away his car keys. Got 'im lined up for an AA visit later today. Road crew's out doing a bit of sanding. We got a dusting. Snow melts pretty fast but the roads're slick. Mayor Shevlin's got the flu. Let's see, what else? Oh, yes. Your lady friend, staying up at the house, entered a flower arrangement in the Ladies' Club Fall Flower Fair and won a blue ribbon. Maureen was a bit disappointed. Her arrangement only took third. Not bad for a foreigner, whaddya say?"

"She's an American citizen, Mort. She just lives in France."

"Well, she's from away," he said, using the

Maine expression for anyone who lives out of state.

"That's true. How's Seth?"

"Saw Doc Hazlitt last week. Got himself a little putting green set up in his office. You know, some of that green indoor-outdoor carpet, and a little plastic cup. He says now that Dr. Jenny is working with him, he figures to practice up on his golf game so he'll be ready by the spring."

My good friend of many years, and Cabot Cove's only doctor for most of that time, had taken in a young partner in Dr. Jennifer Countryman. Seth wasn't quite ready to retire yet, but the presence of Dr. Jenny was giving him some well-deserved time off, even if he chose to spend most of it in his office in case she needed him.

"Please say hello for me," I said.

"Be happy to. So what can I do for you, Mrs. F?"

"I'm hoping you can find the parents of a young woman I've met here." I gave Mort a recap of the situation, as well as the number of Mallory's passport and the issuing office.

"Sounds like this young'un's got herself in a deep lot of trouble," he said.

"Her uncle is probably somewhere in France looking for her," I said. "Her parents should know how to contact him. I'd like to tell them what's happened before they hear it from the authorities, but I doubt we'll be able to reach them in time."

"Do you think she's guilty?"

"I honestly don't know, Mort, but it doesn't look good. Even if she is, she's still only fifteen. I'd feel a lot better if her parents or uncle were here, someone to represent her interests and protect her rights. As it is now, I'm the only adult watching out for her."

"I'll see what I can find for you. We've got a pretty good computer setup, and I can always call down to my buddies on the force in New York City. They'll know how to track down her parents if I run into any snags from up here."

I thanked him, asked him to send whatever he could find to Mme Roulandet's fax machine, and gave him her number.

"Always fun working with you on a case," he said. "Sure you don't need me to come over there and help out in person?"

"Do you speak French?"

"I speak a little pig Latin."

I laughed. It was good to laugh. There was so much to frown about.

Chapter Sixteen

The ride to Les Baux was a quiet one. I'd called the Thomases, told them about Mallory, and asked if they wouldn't mind taking me to Les Baux anyway. It wouldn't be as carefree a day tromping around the ruins as we'd planned — hard to be cheerful in the face of such gloomy news — but the trip could prove useful in my pursuit of the case. I was eager to track down René Bonassé at his aunt's house and question him more closely. Craig was on to my true purpose, and seemed as enthusiastic to watch a "crime writer," as he called me, investigate a murder as he was anxious to see the remains of the feudal stronghold.

We drove through Saint-Rémy-de-Provence, a pretty town that reminded me of a smaller version of Carpentras. The day was cloudy and raw, with rain threatening. At intervals, a damp wind thumped the side of the car, making it wobble. Outside St.-Rémy, we continued south along straightaways with tall trees arching over the two lanes of traffic. Farther along, the road began to curve, and we found ourselves climbing up into the Alpilles mountains. We passed forests of pine clinging to the rocky soil by their roots, their trunks bent at a precarious angle on the steep slopes as they reached for the sun. Then the forests thinned, broken up by boulders of white rock that had tumbled from the craggy hilltops, littering the ground. We crested the mountain and descended into an upland valley of olive orchards girdled by limestone cliffs. The olive trees, short and full, stretched out on both sides of the road, a sea of silvery green leaves.

The oil made from the olives grown in Les Baux was excellent, M. Telloir had informed me. In fact, it had been awarded special status, *appellation d'origine controlée,* just like a fine wine. But you could not put it away for the future, like wine, he'd said; instead of improving with age, it would spoil. I'd promised myself I'd buy a bottle to see if my palate was sensitive enough to discern the difference in taste.

As the road wound through the orchards, the naked outcroppings of rock along one mountain ridge began to take on distinctive shapes. Were those rectangular gaps caused by natural erosion or carved out by early settlers? The closer we came, the more clearly the hand of man could be seen in the shaping of the rock. The view disappeared and reappeared as we drove up a road that twisted around the side of the mountain.

"Isn't this exciting?" Jill said, reading to us from her guidebook. "It says the site may have been occupied as early as the Bronze Age. The tenth-century citadel was built on top of the rock cliffs, and the lords who occupied it traced their lineage back to one of the three magi, Balthazar. The buildings in the village itself date from the sixteenth and seventeenth centuries. After Louis the Thirteenth tore the fortress down in the sixteen hundreds, the population of the village gradually moved away and it was totally deserted for two centuries."

"I wonder what revived it," I said.

"Probably tourists," Craig put in.

"Not at first," Jill said. "It was the discovery of aluminum ore deposits, bauxite, named for Les Baux."

"What does it say about lunch?" he said. "I'm hungry."

"There are all kinds of shops and restaurants in the summer," Jill replied. "I'm not sure what's open out of season."

"We'll soon find out," he said, pulling up to a line of vehicles parked along the edge of the road. "No cars are allowed on the streets, so we'll have to find a space and walk there."

We left the car midway up the hill and gave our calf muscles a good workout hiking to the village.

"Glad I wore my track shoes," Jill said, stopping to catch her breath. "It would be easy to twist an ankle on these cobblestones."

At the bottom of the village, most of the shops were shuttered. Only one was open, its shelves filled with aromatic soaps and candles, linens and dishware in the colorful Provençal designs, as well as regional cookies and candies, and bottles of oil and vinegar with sprigs of herbs floating inside.

"You probably can ask in there if they know

where to find René's aunt," Jill added. "It doesn't look like many people live here in the winter."

The young salesgirl didn't recognize the name of René's aunt. "I work here part-time," she said. "The owner, she knows everyone in the village."

"Is she coming in today?" I asked.

"*Non.* In the summer she lives here," the girl replied, "but now she comes only on the weekends."

We wandered up the main street, peering through dark windows, ducking into the occasional store open for business, more to escape the chilly wind than out of interest in the wares. I tried to imagine the village besieged by the one and a half million visitors it received every year, most of them crowding the narrow confines of the streets from May through September. It would have been impossible to find anyone in such a throng.

"There's a *crêperie* up ahead," Craig said, his eyes lighting up. "Let's fortify ourselves before we continue the ramble."

We climbed a short flight of stone stairs and entered the little café that specialized in making crepes. The only other diners were four young people from Germany chatting with the waitress in broken French. We took a table next to a window and piled our coats on an empty chair.

"Egg and cheese sounds good to me," Craig said, scanning the paper menu that was divided into luncheon crepes and dessert crepes.

I ordered a spinach-and-cheese crepe and a small side salad. Jill did as well.

"What are you going to ask his aunt when you find her?" Craig asked.

"I'm not sure," I said. "I'm really hoping she'll tell me where to find René."

"He may not be very cooperative, you know," he said. "Didn't strike me as the forthcoming type."

"He didn't strike me that way either," I said, "but we were coming here anyway. It's worth a try to see if he'll speak with me."

"There was something going on between René and Bertrand during the class," Jill said.

"I noticed it, too," Craig said. "Bertrand seemed to be taunting him."

"Madame Poutine thought René had been sent to rate him," I said. "She was trying to read his notes, and cautioned Bertrand to be careful around him."

Jill and Craig looked at each other and a silent message passed between them. Did they know more about René Bonassé than they were letting on?

"Why are you interested in René?" Jill asked. "If Mallory had the knife and the police are looking for her, doesn't that mean they think she's the killer?"

"They probably do," I said. "But they still have Claire in jail, as far as I know. Evidently they're not sure."

"How many people can they hold for the same crime?" Jill asked.

"Good question," I said.

The waitress brought our plates and we ate the simple fare in silence. It was pleasant to have a light meal. I wasn't quite ready yet to follow the French regimen of four-course meals at both lunch and dinner.

Craig broke the silence. "Where does René come into this?" he asked.

"He may not come into it at all," I said. "But his time is unaccounted for during the period when Bertrand was killed."

"He said he had a phone call to make, and was going to his room," Craig said.

"Which may be the truth," I said. "I just want to ask him a few questions about the chef. He'd taken the cooking class with Bertrand before. Perhaps he can give me some insight into the man."

"If he's willing to talk with you at all," Jill said.

"Yes," I agreed. "If. And if his aunt can tell me where to find him in the first place."

"You'll want to speak with them in private, I assume," she said.

"I would appreciate that."

"We'll go up to the Château and wander around the ruins," Craig said. "You can meet us there when you're finished."

On the way out of the café, I showed the waitress the paper with the name and number of René's aunt and asked if she knew her.

263

"*Ah, oui*, Jeanne Bonassé," she said. "She has the restaurant up the street, next to the Hotel de Ville."

"Had we known, we could have eaten there," Jill said.

"No harm done," I told her.

We parted company in front of Jeanne Bonassé's restaurant, the Thomases going on to the ancient ruins at the top of the village. I walked up three stone steps, through an archway to an empty stone courtyard that doubtless was filled with tables in the summer. A lion's-head fountain, now dry, hung on one wall, and empty flower boxes lined the others. The glass door to the restaurant was locked; a curtain concealed the view inside. A sign said *fermé*, closed. I knocked. A minute or so later, a man in shirt-sleeves responded to my rapping. "*Bonjour, madame.* The restaurant is only open for dinner. Would you like to make a reservation for to-night?"

"I'm here to speak with Jeanne Bonassé," I said.

"She requires that salespeople call in advance. Do you have an appointment?"

"It's a personal matter."

The gentleman's eyebrows lifted, but he opened the door wide to allow me to pass inside. "Is anything wrong? Any trouble?"

"Not at all," I assured him. "I just want a few minutes of her time."

"May I tell her what this is about?"

"It's about her nephew."

"René?"

"Yes."

The man pulled out a chair, invited me to sit, and disappeared through a swinging door into the kitchen. I unbuttoned my coat, but left it on. This might be a short interview.

The restaurant was small, no more than twenty tables. I admired the simple country decor, most of the material available from stores around the village. On each round table was a long yellow-and-blue paisley cloth covered by a square of white linen. Blue napkins bloomed from the heavy glass goblets, and rough pottery plates the color of egg yolks made up the place settings. The walls were the same gray stone seen everywhere, but the bottom two-thirds had been plastered and painted a soft sky blue. The effect was both cheerful and elegant, an unusual combination.

The door from the kitchen swung open and a woman in her mid-fifties emerged. She was simply dressed in a beige cashmere sweater and skirt. Her dark hair, streaked with gray, was shoulder-length and held back on the sides by two combs. In her right hand she held a handker-chief with lace edging.

"Madame, I understand you wished to speak with me." She walked to where I was sitting and stopped behind the chair opposite mine.

I stood and extended my hand. "Yes. I'm Jessica Fletcher," I said.

She shook my hand tentatively, transferring the handkerchief to the other hand.

"And how may I help you, Madame Fletcher?"

"Won't you sit for a moment? I won't keep you long."

Reluctantly, she sat down. She rested her hands in her lap, the handkerchief held loosely between them.

"I'm looking for your nephew," I said, "and someone in Paris told me he was visiting you."

"And what would you want with my nephew?"

"Just to speak with him."

"Are you a reporter?" She started to rise from her seat.

"I promise you I'm not."

She sat again, but stayed on the edge of the chair. "Does he know you?"

"We've met before. Yes."

"And why do you wish to speak with him?"

"I don't know if you're aware of what occurred in Avignon last week."

"You mean the murder of Emil Bertrand?"

"Yes."

"Of course I know about Emil. All France knows about Emil. It has been on the television, in the newspapers. They have arrested his lover. She killed him."

I realized I'd been out of touch with the news media since I'd come to France. Martine didn't have a television, and although she did have a radio, I hadn't thought to turn it on. "They ar-

266

rested her, it's true," I said, "but I'm not sure she killed him."

"And what would René know about this?"

"He was in Bertrand's class that morning."

She seemed shaken by that revelation. "That doesn't mean anything."

"I'm not accusing him," I said quickly. "I'd just like to talk with him and see if there was anything he noticed that could be helpful in the investigation."

"What do you have to do with the investigation? You are American, are you not?"

"I'm giving the police a little assistance in the matter," I said. It wasn't exactly a lie. I *was* giving the police assistance, or at least I would be when I had useful information for them. That they didn't want me to assist them was irrelevant right now.

"He has spoken to the police already," she said. "And they know all about it."

"All about *it?*"

"Yes, of course. He had to tell them. If he didn't, they could have found out later. And then there would have been trouble."

"True."

"They promised not to release it to the newspapers. We would have no peace if they did. That's not the kind of publicity one wants."

"Certainly not." What was she getting at?

"And they might have made him a suspect," she said. "I advised him to let the police know right away."

"Why do you think he would have been a suspect?" I asked. I noticed that her hands no longer lay quietly in her lap. She'd begun twisting the handkerchief.

"Well, of course he would have been a suspect. It's obvious."

"Not to me."

"There was bad blood for years."

"Why was there bad blood?"

"Why? Because until recently, Emil never acknowledged him."

"Acknowledged him," I echoed.

Her voice grew bitter. "For all the years of René's growing up, Emil never acknowledged him. His only son."

"His son!" I tried to keep the surprise out of my voice, but wasn't completely successful.

"Of course he's Emil's son. Didn't you know? Isn't that why you're here?"

Chapter Seventeen

"He looks a lot like him," I said, realizing as I spoke that it was true. Emil Bertrand and René Bonassé shared the same vivid blue eyes. They both had ebony hair, although Emil's had been shot through with gray. The son had cut his hair in the close-cropped style his father favored, but whether that was a deliberate imitation or simply a coincidental preference I didn't know. René was also the same height as Emil, with the same broad chest and muscular arms. He would have had the strength to kill; did he have the desire?

"Why does René use your last name and not Bertrand?" I asked Jeanne Bonassé.

"Emil abandoned him when René was a small boy," she said. "My husband and I raised him. For a child, it is much easier if he has the same last name as his parents."

"What happened to his mother?"

"My sister was not a strong person. When her husband left, she could no longer cope with the responsibilities."

"She left as well?"

"*Non.*" There was a long pause before she said, "She took her own life."

"How awful. I'm so sorry. It must be distressing for you to speak about it."

She sighed. "It was a long time ago. The hurt, it never goes away, but for me the pain is not so intense anymore. For René it still lingers."

"I'm sure it must," I said.

"His *maman* would have been so proud of him." She blinked back tears. "He could have stayed right here, joined us in the restaurant. We would have been happy if he did — he is our only child. But he dreams of a bigger stage. He goes away to school. He works hard. *Et voilà!* Success, it comes to him. He is in charge of his own department."

The banker, Bertrand had called him. I visualized the sober young man with his starched shirts and stiff comportment, and easily imagined him a corporate executive in a boardroom. Where I couldn't picture him was behind a stove.

"Is he still in Les Baux?"

"Oh, yes, he will stay till after the funeral, and perhaps longer. After all, there is the matter of his inheritance."

"Of course," I said. "Where can I find him now?"

"He is up at the Château," she said. "He goes every day. I think it comforts him to wander among the old ruins. His mother, too, was very fond of the place, and used to bring him there as a child. I guess that's why . . ." She trailed off, her eyes seeing a picture denied to me.

I stood. "Thank you for speaking with me, Madame Bonassé."

"*Je vous en prie.* You're welcome," she said. "But you must promise not to let the newspapers know René's secret. It will come out soon enough, I'm sure. For now, he needs time to mourn in private."

"They won't learn it from me," I assured her.

While I had been inside, the temperature had dropped and the wind had begun to kick up. I buttoned my coat, pulled my scarf over my head, and trudged up to the entrance to the Citadelle de la Ville Morte, Citadel of the Dead City. A few hardy souls passed me on their way downhill, their cheeks red from the blustery weather.

I paid the entrance fee, declined to take a handheld electronic tour guide, and stepped out of the shelter of the small exhibit introducing the site onto a broad plateau. To my left was a little chapel. I could hear music from a slide show that played inside. A rocky plain sprawled before me, reaching a hundred yards out to an iron railing that marked the edge of the cliff. Dropped into the barren field, at wide intervals, were medieval engines of war, siege machines, crouching like huge insects, their wooden skeletons stark against the leaden sky.

Not another soul braved the coming storm to stand at the railing and gaze south across the valley floor to mountains miles away. No awestruck child gaped at the catapult or its sister weapons. I was alone with the wind. It swirled around me, whipping my coat against my legs, blowing up my sleeves, tearing my scarf off, threatening to carry me away, along with everything else that challenged its rule. I put my back to the tempest, pulled the scarf tight, and stuck close to the crumbling ruins, following the path to the remains of chambers that once housed the lords of Les Baux and their vassals.

I rounded a corner where the remnants of walls offered a respite from the squall. Tiny compartments, like pigeonholes, were cut into the stone. I stared, fascinated. Was this an ancient larder? What had the feudal inhabitants stored in these little containers? I wandered from room to room, my imagination conjuring the lives of these long-ago residents in the castle they had carved from the rocky escarpment.

Reminding myself that I was not here to play tourist, I searched for René Bonassé among the small number of visitors I encountered as I explored the ruins. He wasn't there; nor were the Thomases. And it was starting to rain.

Following the path along a towering wall, I came upon a stairway cut into the rock, leading to the top. Modern civilization had provided an iron banister, which ran down one side of the flight. The stairs themselves had been gouged out by centuries of rainwater cascading down, leaving a notch in the middle of each steep step. I grasped the iron rail and ascended slowly, pulling with my arms as I climbed up, keeping my feet on the edges of the wet stone away from the jagged centers. At the top I battled the wind and the slippery boulders underfoot to grab a bar on the parapet. A lone figure, buffeted by the gale, stood at the other end of the wall. I fumbled in my bag for a pair of sunglasses to shield my eyes from the wind, and squinted, straining to see the figure more clearly. Was that René? It looked like him, but the walk to where he braced himself against the parapet would be hazardous. Should I wait till he returned?

Patience has never been one of my virtues, nor prudence, truth to tell, which I've demonstrated on any number of occasions. But I hoped I wasn't foolish into the bargain. I didn't want to twist an ankle skidding on the slick stones or get caught by the wind and knocked over the low barrier to tumble down the wall and the mountain on which it was perched. I held on to the bar and waited, hoping René would tire of the pounding the wind and rain were giving his body, and make his way back toward the stairs. Eventually there was a pause in the storm, and I saw him push away from the rail. I edged forward as he started back, timing my pace so that I blocked his progress at the narrowest point of the battlement.

He raised his eyes and started when he recognized me. "Madame Fletcher. What are you doing here?"

"I could make up a story and tell you I'm merely visiting the tourist attractions," I said, "but I really came here to speak with you."

He didn't respond. He tucked the ends of his scarf into the front of his jacket, and shoved his ungloved hands into his pockets.

"I've spoken with your aunt," I said, "and I

know." I waited, hoping the same strategy that had drawn out information from Madame Bonassé would work on her nephew. But he was not easily led.

"What do you *think* you know?" he said.

"I know you're Emil Bertrand's son."

"Biologically perhaps, but not in any other sense."

"Why did he acknowledge you after all these years?"

He snorted. "Who knows? Maybe he was feeling the approach of death." His bitter smile never reached his eyes. "Maybe his ego required a successor, one related by blood instead of talent."

"What do you mean?"

"He wasn't interested in me as a child, but the idea of that child as an adult, *that* had possibilities." He leaned against the iron railing, his arms crossed in front of him, his back to the steep drop. "As if I wanted any attention from him," he muttered under his breath.

"What did he want from you?"

"I never figured that out." He dropped his head and stared at the ground.

I let the silence grow, hoping his need to sort out his feelings would spur him to continue.

He sighed and frowned, his lips compressed in a thin line. Eventually he raised his eyes. They were angry and hard. "He wanted me to join him in business. Can you believe him?"

"You mean his restaurant?"

"And whatever else he planned to pursue. Obviously someone didn't like that idea."

"You think one of his business partners —"

"Of course, there was a price," he spat out. "Emil Bertrand never did anything without a price. He asks favors and then makes demands." He pushed off the railing and began pacing in the narrow space. The wind picked up and blew the end of his scarf into the air.

"What was the price?"

"The price?" He looked confused.

"You said he never did anything without a price."

"The price was too much." He raised his fists. "He wanted me to change my name."

"Change your name to Bertrand?"

"I told him he could burn in hell before I'd do that," he shouted to the leaden sky. "The bastard. I imagine that's where he is right now." His voice dropped to a growl. "It gives me great pleasure to think of him there, after the hell he put my mother through." He drew his lips back over his teeth like a wolf contemplating its prey.

"Did you turn down his offer to join the business?"

"Why should I turn him down? Let him pay. Let him pay for what he did. Let him pay with his life." He turned on me, his eyes flaming. He grabbed my shoulders and shook me.

I dropped my handbag and tried to wrest myself from his grasp.

"Do you know what a monster he was? She

killed herself because of him. She threw herself off this wall." The wind began to howl. He pushed me ahead of him, dragging me to the railing. "Look! Look down there," he yelled, thrusting my shoulder out over the railing. I tried to twist away, but he was too strong. "That's where they found her body, all broken." The railing was biting into my hip. He gripped my shoulders and forced me to lean out beyond the iron bar. "Look! This was the last thing she saw." The wind rode up the wall and blew into my face, taking my cries and carrying them away. "You think anyone can survive that plunge?" I could barely see, but the view was not one I wanted anyway. "Look! It was days till they could recover her body." The vertical drop of the wall was extended by a steep slide of sharp rocks, bare brush, and torn tree trunks. "Look!" he screamed. My right foot was off the ground, and half my body hung over the precipice. "Look!"

"Oh, Jessica, that's where you are," Jill called out from the top of the stairs.

Abruptly René pulled me back and gave me a shove in Jill's direction. He shouted a curse and stomped past me. Jill ducked out of his way, and he ran down the stairs, taking the last five in a single leap.

"Are you all right?"

I shuddered. "I think so," I said, straightening my coat and picking up my bag from where I'd dropped it. My ears rang with the force of the wind, and my scarf and hair were wet. I looked around for my sunglasses. Hadn't I had them on? They must have fallen off when René Bonassé, né Bertrand, forced me to look over the wall.

"I'm all right," I said, "but I'm ready to get in out of the storm."

Chapter Eighteen

The Brasserie St. Marc was busy but Jill, Craig, and I found an empty table among the ones set up outside the restaurant. The village could have been in another part of the country, so different was its weather from the wind and rainstorm we'd encountered only two hours to the south in Les Baux. The late-afternoon temperature was mild, the wind calm, and a setting sun was peeking out from behind streaky clouds. Only the blare of sirens down on the main road marred the tranquil atmosphere. I thought of Mallory, but she would be far away by now, wouldn't she?

The waiter set down his tray on a stand, and placed three large bowls of fish broth on our table along with three bowls of garlicky mayonnaise, a platter of fish that had been cooked in the broth, and a basket of toasted slices of baguette.

"This bouillabaisse is famous around here," I said, passing Jill the basket of bread. "According to Marcel, people come from all the local villages when the chef is making it. We're lucky there was any left over from lunch."

"Smells wonderful," Craig said, leaning over his bowl and inhaling deeply. "Whose idea was this anyway?"

Jill and I laughed. "Yours," we said together.

"How is it?" I asked after Craig had dipped in

his spoon and taken his first taste.

"Brilliant!" he said. "I hope you appreciate my genius for finding great food in France." He looked at his wife.

"You haven't steered us wrong once," she replied. "Of course, it's almost impossible to get a bad meal in Provence, unless you have the misfortune of going into one of those American 'fast-food' establishments that shall remain nameless. Begging your pardon, Jessica, if you're fond of them."

"I much prefer this," I said honestly.

"Have to remember the name of this place," Craig said as he smeared the garlic mayonnaise on a slice of the toast. "It's worth a detour if they're making bouillabaisse." He dropped the toast into his soup. "Did you get what you needed?" he asked me.

"No. The bakery is closed," I said. "I was hoping a fax had come in for me. The baker is letting me use her fax machine; I'm expecting some papers from the States. But the shop was locked. I slid a note under the door, and I'll call her tomorrow."

We had stopped at the bakery on the way back to Martine's, but we'd never made it to the farmhouse after Craig had spied the blackboard hanging in front of the brasserie with the words *AUJOURD'HUI, BOUILLABAISSE* — Today, bouillabaisse — printed large in chalk. It was just as well. It would have been late if we'd waited for dinner until we were back in Avignon.

The Thomases had urged me to return with them to the hotel, at least for a few days or until the authorities had found Mallory, if they were able to find her. It hadn't taken much convincing on their parts. I wasn't worried about staying alone, which had been their chief concern. I didn't think I was in any danger from Mallory. But I'd already decided it would be much more convenient to be in the city for any number of reasons, not the least of which was my plan to return to the real estate office of P. Franc and M. Poutine. And I thought it was time Captain LeClerq and I had a heart-to-heart.

When the waiter brought a tray of selections for the cheese course, Jill took out a small leather journal and began making notes. "Provence is *chèvre* country," she said, referring to the white goat's-milk cheese that is popular the world over. "The native cheeses are mostly made from goat's milk or a combination of milk from goats and cows, sometimes even sheep," she added. "My goodness, what is all that noise about?"

The insistent wail of the sirens down the hill all but drowned out conversation.

"The police have found the dognappers — that's what they're saying in the kitchen," the waiter confided, raising his voice to be heard over the din. "The thugs who've been stealing our truffle dogs and selling them on the black market. Someone said they arrested the ringleader today."

So it wasn't Mallory. I released a breath I

hadn't realized I'd been holding. While I didn't like the idea of her wandering alone, a fugitive from the law, I also ached at the thought of her under arrest, frightened and friendless.

The keening sirens faded, and we returned our attention to food. We chose three cheeses, a *Picodon,* a *Poivre d'Ain,* which had been rolled in the dried leaves of wild savory, and a *Lou Pevre,* which was covered with coarsely ground black pepper. As I nibbled on the cheese, enjoying the subtle differences in flavor, I watched as Craig and Jill sampled each one and argued their relative merits, with Jill recording their impressions in her book. The Thomases were more sophisticated about food than I'd realized.

When Jill caught me observing her, she blushed. "The family are always asking us for recommendations of where to go in places we've visited," she said. "It helps us to remember if we've written down our experiences."

"That sounds like a smart thing to do," I said.

Following our meal we drove to Martine's, where Craig and Jill admired her paintings — Jill making more notes in her journal — while I ran upstairs and packed a bag for my hotel stay.

"It's too bad we'll be leaving before she returns," Jill said to me as I pulled on the door and jiggled the key in the lock to make sure the house was secure before we left. "I would love to buy one of her paintings."

"They are wonderful, aren't they?" I said. "It's a shame it's too dark to see her studio today. Perhaps another time."

"We'd love to," Craig said. "Maybe we can write to her when we're home and have her send us a catalog."

I knew Martine had exhibited her paintings in galleries, but I wasn't sure she'd ever had a catalog made of her work. But with both sides eager to do business, I was sure they'd find a way to communicate.

The Hotel Melissande was quiet when we opened its glass door and walked inside. No one was in the atrium or the bar, or the beautiful lounge next door. Only five tables were occupied in the dining room, notwithstanding the late hour favored by French diners.

"This place was jumping last week," Craig said. "Nothing like a murder to excite curiosity. The bar was full right through the weekend. Couldn't get a reservation in the restaurant. Now look at it."

"This is probably more normal for November, dear," Jill told him.

"Would you like to join us for a nightcap, Jessica?" he asked. "Could do with a cognac to top off that wonderful meal."

"Ask me another time, please," I said. "I'd like to unpack and make it an early night." I was beginning to feel the effects of my adventure in Les Baux.

The Thomases retrieved their room key from the front desk, bade me good night, and wandered off to the lounge. The bellman took my small bag and escorted me to my room on the second floor, the same one I'd been given the previous week. It was very comforting to be in familiar surroundings.

Although the room was considerably smaller than the farmhouse in St. Marc, it was spacious enough for me to spread out. The high ceiling gave it the feeling of a much larger chamber. The king-size bed was appealing, and the bathroom was designed for Americans, according to the bellman, who told me that visitors from the States prefer hotel bathrooms that are large, well lighted, and with plenty of marble and mirror. What *I* liked about it was that it was sparkling clean. I ran a hot bath, poured in a whole bottle of the scented bath gel, and sank gratefully into the bubbles.

My experience with René had jarred my senses, and as the heat relaxed my sore muscles, my mind went to work. Would he have let me fall over the wall if Jill hadn't arrived? Could his roughness be attributed to his heightened emotions over the loss of a father he'd never really known? Or had his troubled childhood created a disturbed man, one so volatile he could explode in violence, given motive and opportunity? When I'd gone to see if Bertrand was indeed dead, René had emerged from the elevator. Was he coming down from his room, or going up from the scene of the crime? Had his been the voice Claire had heard? And who else had motive and opportunity?

Could the police keep Claire indefinitely without any firm proof? Madame Poutine's testimony would provide only circumstantial evidence. She'd seen Claire with the body, but hadn't seen the murder itself. Now that the police had the murder weapon, would Claire's fingerprints be found on it? Was she as innocent as she claimed?

And what about Daniel and Guy? Did their alibis hold up? Had the police even investigated them? And Mallory, where was Mallory? I ached for that child, a fugitive from the law at fifteen.

I stayed in the tub, turning over what I knew about the case, until the bubbles disappeared and the water cooled. Weary in both mind and body, I succumbed to the enticement of a nice big bed, and gratefully fell asleep.

The next morning, over fruit and croissants in the atrium, I learned what had happened to Mallory. I'd just taken my first sip of the hotel's marvelous coffee when I saw her face before me. It was a photograph on the front page of the local newspaper being read by a gentleman at the table across from mine. I hurried out to the front desk, bought a copy of the paper, and struggled to translate the French idioms in the article as I finished my breakfast.

As I understood it, the knife Mallory had hidden was "an exact match" — *exactement de la même forme,* for the fatal wound on the chef's body. The teenage American suspect had been apprehended in the woods around St. Marc near where she had been staying with an American writer. Efforts to reach the writer, J. B. Fletcher, for comment were unsuccessful. Police had initially gone to the area to break up a ring of thieves that specialized in stealing truffle dogs, and had found the accused hiding in a barn that housed the stolen animals on the property of Albert Belot. Police had had Belot under surveillance for some time. Known as the Truffle King, Belot had dug up his land some years back to plant oak trees to cultivate the fungus *T. melanosporum*. His success in gathering the tuber strangely coincided with the disappearance of dogs in the neighboring villages around his farm, and an increase in reports of trespassing on private properties. It was not known if the young American was part of the ring of thieves.

The police had detained her for questioning, and a relative had arrived, John Cartright, the young lady's uncle, who had already hired a lawyer to defend her. The hotel clerk originally arrested for the chef's murder had been released, the article said, and was recuperating from her devastating experience at home in Avignon. The rest of the report was a summary of Bertrand's career, comments by the police on how they had tracked down the fugitive — *"La Jeune Tueuse Americaine,"* they called her; the young American killer — and ended with statistics on teenagers and violent crime.

Thank goodness her uncle had arrived. Mallory would be grateful, too, I thought, to see someone from home.

"Are you Madame Fletcher?" asked the bellman who'd come to my table.

I put down the newspaper. "Yes, I am."

"A gentleman by the name of Marcel Oland instructed me to give these papers to you right away."

"Merci beaucoup."

Marie Roulandet had received the fax I'd been waiting for. I signaled the waiter for more coffee, and tore open the thick envelope she'd sent to me via Marcel.

The top sheet was a note from Mort, saying he'd gotten the telephone number of Mallory's parents, who lived in Cincinnati, and had called them. They informed him that they'd received the news earlier from the international police and had alerted Mr. Cartright's brother, who was searching for her in France. The Cartrights were both business executives who held high posts in major corporations; their daughter had refused to return to school, they'd told Mort, after an incident in which Mallory had been accused of lying to police during a drug investigation.

Mallory's inability to hold fast to the truth had trapped her once before. Why would a child from a well-to-do home become a compulsive liar? Was it a cry for attention? Or was her prevarication a sign of a much more serious mental condition?

The rest of the papers Mort had sent were copies of stories from her hometown newspaper in which Mallory's name had been mentioned. She'd won a blue ribbon for a school science project in fourth grade; she'd sung in the chorus that had performed for the vice president on a campaign swing through the state; and she'd made honor roll her first year in high school. From all outward appearances she was a normal teenager. But inside, in the psyche of the fifteen-year-old girl, there were problems, serious problems. Had they manifested themselves in murder?

A taxicab delivered me to the building from which I'd fled three days before. There was no man in a trench coat following me this time — at least not one that I saw — and although there were few pedestrians about, the sun had chased away all the shadows, and the commercial area of Avignon looked positively quaint and cheerful. I entered the vestibule of the building and pushed on the painted glass door. It was still unlocked. Several of the office doors on the first floor were open, inviting their customers to walk in. Those that were closed were occupied nevertheless; fluorescent fixtures inside illuminated the glass panes on the doors, indicating they were open for business.

I took the elevator to the second floor and walked to the end of the hallway. The door to the real estate office was open and I entered unannounced. A young woman sat at the reception desk in the center of the large room, which was decorated with file cabinets and a row of straight-backed metal chairs lined up beneath a map of the city. Behind her desk on the left and right were doors, which I assumed led to two inner offices.

"*Bonjour, madame.* May I help you?"

"Yes. I believe so." I debated briefly which of the partners I wanted to speak with first, and decided M. Poutine was the logical choice. "Is Monsieur Poutine in?"

"Have you an appointment?"

"No."

"May I tell him the nature of your business?"

"I'm interested in L'Homme Qui Court," I said, calculating that the disposition of the restaurant would be more likely to open one of those two doors than a discussion of murder.

The receptionist picked up the telephone and called M. Poutine. "He says for you to go right in." She pointed to the door on the left.

I twisted the knob and entered a small office, half the size of the reception area.

"*Bonjour, madame.* I am Marius Poutine." The speaker was a short, stocky man in a skillfully tailored suit that was flattering to his physique. He had thick white hair and a brush of a mustache beneath a straight nose and brown eyes. He stood behind his desk and leaned forward to shake my hand, smiling warmly.

"Jessica Fletcher," I said.

"Enchanté." He pointed to a chair in front of his desk and we both sat down. "How may I help you today?"

"I understand your colleague is a partner in the restaurant L'Homme Qui Court."

"My colleague?"

"P. Franc? The other name on your door?"

"Ah, my colleague, *oui. C'est vrai*, that's true."

"Are you a partner as well?"

He nodded slowly, keeping his eyes on mine.

"I was wondering what plans are being made for the restaurant now?"

"May I ask your interest here?"

"I was in Monsieur Bertrand's class the day he was killed."

"Ah, madame. How terrible. What a tragedy. And we had such plans for him. We are most distressed. My wife mentioned that there were Americans in the class. I did not make the connection when you came in."

"I wouldn't expect you to."

He shook his head. "Many years we know Emil. So sad. To die because of a foolish young girl."

I didn't know if he was referring to Claire or Mallory, but I let that go. "What plans did you have for him?"

"My colleague, as you say, has connections in broadcasting. We had hoped to produce a television show with Emil. He was handsome, no? And very good charisma. It comes across on the camera. But we will defer this now."

"When he died, he was holding a letter from your partner."

"He was?"

"Yes. Do you know what was sent to him?"

He gave a slight shrug. "It could be a monthly report, nothing of great importance, I assure you."

"Had you been in business with him many years?"

"For ten years at least. He wanted to buy our building for his restaurant, but was not quite ready, if you take my meaning. We make a deal for a percentage of the business. That way everyone is happy."

"What will happen now?"

He shrugged again. "A restaurant without a chef is not valuable, you understand. But that will be rectified shortly."

"You have someone in mind?"

"*Certainement*. And we anticipate keeping the Michelin star it has been awarded."

"Isn't it the chef who earns the star?" I asked.

He nodded. "It is the chef's cooking that is judged, yes," he said, sitting back in his chair. "But the management of the restaurant is important as well, the service, the decor, how well the room is run. We are very good with this. And the chef we are hiring is excellent. And very photogenic."

"Photogenic?"

"It is necessary for television. He just needs an opportunity to expand his repertoire in the kitchen, and we can provide this."

It seemed to me that Emil Bertrand's death was not such a tragedy for his partners, who were already making plans to replace him and move forward.

"So you own the restaurant now?"

He nodded again. "We are the surviving partners. So yes."

It was my turn to nod. "And if an heir is named in the will?"

"Pardon?"

"What happens if Bertrand has an heir?"

He waved a hand in front of his face. "Emil never mentioned any family. There may be a cousin somewhere, but I am sure we can negotiate something equitable."

"He has a son."

"A son! *Mon Dieu!* Why do we not know this?" He pushed a button on his phone.

I heard the door swing open behind me.

"Madame Fletcher," he said, "I believe you've met my partner."

I turned around. "Indeed I have. How do you do, Madame Poutine."

Chapter Nineteen

"We had to let her go."

"Mallory?"

"*Oui.*"

"Why?"

I was sitting across the desk from Captain LeClerq in his office at the police station. He appeared harried. His tie was askew. There were shadows beneath his eyes. His desk was strewn with papers, no longer the model of neatness I'd seen earlier.

"The lawyer insisted we had no evidence and the magistrate agreed."

"But the knife?" I asked. "Yesterday's newspaper said it was an exact match to the wound."

He moaned. "The newspapers. Don't mention those vipers to me again. The reporters, they are outside my door every morning when I leave, and they are still there at night when I return."

"The knife?" I reminded him.

"The knife. Yes, it was an exact match, but the blood, it was not."

"I don't understand."

"The blood on the knife was not his."

"It wasn't?"

"No. It wasn't even human blood."

"Ah," I said. "Rabbit blood?"

"How did you know?"

"It's obvious, really. If it wasn't Bertrand's blood, it must have been the knife he used to cut up the rabbit for the dish he was making. There were only two knives like it."

"What do you mean?"

I explained to him about the special knives that had been made for Emil Bertrand twenty years ago, and that they were his favorites.

"So you're back to looking for the murder weapon," I said.

"It is a disaster," he said. "We tested every knife in the hotel kitchen and found nothing. I'm being made to look like a goat. Everyone in the station here, they are laughing, but the magistrate, he is not laughing. And I am not laughing."

"I don't imagine you are," I said. "I'd like to offer my help, if I may."

He sighed. "I have chastised you for pursuing this case, I know. But I need every bit of information you and anyone else has."

"I'll do what I can, Captain. After all, we both have the same goal."

He coughed. "I am most grateful."

"While we're sharing information," I said, "I may as well ask about the man who followed me. You wouldn't know anything about him, would you?"

"Only that he was embarrassed you were able to slip away from him."

"I had a feeling he might have been one of yours."

"Not a very good one, however."

"Good enough to give me a scare," I said.

"I will tell him. He will be happy to know he was not a complete failure."

"Before we talk about the case, I have a favor to ask."

"Yes?"

"I'd like to see the papers that were found with the body. Do you still have them?"

"Of course." He picked up the telephone and dialed. "Thierry, bring in the file on Bertrand, and the evidence bags."

"*Bonjour,* Claire."

"*Bonjour,* Madame Fletcher. It is good to see you again."

"I'm pleased to see you, too," I said. She was looking much healthier than the last time we'd met, still a bit frail from her time in prison, but her color had returned and her hair was washed and shiny. The hotel had given her back her position. She stood behind the desk, her hands resting on the computer keys she'd been tapping before I'd interrupted her. "Have you seen Captain LeClerq today?" I asked.

"*Non,*" she said, paling at the mention of his name.

"I'm expecting him," I said. "I'll be in the atrium. Would you please let him know where I am?"

"*Certainement.*"

I took a seat in the atrium and ordered a pot of

tea. It was a chilly day outside, but inside the sun shone through the skylight, and everything touched by its rays was warmed. The atmosphere in the room was sleepy and peaceful — guests lingering over afternoon tea and pastries, belying the violence that had taken place last week only one floor below. There were a few details I wanted to clear up, connections I needed to make, and if I was correct in my suspicions, Captain LeClerq would arrest the killer today.

"Madame, I owe you an apology." René Bonassé, very red-faced, took the chair opposite mine. "May I?"

"Of course. And yes, you do."

"There was no excuse for my behavior," he said, sitting on the edge of his seat. His broad shoulders were hunched and he leaned his forearms on his knees. "I was a madman. You would have been justified in calling the police and having me arrested."

"I considered it."

He nodded. "With good reason. I can only tell you I have not slept for two nights. I have been looking everywhere for you. Each time I picture it, I am aghast at my actions. I hope you know I would never have . . ." He trailed off, his eyes pleading for understanding.

"I wasn't sure at the time."

"I know, I know." He shook his head. "I behaved horribly, and can only throw myself on your mercy and hope you will forgive me." He held himself very still, eyes downcast, as if his entire future rested with my decision.

"I'll forgive you," I said lightly, "if you answer some questions."

He raised his eyes; his lashes were damp. "You may ask anything. Anything at all. My life is open for you."

"Then I forgive you," I said.

He sighed and sat up straight. *"Merci milles fois."* It wasn't necessary for him to thank me a thousand times, but I didn't say it. "Please ask me what you like," he said.

"I've been wondering," I said, "given the feelings you had for Bertrand . . . for your father . . ." He looked away. "Why did you attend his cooking classes?"

He stared off into space before replying. "He had discovered what business I'm in." His eyes met mine. "He pressured me to visit his restaurant and attend his classes."

"And what business is that?"

"Investment banking. Venture capital."

"Was he looking for you to lend him money?"

"In a way." He ran his hand over his short hair and moved back in his seat, keeping his posture erect. "He wanted financing to create a new corporation without his partners. He had ambitious plans to open other restaurants, and he didn't want them holding him back."

"Holding him back?"

"That's what he said."

"His partners told me they wanted to put him on television with his own cooking show," I said.

"It doesn't sound like they wanted to hold him back. If anything, they wanted to promote him. He might have become famous and made a lot of money. Why did he go to you instead?"

"Poufft!" he said, sounding annoyed at my lack of comprehension. "Fame without the respect is worthless. You don't understand the business."

"Then enlighten me," I said, thinking René had inherited more than his athletic build from his father. He had a bit of his arrogance as well.

"A master chef does not want to cater to the masses. It is the act of creation that is important, finding the unique combination of ingredients, putting together the perfect dish, the extraordinary meal. For this you need an audience who appreciates the subtleties, connoisseurs, not couch potatoes, as you say in the States. He already had one Michelin star. He was aiming for three. And then" — he clapped his hands — "the world comes to his door."

"So he asked you to come to Avignon to evaluate his business, and you did?"

He shook his head. "I wouldn't have come at all. But he was clever. He sent his proposal to my supervisor, suggesting that someone with restaurant experience be sent to appraise his potential. Since a few of my colleagues knew I'd grown up in the business — my aunt's restaurant — I was designated."

"Did your father's partners know who you were?"

"I didn't tell them. I doubt if Emil did."

"And would you have recommended the investment?"

"I already had. After last week's class, I went back to my room and made the call."

"To approve the financing?"

He nodded. "If I hadn't, I would have wondered all my life if I had turned him down because I hated him, if I had allowed our relationship — or lack of relationship — to rule my decision rather than the true potential of his business. He had contacts all over the world. And he was a brilliant chef. I always knew that, but never wanted to believe it. He could open a restaurant in any city and succeed."

I thought about René's aunt and her comment that his mother would have been proud of him. It is a rare person — young or old — who can set aside strong negative feelings and make rational decisions based on logic and facts. He held the promise of becoming a man to admire, a son to merit his mother's pride, provided he acquired some humility and learned how to channel his emotions so they would never overwhelm him as they had in our encounter on the parapet.

I caught sight of LeClerq across the room and waved to him. René Bonassé stood. "Have I answered to your satisfaction?"

I stood as well. "Yes," I said. "You've been very forthcoming. Thank you."

"It is I who thank you. I won't forget your generosity in forgiving me. I don't deserve it." He walked away.

"Ah, Madame Fletcher, my apologies for being late," LeClerq said, shaking my hand. "I hope I have not inconvenienced you."

"Not at all. Our guest has only just arrived behind you."

"Madame Poutine?"

"Yes. There she is."

I pointed with my chin over his shoulder to where Mme Poutine had paused in the entrance, before her eyes found us across the room. Elegant as ever in a black silk suit and peach-colored blouse, she had pulled her platinum hair into a soft twist at the back of her head. Every man and woman in the atrium watched as she strode purposefully toward us, ignoring the stares, her expression deliberately blank, as if to smile or frown might crack the carefully constructed mask of the beautiful woman.

"Captain," she said, addressing LeClerq. "I am here as you requested, but I'd like to know why this woman is here as well." To me, she said, "I thought I'd seen the last of you."

"You were both students in Bertrand's class," LeClerq said mildly. "I thought it easiest to question you together."

"There were other students in the class," she said. "Where are they?"

"You missed René Bonassé," I put in helpfully.

She gave me a furious glance.

I noticed that people in the room were still watching her. "Why don't we go downstairs?" I suggested. "It's a little more private there."

LeClerq looked around and nodded. "Yes. Downstairs is better." He beckoned toward the desk, motioning for Claire to join us. She walked across the atrium to where we were gathered. He extended one hand toward me and put the other under Mme Poutine's elbow, guiding her toward the elevator. "I have visited with the Thomases," he told her, "and Mademoiselle Cartright."

She looked surprised. "Mademoiselle Cartright? Isn't she in jail?"

"Not at the moment," he said, ringing for the elevator.

We stopped at the entrance to the medieval dining room, each of us no doubt envisioning the scene we'd witnessed the afternoon of Bertrand's death, his body slumped against the archway door to the right, his papers scattered on the floor. Ahead of us, in the school kitchen, Daniel and Guy were preparing for the next day's classes, piling wood next to the old stove, assembling the requisite pots and pans, and setting out the knives and cutting boards. A stack of empty folders sat next to a pile of recipes and directions on the scrubbed table.

"*Bonjour, messieurs,*" LeClerq said, escorting us into the room. Mme Poutine and I took seats on opposite sides of the table. Claire sat next to me, her eyes darting around the room.

The chefs looked at us in surprise. "Would

you like us to leave?" Daniel volunteered.

"*Non.* In fact, I prefer if you stay," LeClerq said.

The two men halted their chores and glanced questioningly at each other. Guy shrugged, pulled out a stool, and sat, drawing papers and folders in front of him. "Is it acceptable if I keep working?" he asked.

"Perhaps you can wait a few minutes," LeClerq answered.

Daniel took another stool, and looked from face to face.

LeClerq closed the door and remained standing. "If you have not heard — and Madame Poutine has not — then I will inform you now that the knife we recovered from Mademoiselle Cartright was not the murder weapon."

Neither chef said anything. Daniel's eyes were on LeClerq. Guy focused on the papers in front of him; his fingers played with a corner of a recipe sheet.

"What has this to do with me?" Mme Poutine demanded.

"Patience, madame," LeClerq said. "We will come to this." He addressed the two chefs: "Messieurs, we know what knife we look for, one that was made particularly for Monsieur Bertrand many years ago. Have you seen this knife?"

"You took every knife in my kitchen," Daniel said. "If you didn't find it, how should I?"

"Guy," I said, "when you were cleaning up

after our class, what did you do with the knives Chef Bertrand used?"

Guy cleared his throat and looked at me. "Madame, I don't pay attention to each knife and fork. I only gather up all the dishes and utensils that are soiled and take them to the kitchen to be washed."

"This is ridiculous," Mme Poutine huffed. "Why am I here?"

"I am coming to this now," LeClerq said. "There were many papers on the floor around the body. Hmm? However, the deceased himself was holding a letter when he was killed." LeClerq paused, eyeing his captive audience, and held up the letter. "Does the name P. Franc mean anything to you?"

"Don't be stupid," Madame Poutine snapped. "Of course it does. I'm Paulette Franc. My husband and I were Emil's silent partners."

Claire looked up in surprise.

"This was a very angry letter, madame," LeClerq said to Mme Poutine. "You were threatening him with lawsuits for backing out of his agreement with you."

"We stood to lose a lot of money," she said. "We had worked for months to arrange for a television show for him, and then he tells us he has investors in Paris and doesn't need us anymore. Going to Paris was our idea in the first place. All the years working together meant nothing, the sacrifices we made for him, the —"

"A motive for murder, perhaps," LeClerq

said, one eyebrow raised.

She dismissed him with a flip of her hand and an expression usually reserved for slow learners.

"How silent were you as partners?" I asked her.

"What do you mean?"

"Surely," I explained, "there were others who knew of your partnership with Emil."

"I suppose," she said absently, as though it didn't matter.

"Who?" I asked bluntly.

"This is no concern of yours," she said.

"If a murder hadn't occurred, I would agree with you," I said. "But unfortunately, one was committed. Who else knew that you and Emil Bertrand were partners?" I repeated. Before she could respond, I added, "More important, who else knew that he was planning to abandon you and your husband for new partners?"

She started to say something, but kept her silence.

"I did," Daniel said.

"You knew Emil was going to Paris without Madame Poutine's backing?" I said.

"*Oui.*"

"Because you were going with him?" I asked.

Daniel hesitated, cast a furtive glance at Mme Poutine, and said in a barely audible voice, "*Oui.*"

Mme Poutine's nostrils flared, and her dark eyes bored into Daniel. "You would betray me, too?" she demanded. "We were going to make your career, put you in the big-time."

He said nothing.

While the animosity between Mme Poutine and Daniel was compelling, my attention during the exchange was on Guy, who demonstrated no visible response to Daniel's reluctant admission. He stared at Claire, his fingers continuing to fiddle with the corners of the folders in front of him.

I looked to Daniel and said, "Since you were included in Emil's plans, Daniel, you must know that his backing was going to come from his son, René Bonassé."

"I think I have said enough," Daniel muttered.

"What about you, Guy?" I asked the tall, angular chef seated to my left. "It's evident to me that none of this comes as a surprise to you."

"I knew . . . I knew very little, only that Emil expected his son to arrange the financing for his plans."

"And that he intended to take Daniel with him?"

He shook his head.

"You did know!" Daniel said in a strong, challenging voice. "You confronted me about it, Guy. On the day Emil was killed." He turned to LeClerq. "He knew Emil had chosen me to go with him to Paris. Guy screamed at me; he even scared me a little. He . . . he picked up a pair of scissors; I was afraid he would attack me."

"And that would have been before or during your lunch date at Héllas?" I asked.

Daniel glared at me, but didn't answer.

LeClerq, who'd taken the chair at the head of the long table, drummed his fingers on the tabletop. "What about you, Monsieur Lavande?" the detective asked Guy. "Did you threaten Monsieur Aubertin?"

"Threaten him? No. He is not worth a threat."

"But you did know of Chef Bertrand's plans," I said.

After what seemed an eternal period of deliberation, he said, "*Oui*. I knew."

"Which must have been difficult to accept," I said. "You once told me that Emil had promised you a partnership in his future endeavors."

He ignored me and swiveled in his seat to face Mme Poutine. "You were the one who spoke against me," he said, his voice a melding of anger and sadness. "It was always you who told him I was not good enough for him, not . . . not handsome enough for you." He glared at her. "Not handsome enough for television. *Television!*" He spat out the word as though it were a piece of spoiled clam. "Guests in a restaurant want to eat, not make eyes at the chef."

Mme Poutine laughed and said, "Look at him. He is no good for the camera. Daniel, at least, we can train."

"What do you mean, train?" Daniel shouted. "You know nothing about cooking. You are a bookkeeper. You take some classes, follow around a chef, this does not make you an expert on food. And what kind of television connections could you have? You demonstrated makeup to bored housewives."

"Enough!" LeClerq shouted.

The combatants fell silent.

But Guy was not to be silenced. "I served him faithfully for ten years," he said, "cleaning up after him, running his errands, fixing his mistakes, doing his dirty work." He guffawed and looked at Daniel. "You thought *he* put the salt in your sugar canister, didn't you? I put it there, Daniel, so you wouldn't get a star before he did."

Now it was Mme Poutine's turn to vent. She stood, leaned forward with both manicured hands on the table, and said to Guy, "You ingrate! You sniveling, whining ingrate. Emil planned to go to Paris without you and close the doors on L'Homme Qui Court, walk away from it, leave you nothing. I was the one who convinced him not to do that. I told him that if he didn't take care of you, toss you some bone, you'd make trouble. And I was right. What did you think, Guy, that because you were loyal to your master, like some pathetic puppy, you were owed the world? With Emil and Daniel, and with my financial backing and business sense, we were going to build an empire. Negotiations were completed with the television people in Paris. Emil would have had his show, and we were grooming Daniel for the same. And the restaurants opened for them would become the most popular in Paris. Eventually we'd expand to other cities, too." She paused and drew a deep, labored breath. For a moment I thought she might cry, but that was not in character for this strong, ambitious woman. She tamped down her emotions and finished in a cold voice, "Until Emil decided to take advantage of my planning and contacts, and go off on his own. May his soul rot in hell."

Her hate-filled proclamation brought an abrupt end to the fighting. I turned and looked at Guy, whose eyes had filled with tears. He slowly lowered his head and rested it on his folded arms.

I touched his shoulder. "Guy," I said, "I understand. You've been terribly hurt by a man you revered, a man who lied to you and who . . ."

He raised his head, looking at me with red-rimmed eyes.

"He betrayed you with Claire, too, didn't he?"

He nodded.

"Someone you love very much."

"Oh, Guy. I'm so sorry," Claire said.

Guy reached out a hand to her. "He never loved you, but he knew I did. He played with you to taunt me."

Claire pulled her hand away. "No, I don't believe it," she said, but her voice was uncertain.

"How spiteful," I said, sighing. "And you only wanted to protect her, didn't you?" My heart went out to him. He'd been beaten down by all around him, dismissed as too homely to be of value to the Poutines, betrayed by the man he trusted and to whom he'd given his loyalty and his friendship, and rejected by the one he loved.

"She is so innocent," he said, watching Claire's face. "And he treated her so poorly, like some common piece of fluff. He knew she found him appealing. Why, Claire? I'll never understand."

Claire bit her lip and kept her eyes cast down.

"It's not so hard to understand. A young woman's infatuation with a powerful older man," I offered. "He was very charismatic and Claire is very young. She would have outgrown him."

"I like to think that," he said. "It is comforting to think that."

"You've always looked after her. When you saw her pull the knife from Bertrand, your first instinct was to protect her again by hiding the knife."

He looked at me quizzically. "How do you know this?" he asked, wiping his eyes with the back of his hand.

"I didn't know for sure until you said you don't pay attention to every knife and fork. That isn't the Guy Lavande I've come to know. The real Guy Lavande knows the location of every knife and fork, plate and pot and pan. Remember? You told me that in a kitchen, it's important to be precise, to know where everything is. And that's why you're such a wonderful sous chef. Emil relied on you to have everything perfectly prepared for him, to know what needed to be brought in next, to have his special knives ready. Besides, Madame Poutine said she saw Claire standing over Chef Bertrand's body. Who else would care enough to put himself at risk to help her by concealing the murder weapon? That's a crime where I come from. No, I felt it had to have been you. And I was right."

A look of calm swept across his face, as though a suffocating weight had been lifted. He said earnestly, "Her fingerprints were on it. I was going to warn her but then she . . ." — he gave Mme Poutine a fierce look — "but then *she* came downstairs and screamed and made Claire run away."

"But you helped her all the same. After Madame Poutine left, you hid the murder weapon, and then you put the knife with the rabbit blood on it in Mallory's backpack to throw suspicion on her, and to protect Claire."

Claire made a small noise of distress, and looked at Guy.

"*Oui,*" he said.

"But my men searched this room," an irritated LeClerq said.

Guy looked away. "They did," he said. "I waited till the officers were preoccupied with removing Emil's body. While they were outside, I sneaked back in."

"It worked out, didn't it?" I said gently. "The police arrested Mallory."

"And let Claire go," he said, a tiny, satisfied smile crossing his lips.

"You shouldn't have done that, Guy," Claire whispered.

LeClerq's nostrils flared. "Where did you hide the knife, Monsieur Lavande?"

I pointed to the row of olive jars on the shelf above the stove, their designs, called hermines, all perfectly aligned. "Up there?" I asked Guy. "The one you straightened the other day?"

He nodded. *"Oui,"* he replied. "It is up there. I will get it for you."

LeClerq jumped up and grabbed Guy's arm. "No, monsieur," he said, "I will get the knife."

We all watched as the detective pulled gloves from his pocket and used them to grasp the jar. I went to help him, but he held on to the jar himself, placed it on the table, and removed the lid. I looked into the jar and saw the handle of one of the two knives specially crafted for the master chef Emil Bertrand. LeClerq extracted the knife and laid it on the table.

Everyone stared at the knife except Claire, who gazed through the window into the medieval courtyard where Bertrand had been killed.

"Ah," said Mme Poutine. "You now have the murder weapon *and* the murderer."

All eyes went to Guy.

He realized what was behind those eyes, the accusation that he had killed Bertrand.

"No, no," he said, raising his hands as though to shield himself from those thoughts. "I did not kill him. I hated him, yes. I may be guilty of concealing a murder weapon, but I am not a

310

killer. You are wrong."

"Your protestations are not very convincing, Monsieur Lavande," LeClerq said.

"You don't understand," Guy said, this time extending his hands palms up, in a gesture of pleading. "Please believe me. You must believe me." He looked from face to face.

"I do," I said.

"Then it must be her," Daniel said, pointing at Mme Poutine.

"Watch yourself, or you'll be out of a job," she snapped. "There are other chefs we can hire."

"It may not be your decision to make," Daniel replied. "René will inherit his father's restaurant."

LeClerq interrupted their exchange. "It seems everyone in this kitchen had the motive to kill Chef Bertrand," he said.

"Not me," said Daniel. "He was taking me with him."

"No, he wasn't," Madame Poutine said. "He was leaving everyone behind — me, you, Guy and Claire — everyone. He was planning to dump her, too. She may be a pretty little thing by Avignon standards, but she's no match for Parisian ladies." She laughed at her observation.

Claire glared at Mme Poutine. "You were always jealous of me."

"You! I have no need to be jealous of you. What do you have I should be jealous of?"

"I had Emil."

"You did not. You only thought you did."

LeClerq had heard enough. He picked up the knife, put it in an evidence bag, and announced, "You are under arrest, Monsieur Lavande, for the murder of Emil Bertrand."

"No," Claire wailed.

Guy turned to me. "Madame Fletcher, please help me. You believe me."

"Then tell him, Guy," I said.

Guy turned to LeClerq and again started to protest his innocence, but I interrupted. "Tell him, Guy. You know who the real murderer is."

"I can't do that."

"You can. You tried to protect her, but you can't anymore."

"Who, Madame Fletcher?" LeClerq asked.

"Claire," I said, addressing the young woman. "Are you going to let Guy go to jail? Are you going to allow him to continue trying to save you from your own mistakes? Could you be that cruel to someone who loves you?"

Guy jumped from his seat. "No, she didn't do it. I did it. She's innocent. He deserved to die. He was abandoning her, leaving her behind."

"Claire," I said. "If you don't confess, Guy will be charged with murder. He has already committed a crime for you. If he wiped your fingerprints from the knife, chances are he left his own on it. Think about it, Claire. Could you live with yourself if he had to spend years behind bars for you?"

"Claire, don't say anything," Guy shouted. "I did it. I did it."

Tears coursed down Claire's cheeks and she shook her head. "I can't let you do this."

"Yes, Claire," he pleaded. "Let me do this. I love you."

"I wish I loved you instead," she told him.

He slumped down in his seat and plowed his hands into his hair.

Claire raised her eyes to mine and I saw determination there. She pushed up out of her chair, cleared her throat, wiped her eyes, and began speaking. "Emil wasn't only walking out on me. He was abandoning our baby." She placed a trembling hand over her stomach. "Our child, a sign of our love. I was so happy when I discovered I was pregnant. Now, I thought, we would be together forever. And then she" — she glared at Mme Poutine — "she had to tell me how he didn't really care for me. He was only playing with me. She . . . she dirtied our beautiful love." She shuddered. "I went to tell him what she said. I knew he would deny it. He was arguing with Guy. I waited till Guy went back to the kitchen and then threw myself into his arms. He pushed me away. He waved around a paper and said he had work to do, I was disturbing him. I said, 'No, listen to me,' and told him about the baby and he . . . he said he didn't want it." She began to weep again. "He . . . he told me, 'Get rid of it.' I couldn't believe he could say that. It was our baby, the baby we made when we made love." Her voice hardened. "I . . . I wanted to hurt him the way he hurt me. And the knife was right there on the table. I stabbed him, and he was so surprised. He just kind of sank down to the floor." She gasped and covered her mouth with her hands, reliving the scene. "And then I realized what I'd done. I was horrified, and I tried to take it back. I pulled out the knife. But it was too late." Her voice quavered. "All the pretty words. I'd believed all his pretty words, and they were all lies." She looked desperately around the room. "Why? Why didn't he love me?"

To my surprise, Mme Poutine walked to Claire and embraced her. The young woman collapsed, sobbing in the arms of her older rival. Mme Poutine crooned to her as if she were consoling a child.

Guy crossed his arms on the table and lowered his head. Daniel stood behind him and squeezed his shoulders. Captain LeClerq caught Mme Poutine's eye and cocked his head toward the door. Together they walked Claire out of the room, across the medieval courtyard where Emil Bertrand had betrayed his young lover. Together they took Claire away, while Guy wept quietly in the kitchen.

Chapter Twenty

"I suspect," I told the Thomases, "that a French court and jury will take into consideration Claire's youth, and the circumstances that brought her to the point of lashing out at Bertrand."

"He was such a bastard," Craig said.

"I'll bet Guy will stand firmly with her through everything," Jill said.

"I'm sure you're right," I agreed.

"But why didn't Mallory tell you about the knife as soon as she found it?" Jill asked.

"Yes," Craig added. "Why didn't she?"

The Thomases and I were sitting in the restaurant Christian Étienne, owned by the chef of the same name. An up-to-the-minute restaurant in a fourteenth-century building, Christian Étienne was characteristic of the juxtaposition of past and present that marked so much of modern-day Avignon. I recognized the symbol of Anne of Brittany, the hermine, stenciled on the beams above us and on the hand-painted wall that dated to when the queen of France had visited the walled city. It was the same image painted on the olive jars, into one of which Guy had dropped the knife Claire used to kill Emil Bertrand.

"Mallory was afraid of the police," I said. "She'd gotten herself into some trouble at school and had left others to take the blame. That's why

315

she was running away. She didn't want to go back and face the consequences. Her friends were furious with her, and she was fearful of admitting her guilt to the authorities. She told everyone she was eighteen, thinking people would accept her as an adult and not question why she was traveling alone."

"It must be a great relief for both of you," Craig said, "now that her uncle is taking Mallory home."

"It is," I said.

"Did you have a chance to say good-bye?" Jill asked.

"Oh, yes," I said. "We had quite a farewell."

"I came to say good-bye, Mrs. Fletcher." Mallory stooped in the doorway of Martine's house, picked up the gray cat, and stroked its furry head. She was wearing a flowered skirt and cotton sweater under her ski jacket. It was the first time I'd seen her in something other than blue jeans.

"This is my uncle, John Cartright," she said, introducing the man who stood behind her. "Uncle John, Mrs. Fletcher is the lady I told you about."

"My brother's family and I are very grateful that you were here for Mallory," said her uncle, thrusting his arm forward. "There's no way we can thank you enough."

"No thanks are necessary," I said, shaking his hand. "Won't you come in and sit down? I have coffee and tea."

"We'll come in for a moment, but we can't stay long," he said. "We have a plane to catch in Marseilles, and it's a long ride to the airport."

Mallory put down the cat and we settled on Martine's facing sofas. Mallory sat next to her uncle on one; I sat across from them. I had the feeling that John Cartright wasn't going to let her get more than a foot away until the door closed on the airplane and they were on their way back to Cincinnati.

"Mallory, you have something to say, don't you?" her uncle said.

Mallory fiddled with the end of her braid. She looked confused, then brightened. "We have a surprise for you," she said. "We put it in the garage."

"What's that?" I asked.

"We got you a brand-new bike. And for Martine, of course. It's really hers, I know. It's blue, like the old one, but much prettier, and it has ten speeds and a great big basket in front for your groceries."

"Thank you," I said, "but what happened to the other one?"

"I left it in the woods and someone took it," she said. "I'm really sorry, Mrs. Fletcher."

"That's not all you're sorry about, is it?" her uncle prodded. He lifted her braid out of her hands and placed it gently behind her.

"No," Mallory said, a quaver in her voice. "I'm sorry I was such trouble, Mrs. Fletcher. I'm sorry I lied to you. I'm sorry I took your bike and ran away. I'm sorry I didn't tell you about the knife. And . . . and I'm sorry I was so rude when you tried to help me." She dissolved in tears. Her uncle pulled a white handkerchief from the breast pocket of his jacket and handed it to her. She took off her glasses, wiped her streaming eyes, and dabbed at her nose.

I leaned forward. "I can't say it's all right, Mallory, because it's not," I said as kindly as I knew how. "You're a bright, wonderful young woman with a lot to offer. There's no reason to be dishonest or make up stories. It doesn't improve the way you're seen, and it diminishes your character."

"I know," she said, hanging her head.

"If you lie," I said, "you'll never know if someone likes you because of the tale you tell or if they're seeing through to the real you. You were lucky with me. I have X-ray vision."

She gave me a watery smile. "I know," she said. "You saw through me right away."

"Right away," I echoed.

"I'm going to tell the headmaster what I did when I get back."

"I'm glad," I said. "You'll feel better about yourself when you've taken responsibility. It's an important part of growing up."

"That's the same thing I told her," Cartright said.

"Tell me, Mallory, where did you go when you left here? The police were surprised they couldn't find you right away."

"I didn't go very far," she said, embarrassed. "I went to Madame Arlenne's. I lied to her and told her we'd had a fight and you'd called the police to have me kicked out." She looked at me and blushed. "She believed me and let me hide there."

"And how did you end up in Albert's barn, where the police found you?"

"I got bored hanging around Madame Arlenne's. She kept pressuring me to tell her all about the murder so she could gossip with her friends. I'd already told her everything I knew — except about the knife, of course. So when she went to hang out her laundry, I decided I'd go for a walk in the woods."

"Weren't you afraid you'd be seen if you left her house?"

"I was. That's why I took the bike, so I could cross the road and get up your driveway quickly."

"You weren't concerned about me?"

"Madame Arlenne had seen you leave in the morning. She told me you drove away with a man and a woman. I figured it was the Thomases and you might be gone for a while."

"Go on."

"I walked the bike along the trail and I heard the howling again. Remember, we heard howling at night?"

"Yes," I said. "Monsieur Telloir thought it was a dog."

"Well, he was right. It was a dog — more than one, it turned out. I followed the sound till I came to a farm. I left the bike in the woods and sneaked into the barn. They had at least two dozen dogs penned up, and they weren't being cared for. There was no water or food in the cages at all. They looked so sad. I felt sorry for them."

"What did you do?"

"I let them out." She grinned at me. "They were wagging their tails and jumping on me and scampering all over. Some men came running out of the farmhouse and were trying to catch the dogs and the police arrived and all hell broke loose."

"Mallory, your language," her uncle said.

"Sorry," she said. "Later, the police told me they'd been watching the property but couldn't search it without some proof. When I let out the dogs, that was their proof, and they moved in to arrest Monsieur Belot. I heard sirens and didn't know what to do, so I hid in the loft. When the police found me, at first they thought I was in cahoots with the dognappers." Her smile faded and a frown replaced it. "But then they discovered who I was and arrested me."

"Well, I'm very relieved that you're out of jail and all right," I said.

"Me, too," she replied, smiling again.

John Cartright got to his feet. "We've got a plane to catch, Mal." To me he said, "Thank you again, Mrs. Fletcher. My brother and sister-in-law will want to write or call. Will you be at this address for a little while longer?"

"Yes," I said happily. "I'll be here for another month at least, maybe more."

I walked them outside to their car.

M. Telloir was walking up the drive with two dogs. He waved at us as the dogs raced ahead, barking excitedly. They ran in circles around Mallory, who squatted down to pet them. They jumped all over her, putting their paws on her shoulders and licking her face till she fell backward, laughing.

"Ah, my 'eroine," M. Telloir said, coming up to us.

I introduced the two men. "She 'as made me so 'appy," he said, pumping John Cartright's hand while Mallory got to her feet and brushed off her skirt. "I 'ave my Chasseur back. 'E and Magie are going to be good truffle dogs together." He turned to Mallory. *"Merci, merci, mademoiselle."*

"You're welcome," she said, glowing with pleasure.

"I'm afraid we have to go," Cartright said.

"Don't you want to show Mrs. Fletcher the bike?" Mallory asked hopefully.

"We don't have time, Mal. She'll see it after we leave."

"Okay."

"I'm sure it's a wonderful bike," I said. "I'll enjoy using it."

Mallory flung her arms around me. "Oh, Mrs.

Fletcher, thank you so much. I'll never forget you."

I returned her hug and patted her back. "I hope you take home some good memories, Mallory," I said, releasing her. "And some useful lessons. I expect to hear only good things about you from now on."

"You will," she said. She grinned at me and hopped into the car next to her uncle.

M. Telloir and I waved as they drove away.

"What will you do now, Jessica?" Jill asked. "Life will be pretty quiet without a murder case to unravel."

"Exactly what I'm hoping," I said. "I came to Provence to relax, to read, to cook, to enjoy the culture of another country. I feel I'm starting my vacation right now."

"Will you be taking another cooking class?"

"Oh, I hope so," I said. "The class taught by Christian Étienne was fully booked this week, but I've made a reservation for the next time he teaches."

"I'd like to learn how to make this lobster," Craig said, forking a morsel of the crustacean into his mouth. "It's exceptional."

"It's one of the chef's specialty dishes," I said, tasting mine. "He serves the whole lobster in three courses. Did you try the sautéed chanterelle mushrooms? They're wonderful."

"I'm finally getting the hang of eating in France," he said. "You sample everything, but never finish the whole portion. Otherwise you'll be done for by the end of the first course."

"If you learn to cook as well as you eat, you'll be ready to open a restaurant by the time we get home," his wife said.

"Speaking of restaurants, what's going to happen to Bertrand's?" he asked.

"The Poutines signed a contract with Daniel," I said, "but their agreement with Bertrand made them silent partners. If René, as the rightful heir, decides to take over Bertrand's position, then he will decide who the chef will be, not the Poutines."

"Daniel stands to lose the most if they don't resolve their problems soon," Craig said. "He expected to take over the kitchen at L'Homme Qui Court and resigned from the Hotel Melissande; Guy starts as head chef there tomorrow."

"You've been staying here at the hotel. How do you rate Daniel?" I asked. "Did you give him a star?"

Craig swallowed quickly and began to cough. His wife thumped him on the back. When he recovered his breath, he squinted at me and said, "What are you implying?"

"I won't tell anyone," I said with a smile. "But I'm willing to bet that you're here to rate the restaurants of Provence. *N'est-ce pas?*"

The Thomases laughed. "We'll never admit it," Jill said, "but we're willing to bet you'd win three stars, our top ranking, for solving mysteries."

We hope you have enjoyed this Large Print book. Other Thorndike, Wheeler or Chivers Press Large Print books are available at your library or directly from the publishers.

For more information about current and upcoming titles, please call or write, without obligation, to:

Publisher
Thorndike Press
295 Kennedy Memorial Drive
Waterville, ME   04901
Tel. (800) 223-1244

Or visit our Web site at:
  www.gale.com/thorndike
  www.gale.com/wheeler

OR

Chivers Press Limited
Windsor Bridge Road
Bath BA2 3AX
England
Tel. (01225) 335336

Or visit Chivers Web site at
  www.chivers.co.uk

All our Large Print titles are designed for easy reading, and all our books are made to last.